I0772013

Secrecy and Swooning

E.G. Verot

SECRECY AND SWOONING

ETON COTTAGE
BOOK TWO

E.G. VEROT

Copyright © 2025 by E.G. Verot

This is a work of fiction. Names, characters, places, and incidents either are a product of the author's imagination or used fictitiously. Any resemblance to actual persons, living or dead, events, or locales is entirely coincidental.

All rights reserved.

No part of this publication may be reproduced in any form or by any electronic or mechanical means, including information storage and retrieval systems, without written permission from the author, except for the use of brief quotations in a book review.

Cover Design by GetCovers

Formatting and Editing by Weaver Way Author Services

Ebook - 979-8-9894221-5-9

Paperback - 979-8-9894221-6-6

Hardcover - 979-8-9894221-7-3

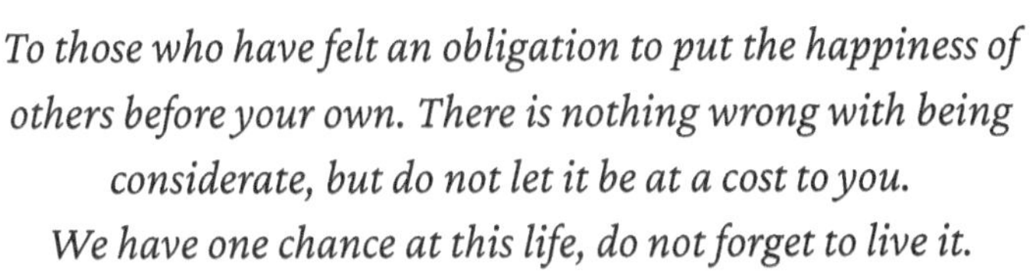

To those who have felt an obligation to put the happiness of others before your own. There is nothing wrong with being considerate, but do not let it be at a cost to you.
We have one chance at this life, do not forget to live it.

AUTHOR'S NOTE

This is the second book of the Eton Cottage Series. It may be read as a standalone, but please be advised it contains many spoilers for book one.. If you would like to avoid the spoilers, please read Hostility and Heartstrings before starting Secrecy and Swooning.

Please note this book contains adult themes and situations. There are some sensitive themes in Secrecy and Swooning that readers may find triggering.

This book contains mentions of a spouse's death (years prior to the story), grief struggles of family members (side characters), parental disappointment and medical emergency.

You will also find loving characters, steamy scenes, and a happy ending.

Thanks for reading!

-E.G. Verot

PROLOGUE

Albert

"You are only a few years from being a gentleman of this society, Albert. You must learn that with our title comes a vast number of duties. Some you will enjoy, others you will endure." My father insists on turning each conversation we have into an opportunity to impart another piece of wisdom upon me. Unfortunately, this day is no different.

Turning away from him, I roll my eyes and vow in my mind that I shall never forgive my parents for forcing me to attend yet another ostentatious wedding celebration.

The late spring heat is suffocating in this small carriage. I scowl at the view outside the window while my father sits silently on the opposite bench, my mother by my side. Of all the ways I could be spending my holiday from school, my mother, Lady Teresa Berry, felt my presence at the wedding of a man I can barely remember is essential. Her words, "The Calderwoods are as good as family to us," echoed throughout our home for the last two weeks as I argued my case to be excused from the celebrations.

As good as family...perhaps to her, but I know my father agrees with me. Lord Nicholas Berry, while he is faithful to his Lordship and the responsibilities that come with it, does not enjoy the social obligations as my mother does.

Even when the elder Lord Calderwood was alive, my father didn't seek out his company. Yet, my mother grew up with Lady Augusta Calderwood, and after the passing of her husband, she has sought out my mother's company far more often.

Now, the new Lord Calderwood, Benedict, is getting married and we must ruin an entire day to celebrate him and his new bride. It's been years since Benedict accompanied his mother while she visited the Berry Estate. More than ten years my senior, at six and twenty, our paths have not crossed since I was a child.

Arriving at the Calderwood family's townhome gives a brief reprieve from the blistering heat as we exit the carriage. I feel the heat lingering under my dress clothes. My cravat sticks to my neck as the sweat from my back threatens to soak through my shirt. I cannot imagine how warm my mother is under so many layers of fabric. The Berry family blends in with London's elite dressed in their finest attire. Yet, what choice did we have but to follow the proper protocol and expectations of appearance for such an event? My mother fusses with her light blue dress that complements her quite well, though my father has yet to tell her and I have given him plenty of opportunities.

"You look beautiful, Mother." I hold out my arm for her as we approach the entrance. She takes it, but not before glancing back at my father, who follows blissfully unaware behind us.

Upon entering the home, we are surrounded by people who have come to wish the newlyweds well. I look around but hardly recognize more than a few people, a true privilege of being away at school most the year. My mother pulls me through the crowds, making quick introductions along the way to people whose names I will surely forget before we take our leave.

Two hours pass as I stay removed from the center of the celebration, now standing at the far wall with my father, eating and speaking minimally with anyone who approaches us. My mother has spent the entirety of the event socializing—it is a surprise she is not dizzy from the number of times she has circled the room. Yet, I cannot blame her for soaking up as much conversation as she can. Surely, she is starved of such attention in our home.

When she finally returns to us, I beg, "May we finally take our leave?"

"Certainly not, Albert. Have you shared your well wishes with the happy couple yet?" she asks.

"I truly have not seen them yet. They are obviously more occupied with the other guests," I scoff.

"Come find me when you have done so, but we must not leave too early," she instructs before rejoining the group of women traversing the room.

"Father, I can't take another moment in this room. May we wait outside? Or perhaps leave and return later to retrieve Mother?"

Unmoving, my father responds, "Albert, as a gentleman in society, we must attend such functions, especially those thrown by such prominent families."

"Well, this prominent family is insufferable. I cannot comprehend the need to flaunt your money and status in such a way. And for what? A wedding? Benedict selecting the prettiest girl he could find and her accepting only because of his considerable fortune is not an inconceivable feat."

"Watch your tongue. We are in mixed company, Albert," my father demands.

"Oh, indeed. Would not want someone to overhear how miserable I am to be in attendance, as if it is not apparent on my face." I huff.

"Then let me excuse myself for a moment. Without an audience, you will have no reason to voice your frustrations," Father tells me as he walks off to the dessert table.

Trying to be discreet, I exaggerate scratching my neck, but in honesty, I am wiping at the sweat that has accumulated under my hairline. The cuff at my wrist is soaked before I bring it back to my side. I check to see if anyone has noticed. How is it that no one else seems to be bothered by the heat in here, all blissfully distracted by the nuptials? I wonder if this marriage will turn out as sour as my parents', which undoubtedly is nothing to celebrate.

"Hem-hem," a soft voice whispers behind me. I turn to find a young woman with the brightest blonde hair pinned with jewels high on her head. The tiara at the top sparkles, but not as bright as the smile on her face. An elegant white gown covers her thin frame. In her white-gloved hands, she holds a small plate with a piece of cake. "Perhaps a piece of cake would improve your experience, Mister...?"

My mind scrambles to find any sense—her presence has overwhelmed me in every way. A moment passes as I struggle to remember my name.

"Mr. Berry." Although, no one addresses me in that way, as I am not yet of age. She certainly is, and the need for her to see me as more than a child of only fourteen years overtakes me. "Mr. Albert Berry."

Her smile grows from proper to genuine, "It's nice to meet you, Mr. Berry. I'm Lily—Lady Calderwood now." She is the bride. "Apologies for not seeking a formal introduction, but it is a pleasure to meet you."

"The pleasure is all mine"—*Lily*—"Lady Calderwood." In an attempt to prove my maturity, I bow and instantly regret the awkward moment. *You moron, now she will always remember you like this.*

"I am sorry to hear you are not enjoying yourself, Mr. Berry." Her eyes hint at understanding as she looks around the room, and her smile diminishes just the slightest.

"Please let me apologize for anything you may have overheard. It was wrong to be so candid." I have only just met her, but I find myself desperate for her forgiveness.

"No apology is necessary. As one of the hosts, I suppose it is my responsibility to see to my guests' entertainment." She looks disappointed. "May I ask about your connection with the Calderwood family?"

"Yes, my mother, Lady Berry, is a close acquaintance of your new husband's mother, Lady Augusta Calderwood. They were close as young girls and remain so."

"Oh, how wonderful. I will be sure to seek out your mother and attempt to make a good impression." She leans slightly closer to me and whispers, "I am worried I was not Lady Calderwood's first choice for her son and could use the support of her friends."

Even in my limited experience, I cannot imagine a woman better suited to be a bride than the woman standing in front of me. "Once she gets to know you more intimately, I believe she will be thankful for her son's choice." My cheeks heat as she looks directly into my eyes. Her smile growing wider with each word.

"Mr. Berry, that is very kind of you. All that truly matters is that my husband is happy with his choice." Her eyes light up at the mention of her betrothed.

"How could he not..." Never having much anticipated marrying myself one day. Living with my parents' unhappy union my entire life had the opposite effect. So much so that I almost forgot I would need to find a bride. Yet, standing in front of Lily, the thought of taking a bride for myself, one like Lily, becomes greatly appealing.

"There is my beautiful bride," a voice booms behind me. I am soon faced with an older version of the young man I remember as Benedict Calderwood. "And who is monopolizing your attention?" he asks while wrapping an arm around Lily's waist, smiling at me without any recognition in his features. Lily looks surprised at the lack of familiarity.

"Albert Berry," I hold my hand out to him, "my mother, Teresa Berry, is a close friend of your mother, Lord Calderwood." Standing taller, with a firm handshake, I attempt to deepen my voice.

"Little Baby Al?" he asks with surprise, and Lily looks between the two of us. Embarrassment floods my mind. Of course, I know Lily and Benedict are married and she could never be my bride, but the thought of her thinking of me as "Little Baby Al" is greatly upsetting.

"I prefer to go by Albert now." The words are firm in my weak attempt to parallel the maturity of the man who is a decade older than me.

"Of course, Albert," he replies with a kind smile. "Thank you for coming. It is great to have you here to share such a special day with us. I see you have met my exquisite wife." *Exquisite she is, but that word is not enough...she is...flawless.*

Before I can answer, Lily lifts the plate she is still holding. "Yes, I was just offering Mr. Berry some cake. It is so rich, I wanted to make sure everyone enjoys a piece." She smiles at me, clearly she does not plan to share what she overheard. Benedict is a lucky man to find such a kind woman.

Lily holds the dish toward me. When I reach to accept it, I brush her gloved fingers and even through the thick fabric, I swear I feel something in my chest. It is a brief tingle, and I wonder if I were not so flushed from the heat of the room, it might have shown on my face. "Thank you."

"Enjoy your cake, Albert." Joy radiates from Benedict as he turns his attention to his new bride. "I wish you the same fortune I have received in finding the perfect wife, my friend. I could not dream of being happier than I am today." He turns back to me as he closes his hand around Lily's. "The moment you find her, make her yours. Do not hesitate once you find true love."

"Certainly." Unable to think of more of a response, his words leave an impression on me. The idea of finding happiness with a woman like Lily fills me with a hope I have not experienced before.

"You must come visit us when you can, Mr. Berry," Lily says with hope in her eyes.

"Not too soon, though," Benedict adds with a wink in my direction. Of course, I am aware of the necessity for privacy for newlywed couples, but this mention of it makes my stomach knot.

"Of course, Lord and Lady Calderwood." I bow in goodbye as the happy couple glide toward the dance floor in the center of the large room.

With a sigh, I enjoy the cake Lily has given me. It truly is delicious. Yet, my heart is heavy since she left my side, knowing there is no one else in this room who could provide such extraordinary company.

As I watch the Calderwoods with longing, I silently forgive my parents for insisting I attend this wedding.

1

PRESENT DAY, 1815

"All arrangements have been made, as per your request, Lady Calderwood," Claire reassures me. She has been my constant companion these nineteen years, without whom I am not sure I would have survived the loss of my husband. Not too much older than me, she has an innate wisdom that has held my homes together.

I have hosted many balls in my time as Lady Calderwood, but this is the first one I have assembled within days. I suppose orchestrating such an event in London is easier than if I attempted to host it here, at the Calderwood family estate, in the country. Both of which I can only consider as mine through marriage and until my late husband's nephew comes of age to claim the title of Lord Calderwood.

If Benedict were never taken from me a mere five years after we exchanged our wedding vows, he would still hold the Lordship. We would continue our lives as husband and wife, waking in each other's embrace each morning, delighting in our shared company every day, and spending our evenings wrapped around one another. Yet, my life played out very differently. I was only allowed to keep him for a very brief time, an unjust, cruel, and unexpected end to our story. The sad truth is that I have spent many more years living in this house as a widow than I did as a wife.

If we had a son, it would have passed to him, yet we did not have any children. How I wish we did. If I could not have kept my husband in this world, having a child with his kind smile or witty sense of humor may have helped fill the immense void he left when he died. We had such hope to fill this massive estate with children, yet year after year passed without any success.

If Benedict were still here, we would have continued our efforts. But he is not, and since the day of his passing, I have felt his loss. I feel his absence in the chilly autumn mornings, remembering the excitement he felt as the leaves began to fall. Each day brings a new memory to remind me of his absence.

Benedict learned as a young child he was not skilled in sporting endeavors and struggled to keep up with the others during games. Yet, his sudden death still came as a complete shock. Doctors said his heart gave out. Since the day we lost him, I have not been able to sleep in his bed since. After our wedding, I refused to live in my own quarters and instead shared the space with Benedict. Now, though, I finally find myself sleeping in the room that was originally intended for me.

When his family visits during the year, his mother insists on sleeping in Benedict's chambers, claiming she feels closer to him when she does. Truthfully, it was the room she shared with Benedict's father before his passing. If she finds comfort there, I have no desire to stop her.

She permanently resides with Benedict's eldest sister, Lady Edith Warner and her large family of six daughters and one son. Edith's son is set to inherit his father's title, so the Calderwood Estate was passed to his younger cousin, Robert Harris, the second son of Benedict's younger sister, Lady Amelia Harris. Amelia, being blessed with two sons, will have the pleasure of seeing both of her children with Lordship titles.

Claire's hand rests on my shoulder. She recognizes when my mind begins to drift and pulls me back to the here and now. "Are there any other preparations we still need to make before your journey to London?"

"You wrote to the chef and made sure the florist was notified?" I ask her, even though I know her answer before she confirms.

"Yes, my lady." Claire is more than a valued member of my staff—she is my friend. Without whom, this unexpected ball would not have occurred. "I shall be traveling directly behind you and take over preparations in London as soon as we arrive."

"Thank you, Claire." I squeeze her hand.

The invitations went out the moment I spoke with

Margo, my dear friend. Miss Margaret Eton's family owns the cottage closest to the Calderwood Estate in the English countryside. She was just a young girl of ten when she and one of the cottage's caretakers, Mrs. Landon, were walking near the edge of our property. Benedict greeted them warmly and our acquaintances grew from there.

It was always a pleasure to share time at Eton Cottage with Margo and the Landons. Yet, it was not until Benedict's passing that Margo and I became true friends. I was devastated beyond words—it was as if my life ended with his. Yet, Margo stayed with me for days, weeks even. Never leaving my side with Claire close by to remind us of meals and to sleep. She gave me a new purpose in life. Without a husband or children to care for, Margo became a younger sister to me, which I never had. My actual sisters are all much older and married off. Suddenly, my life had new meaning. I was able to turn my attention toward her and help the Landons raise the young lady while her parents remained in London, uninterested in her upbringing.

When it came time for Margo to enter London society, her parents were adamantly involved despite their previous indifference and Margo's wishes. While I had my own opinions on the matter, it was not my place to voice them. There were instances when I would let my personal thoughts slip around Margo, but I held steady that she needed to abide by the rules her father set for her. As she was an only child and not a male heir, her father, a close personal friend of the king, made sure she was the rightful heir of the Eton estate. He saw to it that whomever she married would be granted the title of Lord Eton upon his passing.

Having spent the majority of her childhood in the country, Margo never much cared for the thought of joining London society and becoming a wife to a stranger. This feeling of apprehension toward marriage grew exponentially when her father made public the extent of her dowry. Witnessing true love between the Landons and Benedict and myself, she had high expectations of her marriage that she was not willing to compromise on, and none that were met during her time in London society. I never encouraged her to see a connection where there was not one, but I had hoped she would be open to finding a match that would suit her. As I have been so lucky as to find not once, but twice in my life.

Yet, one man always stood out for Margo, Edward Riley. I have it on good authority that Mr. Riley is a good man, but like Margo, he does exhibit stubborn qualities from time to time. The two were friendly as children. When her parents required her presence in the city, I would accompany her. She would return after her father's meetings, sharing stories of how often her friend, Eddy, made her laugh.

When Lord Eton first recommended she join him for business meetings, I was unsure how to prepare her, seeing it was something I had never experienced in my own upbringing. I barely saw my parents in our home, never being involved in my father's business in any way. Like all things she attempts, Margo excelled in that setting. I would listen with great concentration when she shared the items of business that were discussed at each meeting. The information she relayed proved valuable when I found myself in charge of running the Calderwood Estate myself.

On occasion, during desperate times, I would seek Lord Eton out privately for his counsel on particular business matters. I was unsure if he would even reply to my first letter, but he did promptly and continues to each time I write to him. It is only thanks to him that I was able to navigate this estate as a young woman without a husband. While I disagree with his approach to raising his only child, Lord Eton puts business above all else. He firmly believes financial and estate management is a skill all should hold. For that, I am thankful.

We did come across Edward Riley in passing during their childhoods on a few occasions. I never had any concerns about their friendship. Once Margo joined society and through the years following, her friendship with Edward soured, turning to hatred on both sides. She was just as puzzled as I was as to the actual reason they did not remain friends. That all began to change when Edward's younger sister, Evelyn Riley, joined society months ago and immediately befriended Margo.

When Evelyn joined Margo at Eton Cottage for a holiday, I was glad to see her with a new friend. Not that I wanted to share my time with Margo, but it did give me an opportunity to pursue other...hobbies I enjoyed myself. It was not long until I received a letter from Margo notifying me that Edward felt it was his duty to supervise his sister during her visit to the country.

After a few weeks in close quarters, Edward's love for Margo began to ignite, or as I later learned, reignited. Unfortunately, Edward is not the most skilled at professing his feelings and Margo is not familiar with genuine admissions of love. It ended rather poorly. Days later, when Margo discovered proof that Edward Riley had loved her and no others, she acknowledged her feelings, but now it may be too late. As her closest friend, I must do everything I can to help her to win him back.

While I would have preferred the two to settle this matter with more ease and in the country, I should have known nothing is ever simple when it comes to Margo. It was decided that a ball would be held at my home in London, where Edward is currently hiding and most likely sulking. The ball is an attempt to get the two face-to-face. We have invited him and his family with the hopes he will speak with Margo again. I have encouraged her to write to him, as he did for her and express her feelings, which might entice him to attend this evening.

With the last of my bags packed, I head down the grand staircase to the front entrance of my country home. There waiting for me at the door is a man who is not my husband but has loved me just as strongly as if he was.

Mr. Albert Berry is a gentleman, a good man, a great friend, and an exceptional lover.

I met Albert on my wedding day when he was but a young man. His family were longtime friends of the Calderwoods. We saw each other occasionally during my marriage, and he wrote to me after Benedict's passing to share his condolences. We would share correspondence sporadically in the following years while he traveled. It was not until Margo's first night coming out in London society that we met in person again for the first time in over seven years.

"Margo, settle yourself. This evening will be over before you know it." I attempt to reassure her. In the days leading up to tonight's ball, I've had to remind myself she is a scared young girl—an adolescent—who is not yet skilled in expressing her feelings appropriately.

"This is torture," she huffs, not bothering to maintain a whisper.

I turn toward her, barely able to contain my frustration. "You may complain all you like in the carriage this evening and into tomorrow, but you must keep these comments to yourself in public." I do not want to scold her, but she needs to understand all eyes are on her as the newest young lady to be presented to society. She comes from a highly prestigious family and has a reputation to maintain.

I purposely clear my throat as an approaching gentleman catches my attention. To my great relief, it is a familiar face.

He bows. "Hello, Lady Calderwood, it has been too long. How are you doing this evening?" His kind eyes are unchanged, but his features have long matured since I met him all those years ago. Where once was a smooth chin is now covered in a full dark beard. His wild hair is now longer and styled to fall just at the top of his shoulders.

"Mr. Berry, the evening is now much improved with your company. Let me introduce you to my young friend, Miss Eton." Throughout my time knowing him, he has always been a rational man, one who never held much stock in society's entertainment. Without discussion, I know I can trust him around Margo.

She smiles at Albert.

"Miss Eton, it is a pleasure to make your acquaintance. I would be remiss if I did not ask for a dance this evening." I must find time to thank him. Releasing a breath, I know Margo is in good hands.

"Yes, Mr. Berry, I would be honored." She smiles nervously back at me and I give her a nod of reassurance.

The musicians began picking up their instruments to resume playing. I watch from a corner as the two of them dance and speak quietly between themselves.

As I reach the bottom of the stairs, Albert is there waiting with a hand extended for me. "You look stunning, my darling," he says while tucking my hand in his elbow. He places a soft kiss on my cheek and escorts me to the carriage that will take us to Eton Cottage to fetch our heartbroken friend.

While we are not able to take such liberties with displays of affection in London, here in the country, my staff are discreet. They would never share the details of our relationship with anyone else. Truthfully, they have always supported my friendship with Albert and continued that support as our friendship grew into something more, even as I fought against what I wanted most.

Many nights have been spent encouraging Albert to find a young bride for himself. The guilt of having experienced a wedding and a marriage, something he has not, always gets the best of me on nights we are apart. He should not settle for secret affairs with a slightly older widow.

Yet, on nights we spend together, he is sure to use every moment to reassure me I am the only one he desires.

And he can be very persuasive.

2

Albert

The morning air is crisp and the sun is bright as Lily and I make our way to Eton Cottage. Having her to myself, even if only for a few brief moments, I am truly at peace. Lily Calderwood possesses every fiber of my being. She is the source of my joy, the incentive to wake each morning, and the excitement to live each day to its fullest.

When I met her all those years ago as a boy, Lily was the first woman who gave me hope that I could find more than obligation and arguing in a marriage. I searched for years, looking for a bride with similar qualities—one who made me feel as she did. Yet, no other has ever lived up to the standards she set from our first meeting and continued to raise each time we shared company since. It was not until years after the tragic, sudden death of her husband and my family friend, Benedict Calderwood, that I started to realize I never found love in another because I was waiting for her.

Throughout the years, we have each battled personally with the guilt of our affinity for one another and the loss of Benedict. It is a tight rope to walk, but in the end, neither of us can deny the connection we feel. Even now, we keep our love a secret, with the exception of very few close confidants.

The journey to Eton Cottage is brief, the country home of our young friend, Margaret Eton. Truthfully, Margo is not terribly younger than I am, but I have tended to see her as Lily does since the moment we met. At Margo's first ball, after coming into society, I reconnected with Lily. In my eyes, Margo has stayed the same young, naive, and increasingly stubborn girl to this day.

I can say, with all honesty, that I have come to love Margo over these eight years, similarly to how my friend Edward Riley cares for his much younger sister, Evelyn. We have the familiarity to joke and tease, yet we have built a solid understanding and trust between us. Having finally informed Margo of our love just days ago, Lily and I are relieved that we no longer need to censor our behavior in her presence. Not that we were ever very good at hiding it, but thankfully, while we were still finding our way, Margo remained consistently ignorant of our flirting and affections.

Currently, we find ourselves in a situation I have anticipated for some time now. Edward Riley has always been greatly affected when he found himself in close proximity to Margo over the years. He convinced himself it was due to his distaste for her, but no man is ever moved to such emotion by hate alone. Their poor treatment of each other and lack of communication resulted in years of rude looks and innovative insults that I had to moderate so they did not embarrass themselves.

This resolution only came about thanks to Edward's meddling younger sister, Evelyn. As soon as she realized that there may be something between her brother and new friend, Evelyn did not stop until she resolved the problem, ultimately getting what she wanted. I have a feeling this is not the last time we have witnessed Evelyn Riley's headstrong resilience.

As Lily and I foresaw, so much so, we decided to make a wager of how long it would take for Margo and Edward to finally realize their feelings toward each other. She won. I assumed it would take much longer for them to finally come to an understanding. Their malicious banter was so intense, yet now I wonder if it was a part of the foreplay to the emotions that were dying to come to the surface. I assumed they would drag that out for at least a year. We both held our breath when Margo ran Edward out of Eton Cottage after he offered her an abrupt proposal lacking any sentiment.

Lily and I worry for our young friend, Margo, as I worry for Edward. With a deep breath, I remind myself to be patient. This will find its resolution.

As the carriage slows on it's approach to Eton

Cottage, the Landons are waiting outside with Margo and her bags. Lily shared early on with me that Lord and Lady Eton never took much interest in raising their only child. Luckily, the Landons were brought on as the cottage caretakers and cared for her since her infancy. Without such fortuitous events, I would not have ever met the Landons myself. An encounter I am thankful for since I consider them close friends and confidants. They are the only ones who have provided me with their trust and confidence to discuss my love for Lily without concern for exposure.

Speedy farewells are exchanged within our group and we are once again back in the carriage. I place a blanket over Lily's lap and then drape another over Margo's legs.

Margo pulls a letter from her bag and holds it out in my direction. "Albert, you are sure that you will find him before the ball tonight? He did not respond to the invitation. What if he has left town?"

"I am sure I would have been notified if he had left town, Margo." I try to reassure her as I place the letter in my jacket pocket. Edward was heartbroken during the week he spent with Lily and me.

My mind races as I make my way back to Lily's bedroom, where I left her after Claire announced the unexpected early morning visit of a distraught Edward Riley. Foolish me for thinking he and Margo could maneuver a relationship properly. I should know better after years of their hot tempers and endless arguments. Even after falling in love, they still do not understand how to communicate. I feel the ache beginning in my forehead, not because Edward is seeking asylum here but because I cannot think reasonably about how to move forward.

Lily sits in front of her vanity, brushing her soft blonde hair as I come up behind her. Her eyes worry in the reflection of the mirror up at me. "What did she do to him?"

A laugh bursts free and I feel relieved about the situation immediately. "Believe me, my love, he is just as much at fault. Yet, I do not think he is ready for that truth just yet." She turns around in her chair to look back at me as I lean against the wall next to the window.

"He proposed."

Lily's eyes go wide. "So soon?"

"Yes, I suppose he could no longer listen to the discussions of her finding a husband in London." I pause for her to react. A smug look comes over her face, just as I had anticipated. "He did recite his proposal to me and it was one I am sure many ladies would turn down. I am not surprised Margo refused him, believing he was doing it only to secure his freedom as a man who can leave his wife and possible children in the country and continue his bachelor ways in the city."

Her mouth now hangs open as she looks up at me. I lean down to kiss her worry away. Our lips touch for just a moment before she pulls away quickly.

"Should I go to Margo? I can try to help her see Edward's side of things," Lily asks.

"I have a better idea. How about you stay with our

guest, try to comfort him in his rejection. Perhaps you can try to help him see where Margo may be coming from since you know her best. I will travel to Eton Cottage to collect the rest of his belongings and have a talk with Miss Eton."

"What will you say to her?" she asks.

"She could use a reminder that she sometimes misses what is happening right in front of her. Similar to Edward's affection, there is something that has been going on in front of her for years." I watch Lily, waiting patiently to see how she feels about this.

"You want to tell her about us?" She moves to stand in front of me, her hands seeking mine.

"Considering the Landons had us figured out in months, it has been years and she has never suspected anything. It may prove to be a good lesson for her. I will only do this with your approval."

She takes a deep breath. "I think you are right. Yes, share it with her. I have wanted to for years, but now I worry it is too late to tell her myself. It may be best coming from you."

"Then it shall be done, my love." With one last kiss, I grab my jacket and take my leave to visit what is sure to be a very despondent Miss Eton.

Thinking of the state Edward was in when he left Lily's home, I am almost certain he still cares for Margo. If I were a betting man, I would tell her such, but I am not so I shall keep that to myself for now.

"His mother and sister have responded that they will be in attendance," Lily reassures her young friend. I notice Margo observing our closeness. She smiles softly before turning her attention out the window.

"Do you think he told them what happened?" she asks nervously.

"I do not think that they would come if they knew what had happened between the two of you," Lily answers.

"When I saw them off for London, Edward maintained his sprained ankle tale, so much so he pretended to favor it as he climbed into the carriage," I recall.

She nods, still facing the views of the English countryside. The nerves are getting the best of her. Lily reaches over and holds her hand out for Margo's. "There is nothing that can be done right now, Margo. You will do no good by making yourself sick with worry. Try to close your eyes and rest."

Margo tips her head back against the seat, curls the blanket under her chin, and quickly falls to sleep.

With our pseudo privacy, Lily curls into my side, tangling herself into me and resting her head on my shoulder. I place a kiss on her soft golden locks before resting my head atop hers. "I shall miss you this evening," she whispers, sadness in her voice.

While we have endless trust in the staff at her country estate, the city is far more transient with employment, and gossip is as good as gold there. When we are near town, the coachman will knock on the carriage roof to let us know. She will need to move out of my embrace until we can return to the country.

"Each night without you in my arms will be a night wasted." Now is not the time to remind her this could all be different if we were to marry. Those topics are only brought to light in privacy and when there is sufficient time to have a meaningful conversation. Lily has obligations to the Calderwood family and is still weighing the guilt of moving on after Benedict's passing. This is her life and her decision to make. I have declared myself to her on numerous occasions. She knows she need only say the word and I would take her as my bride directly. Even if she never says those words, I will stay by her side. Half a life with her is still a far better life than one without her.

"Hopefully, we can have this matter resolved with haste and return to the country soon."

"Yes, my love." I pat my jacket, "I believe once Edward reads this letter, he will soon be reunited with our Miss Eton and we both know she prefers the country."

"But, will he prefer the country?" she asks with worry.

"Edward prefers Margo above all else. He will follow her wherever she goes," I reassure her.

"That is good, for her...and for us." She nestles against me.

I bask in her closeness—it's been years since we declared our love, yet parting is still painful. We remain close but silent for the duration of our trip, likely thinking about our distaste for living separate lives, but we keep those thoughts to ourselves.

A knock sounds against the carriage roof above us. Lily straightens and stretches beside me before she moves to wake Margo as we approach Lily's townhouse.

The coachmen carefully take the ladies' luggage from the carriage into the foyer. Mine remain on the carriage as I will be heading back to my apartment before beginning my journey of finding Edward Riley.

With a respectful bow to both ladies, I bid them farewell and promise to return as soon as possible. Of course, I plan to see them later this evening for the ball, but it will be different then. The short ride gives me time to contemplate our two parallel relationships. Publicly, we are known as close acquaintances and protectors of the black sheep in London society, Margaret Eton. In private and among the few confidants we hold, we are known as two individuals passionately in love with each other. Our secret love affair does not exist here, we must be on our guard, never to let a look linger too long, to be sure there are no discreet hand touches, and certainly not dancing together.

With my luggage deposited in my foyer, I take a quick assessment of my bachelor lodgings. I have spent so little time here in recent years. Since my friendship with Lily rekindled, the majority of my time away from my parents has been spent in the country, staying at either the Calderwood Estate or Eton Cottage. The life I have established in the country is full of friendship, entertainment, and loving individuals. This lonely apartment is a perfect representation of how lacking my life is in the city.

Moving to change, I notice Lily's scent lingers on my jacket. I set it aside gently, changing everything else before pulling the jacket back over my shoulders. If I cannot be with her this evening, this will have to do.

3

Parting from Albert feels like losing a piece of myself. I will not be whole again until we can be reunited. I thought the more time we had together in the country would make our time apart in the city more manageable, but it is having the opposite effect. My body needs his touch, my mind seeks his sharp wit, and my heart longs to be near its match.

With Margo by my side, I enter my townhouse and am greeted by the familiar staff. Looking around the dark walls, this home reflects the city it resides in. A feeling of business and duty surrounds me. Benedict's mother insisted we not make any interior changes to this home. I believe that to be a contributing factor as to why I have never felt as comfortable here as I do in the country. It could also be that she rarely comes to the country, making her regular visits here. When in residence, I need to have my guard up for any unexpected visits.

I suppose Claire will arrive shortly. Until then I need to speak with the butler, Darcy. As with the other staff in London, we have not disclosed my relationship with Albert to him. He is a good man, but as far as he knows, Albert is a dear friend of mine, nothing more. He could very well be suspicious of more going on between us, but he has never spoken about it. "Welcome back, Lady Calderwood." He bows before turning to Margo. "Pleasure to see you again, Miss Eton." After bowing to her, he turns his attention back to me.

"Preparations for this evening are on schedule. You have received correspondence about tonight's event from the Calderwood family." His expression turns unsure at the end. Something that is not hidden from any of my staff at either residence is Lady Augusta's constant displeasure with me. In earlier years, just the sight of a letter from her would send me into a distraught state. While I have learned to not let them have such an effect on me, the concerning looks have not ceased.

"I will be right with you," I dismiss him to have a moment with Margo before I read how the elder Dowager Lady Calderwood has reacted to news of a sudden ball being held this evening.

I find my friend, Margo, biting her lips and fidgeting with her skirt. "You are worrying." I pull her attention away from the nervous thoughts in her mind.

"Yes," she answers quietly.

"Well, stop." She finally looks up at me, and I continue, "We do not have the time for worrying. There are far too many other things to do. You are not allowed to worry again until everything else has been completed. We must focus on the ball we are hosting tonight."

"I believe that the invitation states Lady Calderwood is hosting a ball, and it does not have the Eton name anywhere on the invitation, Lily." Margo regularly thinks she can outwit me, and I am quick to remind her that she cannot.

"That may be true, Miss Eton, but everyone in London knows we are never apart. I expect you to assist with the hostess duties."

She does not answer but instead rolls her eyes at me. I return a pointed look at her.

"Before you go to your room to prepare for this evening, I have made a list of things that I need you to attend to." I hand her the list I made for her this morning and turn on my heels down the hall. I did not include any strenuous tasks, but she will need to taste the food that the cooks have prepared and sample the wine. I have also given her the responsibility to check that the flowers are fresh. They are all things I can do myself, but I think it is best she is distracted while she waits for Albert and Edward to return.

"Where are you going?" she yells to me.

"I have my own list to complete. See you shortly," I yell over my shoulder, mimicking her loud voice, never once stopping my stride toward the kitchen.

Delicious aromas flood the kitchen as I greet each of the staff and look for Darcy, who is stationed at the back door. Upon him noticing me, he pulls two letters from his suit jacket. One opened and addressed to him, another sealed and addressed to me. Since Benedict's death, the higher-ranking male staff are far scarcer, but Darcy has stayed consistent and has grown more open with me in the years since. I read the letter he received from Benedict's mother.

Darcy,

Why did I find out about a ball being held at the Calderwood townhome by invitation? I have reminded you countless times that I am to be given notice. It is my home. I will not continue to be embarrassed by such ignorance.

I have enclosed a letter for Lady Lily. See that she responds immediately.

I have also included a list of families I want to be sure have been sent invitations. If they were not included on the original guest list, you must correct this matter at once.

"She does not sign her letters to you?" I ask him as I

hand back his letter. I leave it to his discretion if he wishes to reply to her. He is kind enough to share the contents with me. The rest is his decision.

"I suppose she does not feel a need as it is hand delivered by her lady's maid," he mocks.

"And the additional guests?" I ask.

"Already taken care of, my lady," he assures me.

"Thank you, Darcy. I shall find a quiet place to read my letter." I take my leave of the noisy kitchen and spot Margo in the foyer with the florist and Claire. While Lady Augusta has never been discreet about her dislikes of me and how I have served in my role of Lady Calderwood, it does seem to escalate every year, more so since Benedict's passing. How I wish she would not involve the house staff though. I continue until I reach the study. As this room will not be used for the party, I should be unbothered.

Lady Lily Calderwood.

An invitation arrived yesterday for a ball that is to be hosted on Friday at my family's townhome. You can understand why I take this as a great offense. It is quite out of character for you to be so irrational and inconsiderate. I must impress upon you the necessity to share such intentions with me before you take action. If it were not so sudden, I would insist you postpone until I can counsel you on the preparations.

Be that delaying is no longer a possibility, I must inform you I have seen to ensure the proper families have been included on the guest list. Let us hope they are free to attend. There is a reason these events are planned in advance.

You are fortunate that I am not aware of any balls originally scheduled to take place Friday. Let us hope that this will be the only event.

You may anticipate my early arrival on Friday to supervise the final preparations. At that time, I expect an explanation for this poorly planned ball you have decided to have on such short notice.

It seems as if you need to be reminded you are a Calderwood, and your actions reflect on every member of this family, including my late son's reputation. Let us hope next time, you will be mindful of the responsibility you hold.

Lady Augusta Calderwood

Folding the letter, I find a drawer to slip it in. No need to carry it around with me until I return to my room. The glowing amber of the fire is a tempting place to keep it, but I have never been able to destroy letters. I have boxes of each letter I have received since childhood. Unlike these, others I hold dearer are kept in special places. The thought of Albert's love letters warm my heart and provide a brief reprieve.

Surely, Claire will alert me the moment Lady Augusta Calderwood arrives. I cannot be surprised she added to the guest list. I was very particular to keep the Grange family off the list as this event is being held for Margaret, he is the last person she would want in attendance.

How I wish I could break the connection between the Calderwood and Grange families. Only a friendship, in which both parties have been long dead—Benedict's father was schoolmates with Harold Grange's father— keeps them connected. I can be sure if the late Lord Grange knew of Harold Grange's wicked ways he would surely disown his second son.

Margo is fortunate to be blissfully unaware of his dealings aside from being a nuisance to her. Darcy was the first one to shed light on that man's devious activities outside of high society and Albert later confirmed them all. Albert has been particularly forceful when Harold gets too persistent with Margo. I certainly do not want him in attendance this evening, but I must remember Albert will be there and hopefully, Mr. Riley will keep Margo occupied. As long as they arrive in time...

Now, it is I who needs to busy their mind with

distractions. The house buzzes as the staff completes their various duties. They welcome me home as I pass by and share their excitement for the evening. This townhome does not have much opportunity to plan such occasions, with the exception of the yearly dinner planned by Benedict's mother, which is a much more solemn event.

Albert was so confident he would be able to convince Edward to return to Margo the moment he read the letter, though they have yet to arrive. If I am beginning to worry, I imagine Margo must be even more so. Before going to my room to dress, I turn down the opposite end of the hallway toward Margo's room.

I knock softly on her door, not wanting to wake her if she's decided to rest.

"Come in," she calls. When I open the door, she is standing in front of the mirror, sadness covering every inch of her face.

"Margo, your face is so pale. You need to relax, dear," I say as I rush over to her.

"I know Lily. Have you heard from Albert? Is he here?" she asks with anticipation.

I wait with my breath held, hoping she does not elaborate on Albert and me any further. When she does not, I reply with the bad news. "No, dear. Why would he come here so early? He is to arrive with the rest of the guests this evening."

"Of course." She grimaces at first, realizing her words, then shakes her head. It is clear my answer offered no comfort.

"It will be time to dress soon—rest while you can," I tell her before taking my leave.

Walking back to my room, I meet Claire, "I am going to rest and then begin preparing for the evening. I would like a bath prepared when you have a moment."

"Of course, Lady Calderwood. I will have the hot water brought to your room within the hour."

The sound of the main entrance door opening travels up to the second floor. A screeching voice barks orders below, followed by rushed footsteps hurrying across the floor, surely frantic to do her bidding. Lady Augusta Calderwood has arrived. We both shiver as if her presence has unsettled the air around us.

Claire continues, "I will be sure to let everyone know you are not to be disturbed while you are in your room." Years ago, Lady Augusta would demand a formal welcome upon her arrival. I am not sure if she no longer wishes to see me any more than needed or if she expects the fabricated excuses Claire gives her.

Thankful for Claire's interference, I make haste to my bedroom, quickly closing the door behind me.

The sun is warm on my short walk-through town, yet under the shade, there is a distinct chill. Autumn has arrived and within the high buildings in the city, the sun cannot reach us as much as it does in the country. Which is why my girls typically spend these months away from the city. With any luck, I will be able to complete my task this evening, delivering the letter to Edward so that he can attend the ball and we can make our way back to Eton Cottage soon after.

But first, I have one last stop to make. The dark green exterior of the Berry family townhome is offset by the bright yellow curtains draped over the front windows. I approach the matching lemon door, turning the knob, not bothering to knock as I am the heir to this estate.

Griffin, the footman, greets me in the foyer with a polite bow. "Welcome home, Mr. Berry." I hate the formalities, but my father strictly enforces the manners of members of the staff who were here before I was born. How I wish we could drop the formalities and exchange greetings like family members, as is done at Eton Cottage.

"Hello, Griffin. Is my mother available?" I ask. Mother is the only reason I ever dawn this doorstep with freewill. Before he can answer, loud footsteps and a looming shadow fill the door to the sitting room.

"What a surprise to see you, Albert. Has the Eton girl left you without any duties for the day?" My father's snark tone makes my back rise. His current assumption for my still being single is that I am pining for Margo, and she has continued to string me along for years. Admittedly, we are typically seen speaking at the balls in town, but he is not aware of my staying in the country with her and Lily.

Quite frankly, I do not care what he thinks I am doing or who he thinks I am doing it with. Of course, he will see me later this evening, most likely dancing with Margo and I will continue to keep my intentions to myself. "Hello, Father. I am in town for the Calderwood Ball this evening. Can I expect you to be there as well?"

My attempt to steer us toward a neutral topic was unsuccessful. "Oh, of course. You are only in town to enjoy entertainment with a girl who clearly will not have you." He shakes his head, and it takes all of my effort not to roll my eyes at him. "I was patient with you in your younger years, but now it is becoming pathetic.

You need to take your responsibilities seriously. I expect you to be at my side daily."

"We did go through the estate responsibilities, Father. I know what is expected of me and how I will maintain your legacy. There is no need for me to shadow you any longer," I plea with him. I have always fallen short of his expectations. Learning years ago that even doing everything he asks of me will never ease the tension between us and the disappointment he feels for me.

"At the very least, you should be spending your time courting women who want to be courted." He begins to pace and continues with a speech he has clearly been rehearsing for me in his head since the last time we shared company. "As the Berry family heir, you must realize it is also imperative that you continue this family name beyond yourself."

Perhaps he should ask himself why I am not jumping at bringing another child into this family, only for him to berate that child as he does with me. This time, I can not stop myself—my eyes roll as a huff leaves my lips.

"Do not mock me," Lord Berry yells in my direction. Long ago, this display of rage lost its effect on me. In my younger years, he was constantly rushing me to mature—long before I needed to. Always disappointed when I was not tall enough to complete a particular task or when I did not have the vocabulary of a grown man at the age of ten. Devastation filled me when he would make his frustrations known. It was dreadful when he would yell at me or at my mother when she came to my defense. As I grew, I began to meet his demands, yet his anger did not cease. It was not long before I realized there would be no pleasing this man.

"Or what will happen?" Stepping to him. I am my own man, fully grown, intelligent enough to run this estate and familiar enough to do it in my sleep. As for if I sire an heir, that is between myself and my wife, not him.

His head shakes, sweat appearing at his hairline. His breathing heaves. "You are a child masquerading as a man. I can only hope you will take enough liberties with the Eton girl so I will soon have a grandchild."

Fury blazes through me as my mother calls from the staircase before I can offer a rebuttal. "Albert." I turn and notice my mother, her face full of worry, rushing down toward me. "Nicholas!"

Far too often, it has fallen on her to break up the arguments between my father and me. She rushes to separate us, "Nicholas, take a seat. You are going to faint, you look so overwhelmed." I do not believe my father cares much for what my mother has to say, but there are still gentlemanly qualities left within him, and he refuses to act any other way in the presence of a lady.

"Griffin, if you would, please bring Lord Berry a cold drink." My mother's voice is calm and steady, as always. "In fact, could you bring us all some refreshments?"

"Of course," Griffin answers and heads in the direction of the kitchen.

Taking my hand, my mother guides me to sit beside her on the loveseat.

"Albert, darling. It is so great to see you." Her eyes fill with joy. I hope I do a well enough job to let her know just how much I love her as well. "Are you here to escort me to the Calderwood Ball this evening?"

Traditionally, I am happy to stand as my mother's escort during the social season, but tonight, I have other tasks to see to. "I certainly hope so, but I do not want to promise I will return with enough time. You see, I have promised a dear friend I would deliver an important letter on her behalf." Her face falls in just the slightest way. No one, including my father, would notice. Over thirty years as Lady Berry, she has learned to school her facial expressions, but I notice. I have been paying close attention to my mother since I can remember. Watching for each and every disappointment so that I can be sure to make up for it later.

"If only he took his familial responsibilities so seriously," my father interjects. Perhaps my mother's refusal to side with him in his vocal disappointment is another reason for their strained relationship.

"Nicholas, if you can not sit and visit with your son, you are welcome to leave." My mother's continuous patience with my father typically ends once he insults me in front of her.

"As you wish, Teresa." Without another look, Nicholas Berry rises from his large chair and exits the sitting room, no doubt to sulk in his study about his inadequate heir. Griffin returns with the drinks and leaves with one intended for my father on his tray before following him to the study.

"I am sorry about your father. He has been far more on edge lately." I look at her questioningly. "Even when you are not around." She pats my knee. "He is becoming more aware of his age…seeing men held as contemporaries unable to manage as they did before—some have even passed away recently."

"He is afraid of dying?" Certainly, I can understand that fear, if only he could express that instead of twisting it into dissatisfaction.

"Well, yes, I believe that, but he will never admit it. When a man reflects on his life, he tends to think of what he is leaving behind. I believe he may be worried about the Berry family legacy." Her tone is clear; she does not hold the legacy with the same significance.

"I will ensure you are cared for, Mother. As for the estate, I do feel confident in my abilities to maintain our responsibilities as Father does."

"I know, sweetheart." Her hand rubs my cheek, just as she did when I was a child, yet now a large beard acts as a barrier. Yet, that does not stop her warmth from comforting me. "If you are staying in town, it might be helpful for you to attend some meetings with him."

I nod and notice more time has passed than I hoped. I hold out my hand for my mother's, and she takes it. "I must be going now to deliver this valuable letter. I hope to be back before the ball to change and escort you, but if I do not return in time, I want you to go ahead without me."

"Why would you not return? Is the recipient a far distance away? Is there any danger attached to your journey?"

"Oh, of course not, Mother. My destination is relatively close, that is if the person I am looking for is home." I lean in close to her. "Between us, he has been through a bit of a heartbreak recently. He may be avoiding society and, as such, might be a little difficult to track down."

My mother does not question who I am speaking of, "Well, best of luck in delivering your letter quickly, Albert."

With a quick hug, I take my leave and head in the direction of the Riley family townhome, which is conveniently nearby.

Pressing my hand over the left side of my suit jacket, I feel the outline of the letter. It is comical to think how Edward and Margo have spent the last eight years. I am thankful we have finally come to the end of their back-and-forth, love-and-hate relationship. I have no doubt that Edward will run straight to her the moment he finishes the letter. The worry is where to find him.

When Lily informed us that only Edward's mother and sister confirmed their attendance at her ball, I questioned if Edward was in town. I know Evelyn, and I am certain she will ensure his attendance.

Would he deny his younger sister her escort this evening? The smart young lady was well aware something was happening between the two, she interrogated me when I picked her up from Eton Cottage.

"Albert, I know my brother did not acquire a hunting injury and Margo will not tell me anything. You must know something. What happened that caused him to run away from Eton Cottage?" Evelyn says, sitting on the edge of her seat in the carriage.

Thankful for our short ride, I do not think I could withstand her questioning all the way back to London. Although, she deserves to know something. She is an adult now, after all, I suppose I could hint at something without giving anything away.

I sit up, fix my gaze on her, and let my eyes go wide while I barely tilt my head to the side and slightly nod.

She gasps, "Tell me."

I raise my hands in defeat, "That is all I will say."

"You did not say anything." She huffs similarly to her brother. "You only gave me a look."

"Yes, Evey, and that is more than I should have given you."

"I knew something was going on between them!" She sits back, crossing her arms in front of herself. "I read the letters he wrote and then threw away before giving them to her."

"What of these letters?" I ask. Edward had confessed his love for Margo to me, but did he intend to share those feelings with her in a letter?

Evey leans forward, just as I did earlier, keeping eye contact and she shrugs.

Smart girl. I laugh and sit back. I am sure I will discover the contents of those letters soon enough.

"Oh look, there is Lady Calderwood with Edward," she says as we approach the front of the estate. As the door opens, she moves to exit but briefly turns back to me. "Eddy is in love with Margo," she whispers to me and then exits the carriage as if nothing happened. I laugh to myself. What a treasure this girl is.

The Riley's townhome exterior is similar to my family's, with the exception of a dark blue facade and lighter blue curtains in the front-facing windows. It is Theo who opens the door for me. "Hello, Mr. Berry. Please come in."

"Thank you, Theo." As I enter, I hear footsteps above. "Would you be able to tell me if Edward is avail—"

"He has already left, Albert," Evey shouts as she makes her way furiously down the staircase to greet me. Theo nods in agreement and steps away to give Evey and me privacy for our conversation. She is slightly out of breath as she continues. "When I heard Theo mention your name, I ran down here. I was going to seek you out this evening for assistance with Eddy."

"Elaborate, please, Evelyn," I ask.

"He refused to come with us to Lady Calderwood's this evening. I begged him and told him Margo would not have included him on the invitation if she did not want to see him."

"You are correct. She does wish to see him."

"I knew it," she gloats.

"But where has he gone, Evelyn? I need to find him and bring him back to Margo."

"I do not know. When I went to his room this morning, he was sick from drinking too much last night after I showed him the invite. I tried again to persuade him to attend, but he refused and asked me to leave him to himself once his breakfast was delivered. I only know he left because I happened to catch him going out the door."

"He did not give any indication as to where he was going?" I ask.

"No, not at all. His attire is unacceptable for the ball, though, so I can say with certainty that he was not going to Lady Calderwood's early to speak with Margo." She worries her lips, looking at me for reassurance. "You will find him, won't you, Albert?"

"Yes, of course, Evelyn." I squeeze her shoulders. "I must ask you not to share this information with anyone, including Margo and Lady Calderwood, for now. I do not want them to worry."

"I will not tell them." She nods.

"Feel free to meddle in any other way you see fit, though." I wink at her before I make my way to the main entrance and pass the footman on my way out. "Thank you, Theo."

Once I am back in the street, I take a deep breath and look around for any clues as to which direction my misinformed and crestfallen friend may have gone.

5

With our arms hooked together at our elbows, Margo and I make our way down to the ballroom for the evening's festivities. I guide her to the first tray full of wine glasses I see. "Drink one down now, for your nerves, then work on the other as you are greeting our guests. I promise it will help," I instruct her.

She does as I say and deposits the empty glass back onto the tray. Soon after, the front doors open and our guests begin to pour into the foyer. Margo makes herself scarce as I stand just outside of the ballroom to greet each guest and thank them for coming. Lady Augusta Calderwood and Benedict's sisters arrived while I was dressing in my bedchamber and made themselves at home. *It is their home*, I remind myself. Fortunately, they have decided not to join me in hostess duties.

Once the majority of the early guests have made their way to the ballroom, Margo finds me, worry clear on her face. It is getting more and more difficult to mask my concern for her. Albert should have been back with Edward by now. She looks at me as if afraid to speak the words, so I do, "I have yet to see Lady Riley or Miss Riley enter."

"They are not here." Panic lines Margo's voice.

"Well then, do not stress yet, Margo. He may arrive with them."

Without a moment between my attempt at reassurance, the women of the Riley family arrive alone. I stay close to Margo's side as they approach to greet us. Bows and pleasantries are exchanged.

As the hostess, it is my duty to ask, "And how is your family, Lady Riley? Lord and Mr. Riley are well?"

"Yes, thank you, Lady Calderwood. They are doing very well," Lady Riley answers.

"That is wonderful. Please enjoy the evening." Extending my hand toward the dance floor.

Margo leans into me, "Thank you. I do not think I could have asked about Eddy without showing my emotions."

"Of course. Stay close, Margo. I will not leave your side." As this ball was partially my idea, my shoulders strain with the weight of possible repercussions we could face if Edward Riley does not attend. Yet, if he was so against forgiving Margo for her actions that night in the country, surely Albert would have returned and shared that truth with us. I stand straighter with confidence knowing that there is still hope this will be resolved.

From the corner of my eye, a wave catches my attention. Lady Augusta is seeking my company. Could I ever truly snub her? Certainly not, yet, I just promised Margo I would not leave her unattended. At that moment, I notice Miss Evelyn Riley being bored to death by a gentleman near the refreshments table. Once I catch her gaze, I tilt my head for her to join us.

"Apologies, Margo dear, but I have a few things to attend to," I whisper into her ear as Evey makes her way toward us. Margo's face turns to panic, and I assure her instantly. "I found an alternative guard while I am away. I think you will be safe." Turning us so that she can see Evelyn as she interlocks her arm with Margo's, I take my leave in the direction of the women of the Calderwood family.

"Lady Augusta." I bow to my mother-in-law, then turn to address her daughters, "Lady Warren, Lady Harris."

"Lovely occasion, Lily. I am surprised it turned out so well, being planned with such short notice," Amelia says, her eyes scanning the room. She has enjoyed voicing her opinions on the way I have run my home since Benedict passed. It is her younger son who will inherit the title, yet he is still a child and she has her household to run.

"Thank you, I am very pleased with the outcome myself." Unless they plan to ask me the reason for the ball, I have no intention of sharing it with them. I am the lady of this house and I shall do as I please... *for now.*

"Yes, I am thankful that your entire guest list seems to be in attendance despite the short notice," Augusta adds. Looking around, little does she know the two most important guests have yet to arrive.

We held this ball for Margo to reunite with Edward Riley—we need him here. *But I need Albert.* Not just as the person responsible for delivering Edward but because I feel better when we are in the same room. Even if we can not touch, dance together, or let our conversation linger too long. His presence alone is grounding.

It is Edith who pulls me out of my worry, "What beautiful flowers you have selected, Lily." Her compliment is genuine, just as she has always been toward me. With a son to secure her family's legacy and a handful of daughters to care for, she never sought to compete with me. While still missing her brother greatly, I feel she was able to accept her grief in a far healthier manner than her sister and mother.

Before I can respond, Lady Augusta reprimands me. "What have I told you about selecting lilies for your bouquets?" Oh, yes, how can I forget. Her dislike for me expanded to the flower I was named for the moment her son decided to marry me. Yet, it is only since Benedict's passing that she has berated me when using them for events. *"It shows a particular selfishness, Lily. A very unbecoming look for a widow as young as yourself. It is as if you are constantly celebrating yourself instead of grieving for your late husband."*

The guilt his mother has insisted I share with her has truly taken its toll on me over the years. Of course, I was devastated for years after I lost Benedict. But I found a purpose with Margaret by my side and growing into the young woman who needed me. I started to enjoy life and laughter again with her and her caretakers, the Landons, which I did not realize I needed so desperately. I still think of Benedict every day, but I also am sure to live for the happiness in life. Even after so many years, his mother has barely changed since the day of his passing. I know he would want more for her...*and me.*

"Yes, I apologize about the flowers. I will see to it that the mistake does not happen again," I promise her.

"You should have included more roses—you know they were Benedict's favorite," she scolds. "But I suppose you did at least include lemonade, his favorite drink, on the refreshments list." Regardless of the reason for the events I host, Augusta is insistent her son be reflected in each one.

"Yes, and I picked some of his favorite foods for the menu as well."

She ignores my attempt to reassure her and mutters, "If there was an heir, we would not need these small reminders. We would have a child of Benedict's to remember him."

With a deep breath, I try not to let her words upset

me, recognizing it is time for me to walk away. She knows she is being hurtful, blaming me for our inability to conceive. Edith gives me a forgiving smile, but the damage is done. Without another word, I turn and take my leave. For years after Benedict's death, I had assumed the medical condition that stole his life was also responsible for our inability to conceive a child. Although, now I am no longer sure that I am free of blame. While Albert and I take precautions, I worry from time to time that I may be with a child, yet it never comes to pass. Perhaps it is my doing that Benedict never had an heir.

I feel tears rise behind my eyes and seek out privacy in the kitchen away from the guests. Claire is there with a cloth, handing it to me. I will never be able to repay this woman for her kindness. "Thank you, Claire." She nods. "Has Albert arrived yet?" I ask, praying to hear that he has.

"I am sorry, my lady, I have been watching for his arrival, but nothing yet."

"Thank you" is the only response I can give.

As I leave the kitchen and re-enter the ballroom, I notice some of the guests' attention is on the opposite wall. As I move past them, the object of their attention becomes clear.

Margo in the arms of Harold Grange. Fury consumes my being as the awful man has his hands wrapped tightly around her body and his mouth far closer to her ear than he ever should be. Margo's skin is pale and her face has lost its protective grimace. I rush toward them just as she falls faintly in his arms.

I may not have children of my own, but Margo is my friend, my family, mine to protect. "Let her go this instant!" I scream as I pull her out of his arms and into mine. Within moments, Darcy and Claire are at my side, and Darcy lifts Margo's limp body into his arms and awaits my direction. But I am too busy screaming at Harold Grange.

"That is my intended, Lady Calderwood. Know your place."

"Margo will never be your intended."

"Oh, but she already is. I spoke with her father just this morning," he says, the words turning my stomach. Grange is a sly man, but surely Lord Eton should be aware of his reputation and know better than to sentence his daughter to a life with him. Yes, the Etons have rarely been involved in Margo's life, but this is cruelty.

Claire steps between us to pull me away from the horrible man, but it does nothing to calm my fury. She is talking, but I do not register her words until she shakes my shoulders and addresses me by my name. "Lily!" I focus on Claire's desperate eyes. "You have a ballroom full of people. You must compose yourself."

My body heaves as it attempts to breathe in air between my shouting as I drop my arms. I did not notice until now that I was swinging.

More of my staff are now surrounding us, Darcy still holding Margo. I turn to Harold Grange, who has the audacity to fix his jacket as he acts insulted. "You are to leave my home at once." I turn away from him, having nothing more to say to that sorry excuse for a man. My male staff members surround him and begin herding him out of the ballroom and to the front door.

"Lady Calderwood," Darcy pulls my attention back to Margo.

"Please take her to my private parlor, Darcy." Claire follows us out of the room when I hear my name behind me.

"Lily." Evelyn Riley has tears streaming down her face. "I am sorry, Lily, I was with her when he approached. She said to find you, but I couldn't. Then, before I knew it, she was in his arms, and you saw the rest." I grab her hands as her mother comes up behind her.

"Will she be all right?" Lady Riley asks, rubbing her daughter's back while Evey's shoulders heave heavily from her crying.

"You are welcome to come with us to see her. I know you both mean a lot to Margo."

As I am orchestrating the guests' departure, Evey offers to stay beside Margo on the chaise. Her mother looks on from the opposite chair.

I stand in the doorway to the parlor, trying to school my face as the guests take their leave. That is when Lady Augusta approaches with her daughters close behind.

"What on Earth has caused such a ruckus?" Lady Augusta asks. Could she really not see what damage her guest inflicted? My face must show my utter shock.

"Mother was in the kitchen with Amelia when the

incident occurred," Edith begins with a calming voice. "I explained what had happened-"

Lady Augusta cuts her off. "I do not see why any woman would be opposed to becoming Harold Grange's wife. Yet, your young friend is so well known for her obstinate countenance and surely she would rise at such an occasion to faint and gather more attention for herself."

I look up at Edith, and she nods her head. Lady Augusta knows nothing of my outburst, and I am thankful for that. I need to clear my home and get back to the more important matter of my friend.

"Lily, she is waking up," Evey calls to me from the parlor.

"Lady Augusta, Edith, Amelia, thank you for your attendance this evening, I must see to my friend." Without waiting for their reply, I rush back into the room, taking Evey's place.

"Where is Albert?" I whisper. A silent plea as if he can hear.

Margo shudders in my embrace and then begins to cry. My heart breaks for her. I feel water building up in my eyes as I hold her tightly. I blink the tears away before they can fall, needing to appear brave while I comfort her.

"It is all right, Margo. We will find a solution." I pull her up so she is able to meet my eyes and make her a promise, "You will never marry that awful man." I would offer up myself before I would let him near dear Margo. This man must be stopped.

"Is he still here?" she asks with a shaky voice.

"Certainly not. I had him removed and warned to never return to my home," I reassure her. She looks around, I assume concerned about the ball. "You do not need to return. Please stay here and rest."

Evey is still watching, her mother now by her side, pulling her daughter to her, suggesting they leave Miss Eton to rest. Then Lady Riley turns to Margo, "I hope you find a way out of this, Miss Eton. Being married to that man is a fate I would not wish on anyone."

Darcy has stood guard by the door since laying Margo on the chaise. I must thank him for his assistance in this hectic matter. It could have been much worse without him here.

After all the guests have left, Darcy lets me know and Claire brings refreshments. I grab one for myself and another for Margo. Sitting next to her, I ask, "How are you doing?" She appears a little calmer now; her sobs have stopped, but she does not look much better.

She keeps her eyes on her glass and shakes her head. I continue. "It's time for you to rest, Margo. Take your drink with you and prepare for bed. I will be along shortly to say goodnight."

Claire rises and escorts Margo to her room, offering to draw a warm bath for her while she enjoys the rest of her wine. I smile at the two, finally allowing myself a moment to steady my breathing before I retreat to my room. Eager to remove this dress, I take the bottle of wine with me while I think about how we will get her out of this mess and wonder how I can track Albert down.

Gently, I knock on Margo's door. "It is just me," I say softly from the hallway. She lets me in and we walk back and sit side by side on the end of the bed. I knew she was safe in her room, but I feel better now to be beside her once more. I put my arm around her, "You are a strong woman, Margo—you will get through this. We still do not know what kept Edward from attending. Albert has not yet returned, so he may not have found him yet. As for this Grange business—Albert and I will not allow it. I will go to your father myself at sunrise tomorrow. We will convince him to change his mind. And, if we cannot...you will marry Albert."

This is an idea Margo mentioned to me before— before she considered she would ever find someone to love her. A marriage to Albert built on the friendship and trust they shared was the only reasonable option for her. Yet, now she still could find love with Edward... *hopefully*.

"Lily, I could never. You and Albert are together. It is you who should be marrying him."

I shake her head, "I am not sure if that was ever in our future, Margo. It is far more important for us to keep you away from Grange. That is a life that we will not allow for you. I know Albert would agree to this."

After locking her arms around my neck, her tears return. "Thank you, Lily. Thank you for everything. Perhaps we can change my father's mind." It is clear exhaustion from the evening—*with help from the wine*—is finally taking hold of her.

I embrace her as she cries a little longer. I wait for her to pull back, not waiting to break the connection before she is ready. Clearing the hair from her face, I insist, "Get some sleep. We will get things straightened out in the morning," and kiss her forehead. With one last gentle smile and nod from Margo, I leave the room.

Where are you, Albert...

6

Albert

I f I were heartbroken and avoiding the higher society members of this city, where would I go?

To the pub.

Yet, there are so many pubs in London. I suppose it is best to start checking each one until I find him.

Stopping first at the one I brought him to after the last time he danced with Margo in London and lost his mind over his complicated feelings for her. This one is not the most prestigious place in town, but not the most sordid either. I exchange greetings with the patrons in the back corner before they return to the game of cards and I continue to search the crowds for Edward Riley.

Once I am confident my friend is not here, I exit and move to the next. Luckily, this one is located on the next street over. This pub is just like the last, with men playing cards and women fluttering around delivering their drinks. The low light makes it more difficult to identify the slumped-over patrons, but upon closer inspection, I can determine that Edward is not one of them.

As I move further away from the Calderwood Estate and the pubs most gentlemen from society prefer, the state of the establishments I check decreases the further I go. I can only hope I am headed in the direction Edward took. *That is, if he is in London...he may have left town.* No, I have a feeling about this. He is drowning his sorrows.

While I would like to think of myself as an understanding friend to Mr. Riley, my patience is wearing thin. Surely, Lily and Margo must be worrying. The ball is well underway by now. I promised them I would deliver him in time and yet, here I am hours later, traipsing through every grimy watering hole outside of London looking for him. *If only I could get word to Lily, yet, that effort would be pointless.* She likely would not read the letter until the ball ended and I plan to be there before that. These high-society evenings tend to continue well into the night.

My mind wanders to Lily, not that I could offer much relief from an evening with the women of the Calderwood family, but I try to support where I can when these events take place. Surely, Benedict's mother is giving Lily a dressing down about nonsense things such as flower arrangements and not enough attention to the photos of her late son. I would never tell a mother how to grieve for her child, yet I feel she would have only been satisfied if Lily threw her body in Benedict's grave and was buried with him. It is not fair for Lady Augusta Calderwood to dictate the way in which Lily grieves.

I should be there this evening with Lily. It pains me to think of her suffering. In addition to being the hostess of this evening's ball, I am sure she is spending the majority of her evening seeing to Margo's worry.

I could not explain it and did not share my theory with anyone other than Lily, but I always had a feeling about Margaret Eton and Edward Riley. The chemistry they displayed when in each other's presence was undeniable, even if it was not always kind. Edward knew from a very young age that he wanted no one but Margo. However, Margo took years to find her way to the same conclusion.

Loving someone is a journey, not a destination.

Edward and Margaret were meant to be, decided when they were young children, walking into business meetings behind their fathers, trying to make the other one laugh. Yet, that does not mean they were meant to be together from the start of their adult lives. They still had much maturing to do between the two of them. Once I find him and deliver this letter, they will continue on their journey. Being together will not be the end for those two. They will now need to learn to love each other.

Oddly, I have had a vastly different beginning to my journey of loving Lily. When we met, I was just fourteen and she was someone else's bride. I knew better than to pine for a woman I could never have, but I could not stop myself from comparing every woman I encountered to Lily.

The few times I visited with Lily and Benedict, I quickly realized I enjoyed her friendship even more than his. Yet, when word had reached me of Benedict's sudden death, I grieved more than I expected I would. Looking back, I grieved not only for my personal loss but I felt the devastation that would fall on Lily.

Not knowing how to move forward, I spent the next years traveling as much as I could, hoping to distract myself. As my father became more insistent, I returned to London and spent my days learning his duties; the duties, while infuriating, led directly back to Lily.

Our journey has evolved from years of close friendship into a love our bodies recognized even before our hearts and minds caught up. Now, we have no doubt about how we feel but are still trying to navigate how to integrate our shared love with our individual lives. Until then, Lily knows the depths of my love and that will do. She need only say the word and I would be elated to be her husband.

If I could only return to my love, if not to embrace her, but stand by her side in silent support.

The locations of these illicit establishments are getting further apart. While irritation grows, so does my concern. If Edward drank his way through each of these pubs or worse, has been huddled at the same one for hours, he will be in no shape to attend the Calderwood Ball.

The next is particularly empty—he is not here, but I

am getting desperate. "Barkeep, I am in search of a friend of mine. Can you tell me if he has been here?" I ask and describe Edward, yet as I watch the barkeep's face, it is clear Edward does not have many distinct features.

"Is your friend nursing a broken heart?" he asks as he lifts a glass from the sink below and begins to wipe it down with a dirty rag.

"Yes...actually." It seems Edward is seeking counsel in his travels.

"He was here not too long ago. Had something to eat but then said he needed to leave to see the moon or something along those lines."

"How long ago did he leave?" I ask as I make my way toward the door.

"About an hour."

"Thank you," I shout at him while I exit and look around for the next pub he could have entered. When I spot a sign hanging above a door, Miller's Grogshop.

I run to the door and pull it open. I hear "another" slurred from the bar in a familiar voice.

I approach my friend from behind. "Edward Riley... what have you done to yourself?"

"*Albert*! My friend." Edward rises from his stool and raises his arms above his head before wrapping them around me as he loses his balance.

Placing him back on the stool, I look at the barkeep. "He is done. I will settle his tab."

"No need. He makes friends easily. Each person here

who has had their heart broken took pity on him and bought his drinks."

"How kind, thank you." I take the seat next to Edward. "It is time to go home, my boy."

"I can't, Albert. If I go home, Evey will be there. And she will tell me how beautiful Margo looked tonight, and I just...I just cannot hear it." Tears well in his eyes. While he surprisingly seems more coherent than I would have guessed, his emotions are on full display.

I suppose now is as good a time as any to deliver the letter. "Here, you need to read this."

He recognizes his name in Margo's handwriting and her "E" seal and looks up at me as he moves to give the letter back without reading it. "Albert, I don't think I can."

"I know what it contains, trust me." I push it back toward him. He carefully rips the seal.

As Edward reads through Margo's words on the two pages in front of him, I bask in this moment and remember Margo's first ball and how upset Edward had been after they danced together. Now I know it was because he was planning to court and quickly thereafter marry her before she denounced marriage for herself during their dance.

"Edward, I see you are acquaintances with Lady Calderwood and her young friend?" I ask as he leaves the dance floor, noting the redness covering his face.

He seems lost in thought, but when I press, he answers. "No, Albert, I am acquainted with Miss Eton. I barely know her chaperone, Lady Calderwood."

"Everything all right, chap?" I ask, worried about the young man who seems to be breathing heavier than expected after the slow dance he just shared with Miss Eton.

"Yes, I am fine." He pauses. His hand goes to the backside of his neck as he begins rubbing it, while watching Miss Eton return to Lily. His chest rises erratically as his face begins to fall. Suddenly his posture stiffens like a statue, determination on his face as he looks around frantically. I try to follow his gaze that stops at the exit to the ballroom. "Actually, no, I need to leave." And with that, he left the ball.

"We have to find her now. Where is she?" Edward rises and asks as he runs to the door.

"At Lily's, but it is too late now. We can call in the morning," I insist.

"No, I'm not waiting another moment," Edward says as he searches the street, looking for a horse.

"Edward, listen to me." I grab his shoulders. "You can not go to her in this state. You stink of liquor, your clothes are dirty, and you are disheveled beyond acceptability. You must go home, bathe, get some rest, and go to her in the morning."

He nods but does not speak, still appearing so distracted.

"I shall fetch us horses and we will return to your home for the evening," I instruct him.

"Yes, of course." He finally meets my gaze. Relief fills his voice and he smiles. "Thank you, Albert."

"Certainly, my friend."

～

Arriving at the Riley family townhouse, we are greeted by their footman. "Evening, Theo," Edward greets as he runs into the house. "I will need a bath as quickly as you can."

He barely spoke on our ride from the pub. Now I see he was plotting against my directive to wait until morning. He plans to go to Margo this evening. Well, I suppose it is the early morning hours at this point, just much earlier than company is expected.

As Edward runs upstairs, I speak with Theo. He has been the person to visit Eton Cottage with the Riley siblings and is well aware of the situation. "Miss Eton wrote to him."

"Ah," he responds with an understanding nod. "Please make yourself at home, I need to see to Mr. Riley's bath and fresh clothes. I will rejoin you shortly."

In what feels like mere moments, Edward rushes down the stairs, buttoning his jacket as he goes. I must admit, for how quickly he changed, he does look just as he should.

"Are you coming, Albert?" he asks, never stopping as he approaches the door.

Theo is behind him. "I have the carriage ready, sir."

I step in front of him, "Is there any way I can talk you out of this impulsive decision, friend?"

Edward laughs and leans in to say quietly, "Come on, Albert, are you not anxious to see Lily?"

I scowl at him but nod, turn to the door, and make my way to the carriage waiting on the street. Exhaustion overwhelms me the moment I sit down.

Now that I know this matter is about to be resolved, I can finally admit how tired I am. I smile to myself knowing I will soon see Lily. That is if she lets us into her home at such a late hour.

As we approach the Calderwood townhome, I say to Edward, "I think it's best if we try to discreetly wake a staff member to see if they are accepting visitors."

Edward smiles and says, "I have a better plan." The moment the carriage comes to a stop, he jumps out and races up Lily's front steps and begins banging on her front door.

7

BOOM! BOOM! BOOM!

A loud banging sound interrupts my tossing and turning. I wonder if, in my sleep-deprived state, I am imagining it.

BOOM! BOOM!

No, someone is making that noise. I make my way into the hall. Margo is already out of her room and walking toward me.

BOOM! BOOM! BOOM!

We both make our way to the window outside my door, which faces the main road. Pushing it up, a cool breeze rushes in.

BOOM! BOOM!

"MARGO!"

After tightening our housecoats, we give each other one final look before leaning out the window and looking down to find the perpetrators.

"You must stop. I insist. You are going to frighten

them out of their wits." *Albert!* He has finally come and seems to be in perfect health, aside from his unsuccessful attempts to subdue the man beside him, whom I must assume is Edward Riley.

It does not seem as though they are aware of their audience yet. "Mr. Berry?" I whisper loudly, hoping to grab his attention but not cause more of a disturbance. He sees us and throws his hands up.

"Lady Calderwood and Miss Eton. I am so sorry for the disruption, my frie—" Albert goes silent as Edward comes running at him from his position at the door.

"Margo," Edward shouts. Albert struggles to contain his friend and is successful when he closes his hand over Edward's mouth. He whispers something to him that we cannot hear.

Edward nods then Albert releases him before addressing us. "Ladies, my greatest apologies for the late-night intrusion, but I was unable to convince my dear friend to come at a more reasonable hour."

"Stay there," I tell the gentleman before I pull Margo from the window and turn to make my way downstairs.

"What are you doing?" she calls behind me.

"Letting them in. It seems Mr. Riley is insistent on seeing you. We must get them inside so as not to cause a bigger scene," I answer. As I make my way down the grand staircase, I mutter a prayer of thanks that Lady Augusta and her daughters elected not to stay here this evening but returned to Amelia's home after the scene with Harold.

I barely have the door opened before Mr. Riley

bursts through with Albert on his tail. Margo is lighting the candles in the sitting room as I guide the gentlemen in her direction. Edward freezes in place when he spots Margo, but Albert pulls him to the loveseat and sits beside him. Margo and I each take a chair across from them. Fatigue covers Albert's face, still in the jacket he was wearing for our travels this morning.

The room is silent, aside from Edward's weighted breaths and the sound of Margo's letter crinkling in his tight grip. Margo keeps her eyes in her lap as I look at Albert. He leans back in his seat and winks at me. I look around, surprised that none of my staff are present. Could they have slept through our guests' loud arrival? If I could be sure, I would move to Albert, sit in his lap, and fall asleep in his embrace while Margo and Edward have their own reunion. We shared a bed just last night, but once again, I am starved for his touch.

Edward's voice pulls me from my fantasies about Albert. "Margo…" Longing looks are exchanged between the two. How privileged they are to look at each other with such desire without worry about the consequences of being seen. Edward moves to kneel in front of Margo and she calls his name. He beams at the sound.

"May I have this dance?" Edward asks.

Albert takes that as his cue and moves to the pianoforte. With one more cautious look into the hallway, I see not a single soul. Yet, still a risk of being seen, I follow Albert and sit beside him on the bench as he begins to play. As if to get our approval, Margo looks to us before answering Edward's request. We both nod our heads with encouragement.

"Of course," she says quietly.

Not wanting to interrupt their intimate moment, I angle my body away from the happy couple, now wrapped in each other's arms, speaking softly to each other.

"It seems you had a rather exciting evening," I whisper to Albert.

He smirks and continues to play softly, "It felt as if I walked the entirety of England in search of this dejected man. He toured every pub in London attempting to forget the girl he now has in his arms."

"You are a good man, Albert Berry. Going to such lengths for your friends like that."

"They deserve to be happy. If I can bestow a love like ours on anyone else, why would I not? My life is complete with you, Lily. Everyone should experience this in their life." His words are as flawless as the notes he is playing. I do not deserve this man beside me, but I fear I will never be able to release him, either.

"I tried to convince him that coming at this late a time was inappropriate, but there was no stopping his need to be with Margo. I am just thankful he listened to my insistence that he bathe before coming." We both laugh softly and admire our friends' dancing while looking lovingly into each others' eyes.

When Margo pulls out of Edward's arms, she gives me a worried look, I know what is coming. "I would love nothing more than to return to the country, but unfortunately, I have some upsetting news to share," she says loud enough for us to hear.

Albert stops playing and looks at me as I leave his side. "I think we should all sit down to discuss this." Edward looks to Albert, who shakes his head, confirming he does not know the subject of this concern either. Margo joins Edward on the loveseat this time, and Albert settles in an empty chair next to mine.

Margo's pleading glance urges me to share the details of this evening. As I describe the events that took place with Mr. Grange, Margo shudders. Edward pulls her closer while he listens intently to my retelling. Albert's hand finds mine and squeezes it for reassurance. As upset as I am, his touch grounds me and allows me to continue.

All the details have been shared, but I have one more thing to say. "He should have never touched her," I pause, "Yet, we can not go back and change that it happened. We must look for a solution to his claim for Margo's hand in marriage."

Albert leans across the small table that sits between our chairs. A hand soothing my arm as the other remains firmly in mine. "Lily." He meets my eyes and then looks straight ahead to address her, "Margo." Even after knowing Harold Grange was removed from this home hours ago, the sensation remains as both Margo and I have tears in our eyes. "I should have been here. Please accept my deepest apology that I was not."

Edward pulls Margo closer to him, "It is my fault, Albert. If I had not made myself so hard to find, we could have been here before the ball began." He speaks directly to his beloved. "I am sorry." She nods with her face buried in his neck.

Albert is silent beside me, but I can feel the tension in his body. Albert is a protective man. My blood begins to rush as I feel the fury building within him. Having been left alone for so many years, I crave his defensive nature.

Margo sits and clears her throat. "I will go to my father first thing tomorrow. I will fix this," she says to Edward.

"My dear, Margo. Do not spend another moment worrying about Mr. Grange. I know I will not. I have had your father's approval for nearly ten years." Edward's voice is calm and soothing but also firm and resolved.

He tightens his embrace and turns to nod at us. Albert stands, never releasing my hand as he pulls me up beside him before we leave them.

Albert surveys the hallway. When he is satisfied we are alone, he turns me to face him and backs me against the wall.

His touch warms my skin as his hands caress my arms, moving up and then back down to meet behind my back. Wrapping my arms sround his neck, I lace my fingers through his long brown locks. Albert nuzzles my neck, "Is there somewhere we can go?"

"I have just the place." Rolling my body against his before he backs up and I lose contact. Turning down the hallway, I lead him into the study. The room is dark as we enter, but I quickly light a single candle beside the doorway.

Albert closes the door behind us and I hear the click of the lock. His body presses behind mine, his hands roaming over me gently before one comes to the bottom of my neck and wraps around my throat, securing my body against his.

His breath warms my ear as he whispers, "Get on the desk."

8

Albert

After releasing my hold on Lily, she strolls toward the desk slowly, letting her body sway freely for me to admire its entirety. She stops in front of it, turning only her head over her shoulder, eyes wide with false innocence. Her shoulders give away her pronounced breaths as they rise and fall with anticipation. Gliding her fingers across the edges, "How would you like me on this desk?"

After years of worshiping her body, I still feel my skin burn with anticipation, especially when she teases me in such a seductive way.

If we were in the country, without worry of being found and endless time to enjoy her, I would play this out. Giving her directions of how I wanted her, only touching her briefly until she was crazed with need for me.

I smile at the thought but save that idea for another time.

As I close the distance between us, I assess the thin sleeping and dressing gown covering her body and determine the fastest way I can remove both.

My hands lock onto her waist and lift her up to sit on the desk before me, claiming my place between her spread legs. Before I can act, Lily's lips are on mine. The lust between us has created an equal balance of power in the bedroom...or the library...or, in this case, the study.

With barely a night apart, the longing in her kiss ignites my body. No longer do I feel the exhaustion from the day, but a renewed sense of vigor and need that dictates my every action. I deepen our kiss, letting my tongue playfully brush her lips before sliding it between them. Her own ready to tangle with mine.

My hands search for the bare skin around her neck, only a brief connection before Lily pulls my jacket off then moves to the buttons of my shirt as I untie and discard my cravat.

With my shirt completely unbuttoned, my chest bare for her, she reaches to the waist of my britches, but I move back. She is still fully dressed—well, in her night clothes—but I still need to even this out. I grab her wrists, then move to hold them in one of my hands, raising them above her head. My free hand pulls on the tie of her robe, letting it fall open to her sides.

"Lay back." My voice is deep and direct. She does as I tell her while I walk along the front of the desk, with her wrists still bound by my hand. When they hit the opposite end, I give my next directive. "Do not move those."

Lily nods. Even in the low candlelight, I can see the flush of her skin peeking above her nightgown, covering her chest, rising up her neck to her cheeks.

"Albert, I need you," she whispers as her body jostles with need for my touch. I discard my shirt before hovering over her body, deciding where I shall start my devotions. Being we can be caught at any time, perhaps it is best to leave her clothed. I can work around this dress.

I begin running my hands up her arms, sliding them down her side, loving how she squirms for more. I cannot deny her any longer.

The top of her nightgown is soft with a flexible material that lowers to reveal her with little resistance. The sight of her bare peaks, rising and falling from her shallow breaths, snaps my restraint. I lean over, cupping one with my hand while lowering my mouth to the other, nibbling the rigid point. Lily moans as her body pushes into my efforts. With one final bite, not too rough, but enough to make sure she feels it between her legs. I release her and switch to the other, licking and softly nibbling until delivering a bite to match the previous one. Her moan is deeper this time, more pleading as her legs sway on the end of the desk.

When I step back, Lily's beautiful eyes fly open. Her reaction is a response to the lust in my gaze, the animal she knows will take over when I have a taste of her. I leave the top of her dress as is, exposing her breasts to the cool air as I prowl to the other end of the desk. I grab onto her ankles, using them to bend her knees and place her feet at the top of each corner. The skirt of her dress still covers her to the top of her calves. *Unacceptable.*

I could rip it off. How she loves it when I tear her garments to get to her. But again, I remind myself that she will need to walk out of this room just as she entered. With my hands still around her ankles, I grip them roughly and begin to move them over the length of her silky legs. Her skirt moves as I push further toward her center. When the material is all bunched up around her waist, I finally look up at her. I swear her eyes are alight with the fire from her need. Each time we are together, I am reminded how lucky I am to have this woman beneath me, sometimes above or beside me.

While watching her, my fingers move to her heat, never lingering where I know she longs for my touch. Her body tightens as she fidgets, attempting to align my hand with her core.

"Albert," she pleads. "Please..." I love the sounds of her begging, my name spoken with such need and urgency.

As we both enjoy when I take charge, she knows I will never deny any request that leaves those soft pink lips, especially when they are parted from her heavy breathing as if an invitation.

I drop to my knees in front of her, not wasting a moment before my mouth begins to devour her. Her panting fills the small room and I continue lapping, feeling her wetness in my beard as her body begins to thrust against my tongue. I could lose myself in her.

"I need you, Albert." Her words are drawn out, each only escaping her lips on the exhale of her panting. Lily gets whatever she wants.

I stand, making quick work of the buttons on my trousers. Once I am free of them, I let them fall to the floor while I scoop my arms under her knees, lifting her body and pulling it to the end of the desk. Placing one leg over my shoulder as she wraps the other around my waist. The familiarity of our bodies is like a dance we have performed countless times.

I ease inside of her and nothing else matters in this world. Basking in the feel of being surrounded by her for just a moment, then I begin to thrust, increasing my force and strength with each push. The collision pushes her body back and her arms finally move from where I set them above her head. Her hands grab onto my arms as my hand clenches her waist, holding her in place. Her nails dig into my skin—surely they will leave a mark. The evidence of our lovemaking will cover my body. If only I could display it proudly for all to see.

I can feel myself throbbing within her as she matches my rhythm.

"Tell me what you want, Lily."

Her head tips back and her eyes are closed, "Do not stop. I am almost there."

"I am right there with you, my love."

A few heartbeats later, she finds her release. Her

body tightens around me, sending me over the edge as well. I can use every breath I have to tell her how much I admire and love her, yet expressing this love physically feels more powerful than any word ever will.

I lean my body over hers, my head nuzzling in the crook of her neck as we both regain our breaths.

Once my body is ready to move again, I rise above her, first fixing the top of her dress and then moving her skirt back in place before stepping into my britches and pulling them up around my waist.

I hold a hand out to help her stand from the desk. She points behind me. "The settee?"

I turn to see it. I hadn't noticed it when we entered. Quite frankly, the only thing I noticed would be Lily. With my legs weak from our activities, I am thankful to be able to sit and rest.

I move over to the piece of furniture as Lily grabs my shirt from the floor and follows behind me. Once seated, I watch desire return to Lily's features as her eyes move over my body. When she reaches me, she does not sit beside me but straddles my waist and wraps her arms around my neck, her fingers combing through my hair.

"I hope you were not expecting to sleep now, were you, Albert?" she asks, not waiting for my answer before her lips return to mine.

LILY STIRS IN MY ARMS. The settee in the study is not ideal for sleep, but after such excursions, one can find sleep almost anywhere. I lie with her nestled into my side, her head on my chest and her limbs stretched across me. To assess the time, I pull back the curtain and see the faintest hint of sunrise building in the sky. Surely, her staff will be starting their days shortly, and we would both rather avoid any questioning.

"Time to wake, my love." Smoothing my hand down her arm, gently but firmly to bring her from her peaceful sleep.

She runs her face over my bare chest, and her groggy voice greets me, "Good morning."

"The sun is about to rise." At my direction, she leisurely lifts herself to sit, I feel the chill at the absence of her body. Once again, pulling the curtain back to show her the purple and pink light starting to break through the black of night.

"Yes, I shall head to my room." She nods as I move my legs to the ground and allow room for her to do the same. Once standing, she leans down, hands holding my face and gives me one last kiss. We did not expect to have time together here in London. It was truly a gift, yet it does not ease the sting of not knowing when our next kiss will be. With that in mind, I make the most of it. Showing her with my lips, my tongue, my rough hands that embrace her, just how much I will miss her.

When we part, she asks, "And where will you go?"

"With your approval, I shall make my way to the loveseat in the sitting room. No harm in your staff finding me there, sleeping and waiting for my friend." She looks puzzled, and I continue as I button my shirt. "Not you. Mr. Riley is surely still in residence at the moment. No one can fault me for waiting for him."

She nods, "I do worry it may cause some scandal if he is found in Margo's room, even if they are soon to be married. Should I go wake him, Albert?"

"That is your choice, love." I laugh, "As long as you are prepared for what you may be intruding on." I wiggle my eyebrows at her as I tie my cravat.

Lily's laughter fills the room as she swats me on my chest then makes her way to the door. I finally put my coat back on, attempting to straighten out the wrinkles. She puts her ear to the door to check for any noise, but hearing nothing she unlocks it, then slowly opens it. I hold the candle she lit that now barely has any wax left, proof of the blissful hours we stole for ourselves.

Both light on our feet, we move into the hallway and close the study door behind us. That is when we hear it, the not so graceful steps coming from upstairs. Both of our heads turn up as we take a step away from each other. *As if that would make much difference, me in my disheveled state and her in that nightdress. Two steps distance will not rid us of suspicion.*

Thanks to the candlelight he holds, the identity of the loud man is quickly revealed to be Edward Riley. Both Lily and I release a sigh of relief. He spots us on his descent and waves. Ecstasy beams from his being, even in this poorly lit foyer.

"Lady Calderwood," he bows and then turns to me, "Albert" with glee across his face.

"I do believe we are past formalities now, Mr. Riley, especially in private moments such as these. Please call me Lily."

"Then let me thank you, Lily." He holds out his hand, she takes it and he encloses his other hand on top of hers. "Thank you for offering to throw this ball. Thank you for protecting Margo when I could not last evening. Thank you for delivering a happiness I have not thought possible in many, many years."

"You are most welcome, Edward." She pulls her hand out of his. "But, I must be going before anyone wakes. You two should take a post in the sitting room. Let the staff know you came in the night, I let you in, and you decided to wait here to see us first thing."

"Brilliant plan, darling. We shall see you shortly." I watch her move up the staircase.

Just as she reaches the top step, Claire comes bursting out of the door that leads to the kitchen. Lily stops instantly, not knowing who has joined us.

She assesses the scene as Lily turns slowly. Once Lily recognizes Claire, she faces her fully.

She shakes her head at Lily and moves her hands in a shooing movement. Lily does not hesitate and continues up the stairs.

"And what of you two?" she asks.

"We came in the middle of the night, Lily let us in, and we asked to wait the night to meet with them first thing," I explain quickly and quietly.

"As you were then." Her words are quiet, but it still feels as if she is yelling at us. She turns quickly and runs through another door that I am not familiar with.

Edward and I move to the sitting room, he on the loveseat, I in a chair, both in relaxed states as we close our eyes.

A masculine voice alerts his presence before I can find sleep. "Hem, hem…"

My eyes open to Darcy standing between us, arms crossed, with a look of suspicion on his face.

"Good morning, Darcy." He does not return the acknowledgment but waits for my explanation. I suppose I am getting too familiar with the ways of life in the country. This is very peculiar for Edward and me to be here. I deliver the reason as Lily instructed.

"Would you like us to prepare you some breakfast?" he asks. "I can find Claire and have her wake the ladies to join you."

"That actually will not be necessary, Darcy," Edward speaks up. "The waking of the ladies, that is, I think a light breakfast would be much appreciated. Yet, in my hours of slumber, I have since regretted my hasty decision last night. I would very much like to let the ladies sleep. I have some errands to see to this morning. Albert, I am sure would be happy to help with them, and we can come back later in the morning."

"Certainly, I will return shortly with a light breakfast." Darcy bows and leaves us.

"You have plans for this morning?" I ask, moving to the small table in the room. I truly would not exchange the night I had for sleep, but the lack of rest is starting to take its toll. Yet, my friend seems to be in the opposite condition. He jumps up from his position on the loveseat and joins me at the table.

"Yes, there is a wedding to be planned...and hopefully, held this evening." My shock stops him, but only briefly. "I cannot wait another moment, Albert. I have spent years waiting for her to agree to be my wife, now that she has, I will make it happen as soon as I can."

"Does this have anything to do with Harold Grange's challenge?"

"Oh, he can piss off. I signed the marriage contract with her father years ago. I never sought him out to revoke my intentions. Perhaps Grange went and asked for her hand, but I can only assume he inflated Lord Eton's answer." Edward shrugs.

Darcy returns with our pastries and tea. Edward thanks him before asking, "Could you send for Theo at Riley House? Ask him to have the carriage brought for Mr. Berry and a horse for me, please."

"Certainly, sir." Darcy turns and leaves us once again.

"So much to do we need to separate?" I ask.

"That is correct. I wish to marry her this evening at Eton Cottage. Most importantly, I will need you to get urgent word to the Landons. Can you spare a member of your staff to make the journey with this letter, informing them of my intentions? As it is the most distance to travel, it will need to be sent directly." I nod, he continues. "Then if you would, also write to Mr. Landon's brother and his family to request their attendance as well. I believe one of his sons is musically inclined. Could you maybe request he play this evening? Make suggestions on music, perhaps?" It is clear Edward has put much more thought into this than I had planned. Perhaps he did not sleep much last night, either.

"Of course, I still feel as if I am not doing enough. What more can I do?"

Edward leans back, "I will visit the Eton's home here in town myself. Formally announce the union and ask them to join us for the ceremony. Then, I will visit my family and have them prepare to travel at once. Lastly, I will need to have an officiant willing to travel at such late notice."

"I could speak with Claire. Have her leave for the country immediately—she will prepare the Calderwood Estate for visitors. Surely, you will want Eton Cottage to yourself this evening."

"And perhaps a few evenings after that..." Edward's sly smile fades quickly, "Thank you, Albert. I would not be able to arrange this on my own. Shall we meet back here once our tasks are complete to escort our ladies back to the country?"

"Of course, Edward," I say, "We have a wedding to plan, my friend."

9

A knock at the door startles me awake. I did not imagine I would fall back to sleep after parting with Albert and Edward. The bright sunshine coming through the curtains is proof I have slept for hours longer than I had planned. My arms and legs move lazily under the covers as I regain my senses.

Another knock comes through, accompanied by a delicate voice, "Lady Calderwood, it is Claire."

"Please, come in, Claire." I sit to greet her properly.

"I am sorry to wake you, but I did not think you would have wanted to sleep much longer."

"No need to worry, as always, you know me perfectly. I do not wish to sleep late today." I stand and move the mirror with the filled basin to wash my face. "Would not want to keep our guests waiting."

"Yes, my lady, about your guests...they left. Some hours ago, actually."

Her confession pulls my attention as I quickly dry my face to inquire, "Did they say why?"

Claire lowers her voice. "Yes, ma'am. They spoke with Darcy, who believes he was the first to discover them, and I did not correct him."

"Thank you." I will forever be grateful to Claire for her discretion and support of Albert and me.

"Of course. I spoke with Mr. Berry before he left. He has asked me to return to the country and make preparations for guests to be hosted this evening and possibly for the week at the Calderwood Estate." She studies my face but continues when she sees no objection. "It was all Mr. Riley's plan. They have left early this morning to make the arrangements for him to marry Miss Eton at Eton Cottage...this evening."

"This evening?" I ask.

"Yes, ma'am." She giggles, "Mr. Berry said you would have this reaction and asked me to tell you that Mr. Riley just could not wait another moment to make her his wife. And that they will take care of every preparation, with my help, of course. You just need to be sure the bride gets to the country." She smiles and whispers, "He added 'my love' at the end of most statements he asked me to share with you." A faint blush rises in her cheeks.

"And what of Mr. Grange's declaration?"

"Oh yes, he said you would ask about that too. He said to remind you, 'we never trust a word that man says any other day; no need to start now.'"

"How true that is, all right then. I suppose we must

prepare. It will be nice to host guests for a happy occasion." Sadly, the only events that have been hosted in the country have been melancholy ones, held in the name of my late husband and orchestrated by his mother. I suppose the last time there was a grand and joyous occasion was when Benedict was alive, and even then, it was typically intimate parties of ten or so guests.

"Indeed, my lady. The staff will be happy to hear it too."

"Then I guess you should be off, you have much work to do. Before you go, will you send hot water up to both Margo and I for baths?" I ask.

"Certainly." She walks to the door but stops short. "Oh!" She turns quickly as she is pulling something from her pocket. "I just about forgot to give you this." She hands me a folded letter. "It is from Mr. Berry. He did not have time to seal it, but I promise, my lady, I did not read it, nor did anyone see him give it to me for you."

"We trust you implicitly, Claire." I pull her into a hug. Something we seldom do, but I felt the need for it at this moment. "Safe travels. I shall see you this evening."

After she closes the door behind her, I sit at the desk in the far corner of my room and read Albert's letter.

My Flawless Flower,

How I would love to see you when the morning sun warms your skin, yet this morning was like any other that keeps us separated.

For wherever I go, be assured, I bring you with me. You will consume my thoughts throughout my day. Especially on such a day as today, so filled with love, one can not find sadness. Though love takes time and preparation, I do believe by the evening, a new peace will enter our world. For those we care about can settle a long-standing battle they fought so hard for during these last few years.

I look forward to sharing their joy with you and our affectionate family and friends.

I will return in time to accompany you on the journey to our next destination, but if you are fortunate to find more rest, please take it. For who knows when you will have the chance for such uninterrupted sleep again.

-Always,

Yours

Albert is sure to write vaguely when he is concerned his letters may be lost or read by someone other than myself. Typically, when he writes to me while I am without him in the country, he folds letters for me within his letters to the Landons or Claire and requests they be delivered to me.

I take a moment to hold his letter to my chest, as I do with every single one he gives me, hoping the closeness will allow my heart to consume his words and never forget them. A knock comes at the door, "Just a minute," I call as I move to hide the letter in a secret hiding place I have made in my luggage by cutting a slit along the lining.

When it's in place, I silently close the luggage and move to open the door. I am greeted by two staff members bringing in hot water for my bath. Ambrose, a young man carrying the large basin with water steaming from it, and Daisy, who speaks first, "Good morning, my lady. Claire said you would like a bath this morning."

"Yes, thank you, Daisy. And one for Miss Eton too, please?"

"Straight away, ma'am," Ambrose says and bows before he takes his leave.

Daisy prepares the bath with hot water, oils, and fresh flower petals. After checking with my hand to make sure it is no longer boiling, I sink in, feeling the ease of the muscles I overused last night with Albert. *I will be with him again this evening.* I know it cannot last, but I cannot think of that now. I let my limbs sink under the water while the rest of my body is warmed by the steam rising above it. Now is for relaxation and reflection to prepare for the grand occasion that will take place this evening.

NOT ABLE TO WAIT A MOMENT LONGER, I quickly knock on Margo's door, and continue in to see my friend. I must hear about her night with Edward and how she feels to be getting married this evening. "Margo! My dear, dear friend. We have so much to discuss!" My excitement takes over and I have trouble keeping my voice down. Daisy puts the finishing touches on Margo's hair before bowing and leaving us to discuss in private.

"What bliss this new life is, Lily. I do not think I could have imagined what it would feel like to be in love. It is grand. Grand indeed." She smiles so brightly.

I cannot help but to hug her. "To think you've only spent one day in town and already secured a husband, Margo."

"The perfect husband," she adds. "Oh, Lily, how stubborn I have been all these years."

"Yes, that is true, but everything happens for a reason, and at the exact moment it is meant to, Margo." If only I could take my own advice, perhaps then my guilt for being with Albert would subside, and I could love him just as I am meant to.

Ambrose is carrying the last of the luggage downstairs as we descend behind it. Fortunately, not much was unpacked with the preparation for the ball being the priority yesterday, which made for ease of preparing to leave today.

Each in our traveling attire, we follow Daisy to the breakfast prepared for us. I am so thankful she thought of it. With all the other matters on my mind, I completely forgot we would need to eat.

As we follow her from the foyer, we notice a man standing just inside the main entrance, attempting to gain entry to my home. We halt in our step as we recognize Harold Grange. Albert said to pay him no mind, but surely he and Edward addressed this issue. Mr. Grange is not a man who can easily be ignored.

"I am here to see my bride." He pushes past Darcy, who attempts to stop Harold but is met with a physical confrontation. The men scuffle as Darcy tries to subdue Grange's intrusion. He is not prepared when Harold delivers a blow to the side of his head, leading to him being temporarily incapacitated. When Harold notices Margo, he makes his way directly to her. Surprisingly, Margo does not back away or cower as I would expect her to. No, instead, she stands straighter by my side. Her face stays indifferent, showing no signs of fear...I can only guess that is due to the security she now feels from Edward Riley.

"Margaret, my beautiful." He steps incredibly too close to her and rests his left hand on her cheek.

"Do not touch me, Harold." She bats his hand away.

Harold grabs Margo's wrist tightly, using it to spin her so that her back is against his chest as he holds her to him. I know Mr. Landon has taught her to defend herself, but with her arms pinned beneath his, she is without any options. She begins kicking, but he just seems to enjoy it as he speaks into her ear.

"Glad to see you have come around to addressing me informally, Margaret." He lowers his head to kiss her neck and the fury that froze me in place finally sets me free. He continues, "I always knew you had a fight in you. I cannot wait to see how this comes out in the bedroom."

"You disgusting old man, let me down," she yells, but it just seems to delight him.

With no weapons in my house, I pick up the first thing I find to hit him with, "You let her go." I swing the umbrella behind me for momentum before I release it with all of my strength at Harold's head. Margo moves out of my path as I hit my target with a loud thud. It works and distracts him enough to loosen his hold on Margo and she runs away from him. I wind up and hit him once more for good measure. Harold stumbles on his feet, using his hands on his knees to support him. Panting, I hold my pose, ready to strike again if he comes near Margo.

Harold looks in my direction, filled with anger and plotting. Until he notices something behind me, his face changes, still angry but with more apprehension.

"Good swing, my love." His words are a whisper in my ear.

Albert is here.

10

How proud I am of Lily, not only defending herself but also her friend. I wrap my arms around her, pulling her back to my chest. I place a soft kiss on her cheek that is facing away from Grange, "I am here, no need for this any longer." I take the umbrella from her.

"He is insistent she is to be his bride. Please do something," Lily pleads before she runs to Margo's side.

With my girls safe and out of Grange's reach, I can let my rage take hold. Footsteps become heavier as Edward enters and discovers the scene. He meets my eyes only for a moment before turning to Margo, assessing her for injuries, while I keep a close eye on their assailant.

Grange begins to straighten his stance, but I do not allow him to reach his full height. Just like Lily, I use my force and bring the umbrella down on his head. He stumbles before returning to his hunched position. He is a big man—it will take more than an umbrella to knock him off his feet. I happily accept that challenge. I throw the umbrella aside and descend upon him. Using his hunched position to my advantage, I heave my knee into his stomach and step back. "You are finished, Grange."

Edward is frozen where he stands, his attention locked on to his love. Yet, he does not go to her. He keeps his position between the ladies and me next to Grange. Harold turns to face me and I remind him that I am not the only gentleman he has angered by this ghastly display of behavior. "Edward has not addressed you yet; that is how I know you are finished. Before he knocks the life out of you, here is your warning. You are never to look in the direction of these women again. And if you do, I will be sure to find you and end you." Edward turns his head in our direction at the mention of his name.

How I would like to tear Harold Grange apart by myself, but Edward deserves his chance to defend his soon-to-be wife. I cannot walk away just yet. I swing and punch Grange in his face before moving behind him. He is taller than I am, but thanks to my efforts, he is easily dominated. I kick his knees out from under him and enjoy his squeals of pain as he attempts to break his fall.

Edward turns back to Lily and Margo one more time, "Are you both all right?" They nod quickly. With that, Edward reaches Grange in two steps and strikes Harold in the face. But he does not stop after one—he continues without pause. When Grange starts to slump, I assist my friend by pulling his arms behind him, forcing him upright and making an easier target for Edward. Darcy struggles behind us to get up from the floor and moves toward Lily and Margo, standing slightly in front of them. Offering what protection he can.

Harold Grange's skin is swelling under Edward's fists, and colors of purple and red cover every inch of the man's face. Any rational man would apologize to end this beating, but not Harold Grange. No, he foolishly decides to make things worse. "Riley, she is to *be my* bride." It is difficult to tell with his puffy cheeks, but I believe the bastard is smiling.

Edward leans into his prey. "She was never yours, Grange—she has always been mine." Then he turns back to Margo, I can not see their exchange, but I watch as she practically swoons. I meet Lily's gaze and we share a moment of understanding. I suppose Edward has missed out on years of flirtation with Margo and he is now taking every chance he gets to make that up.

Edward turns back to Grange and says with a tone much calmer than his previous statement. "We were married this morning." Oh, my boy is quite a genius. A lie that will surely send Grange running for evidence, yet it will take days for him to prove they were not married this morning. And by that time, they will be married. Thankfully, I am behind Grange and he is unable to see the smirk I give Edward.

Harold Grange's body goes stiff beneath my grasp. "No, i-it can no-not be tr-true."

Edward stands tall with a devilish smirk on his face, addressing Harold Grange. "Yes, it is. And she and I are to become the lord and lady of two of the most prominent estates in this country. More power than you can dream of." Then he extends his hand to Margo, "Wife?"

Margo smiles at his endearment while she moves to him, taking his hand in hers. The two look just as they should, a couple of prominent standing. With Margo this close, I tighten my grip on Grange. He will not touch her again.

Edward longingly looks into Margo's eyes and inquires, "What would you like done with him?"

Margo turns back to Harold Grange with murder in her eyes while she takes a moment to deliberate. I certainly know what I would like done with him, but this is her battle. While she does not have the strength to physically deliver justice for him, giving her the final decision on his fate is honorable.

"Take him to the outskirts of town; leave him there," she hisses while glaring at Grange.

I will be happy to see that her wishes are carried out.

Edward kisses the back of her hand. "Right away, love."

Grange mumbles, "Strumpet." I pull him upright and Edward turns to deliver his worst blow yet. He goes limp in my hold and I let his body drop to the floor. If only Harold Grange could remain in this state of unconsciousness for the rest of his days. If only he had no more days...

Darcy moves toward us, but Edward rushes to Margo, pulling her up into his arms. Jealousy overwhelms me. I steal a glance at Lily while Darcy leans down to be sure Harold is knocked out. She gives me a woeful smile before approaching us.

"What will be the best way to...dispose of him?" Lily asks, looking between Darcy and me for an answer.

"If I give you a name and an address, can you be discreet about it?" I ask Darcy.

"You have my word, Mr. Berry." It seems we are on the same page on this matter.

"Yes then, I shall need to pen a letter to this person as to how we would like him to proceed with this man. He will be sure to pass along our threat to Mr. Grange when he wakes up." Darcy nods and dashes off, returning moments later with the writing materials. I find the nearest piece of furniture and scribe the letter while Lily and Darcy keep a watchful eye on Harold.

You owe me a favor, in fact, a few favors if I recall correctly.

I am calling in your debts. This man is a nuisance, as I am sure you would perceive yourself if you were able to recognize him.

Rest assured, the ladies he attempted to assault this time are safe and are in far better condition than I have left him.

I fold the note, but when Darcy offers wax for the seal, I decline. "It is best not to leave any indicators of who wrote it. I will need you to share my identity with Mr. Jenkins when you hand him the letter." With another piece of parchment, I scribe the address. "Here is where you will take him."

Darcy inspects the address, "I know where this is, I can have Mr. Grange delivered within the hour."

"Good." I turn to Edward, who has yet to release Margo. "Mr. Riley, if you can endure a moment away from your bride, we require your assistance in carrying this oaf to the carriage."

11

The four of us file into the carriage to begin our journey to Eton Cottage. I had not anticipated Albert and Edward accompanying us, but I am glad for their presence nonetheless. If he has any sense left in him, I do not anticipate Harold Grange will be seeking his vengeance...*at least not today.* The gentlemen were sure to leave him in an incapacitated and unrecognizable state.

We exchanged minimal polite conversation for the majority of the trip. Each of us, seemingly in our own minds pondering this afternoon's event personally. Every so often, I notice Albert and Edward rub their knuckles, each only had minimal swelling and did not seem to have suffered any broken bones, which is surprising for how hard Harold's head appears to be.

Margo's eyes look heavy from exhaustion while her brows furrow above them. She woke this morning with such joy to be marrying Edward today, but the pressure she endured only hours ago is still laying heavy on her. To think, at one time, the stress of marrying was just as upsetting to her. A slight smile grows on my face as I recall the day Margo's parents, Lord and Lady Eton, asked Margo and me to meet with them at their London townhome. While I was not a paid member of their household, they acknowledged that I was acting as a governess to Margo and would eventually be the one to present her to London society.

On that day, Margo was informed of the expectation her parents held for her to transform into a woman of society and leave behind the peace and careful life of a child of wealthy parents. To say she reacted poorly would be an understatement.

"Margaret, you are now of age. It is time to take your place in society," Lord Eton commands from behind his large wooden desk with a disinterested tone. Margo sits directly across from him, with her mother and I on either side of her.

"But Father, certainly we could wait another year. Or two, perhaps?" Margo begs, on the edge of her seat. They never had much of a relationship. I do not expect him to be affected by his daughter's pleas.

His gaze moves to his wife. She takes his directive and addresses their daughter, "Margaret, you should be happy to finally be able to enjoy all that being a woman has to offer. You no longer need to hole up in the country. You can reside in town, attend the extravagant balls, and socialize with the other young ladies of your age." When her daughter's expression does not shift to the elated look Lady Eton was hoping for, she continues, "Think of the beautiful ball gowns you will wear and the dancing you will be able to enjoy. Oh, you will have an endless supply of suitors begging for a spot on your dance card each night!"

Margo sits straight in her chair. I recognize her movements. Far too many times, I have been on the receiving end of her indignation. I brace for her next words, as they will surly cause waves I will have to settle before things get out of hand.

"And what if I refuse?"

Lord Eton's head snaps back at his daughter. "You will not refuse. It is your duty as the only heir to the Eton name!" Her father raises his voice. "That is why we agreed to allow your friend, the Dowager Lady Calderwood, to be your escort. So that you would be reasonable when this time came."

To balance her father's strong words, I interject, "You may enjoy this next chapter of your life, Miss Eton." Margo turns and scowls at my use of her formal name. She is fully aware this is a show for her parents, and she clearly does not enjoy it.

"And if I do not?" she asks me but then turns back to Lord Eton, "What is the minimum I must do to fulfill my duties as your heir?"

Pride fills my chest at the memory. Margo took on her very powerful father, Lord Eton, to negotiate an agreement that she could tolerate while appeasing her parents. She was very fair in agreeing to only remain at each ball for two hours if she danced with at least five gentlemen in that time. If only we could go back and tell past Margo what her future would hold...

That was not the only time Margo had very different expectations of her life. Weeks ago, when she visited with me just after Edward's arrival at Eton Cottage and shared she truly believed finding a love match was out of her reach. *Little did she know the man she would marry was staying at her home at that moment.* She shared her plans to marry for friendship instead. The friendship she was referring to was Albert.

At that point, we had not disclosed our connection with Margo. She certainly did not mean any malice but from her point of view. It was a sensible thought.

She leans in to lower her voice. "I'm not pronouncing that I will be taking a husband immediately, Lily. I just want to start taking the marriage market seriously. I still hope to marry for love, but I cannot fall in love with someone if I do not even speak to them outside of a brief conversation during a dance. The only man I have meaningful and pleasant conversations with outside of my family is Albert."

I startle, "Do you plan to pursue Albert?" I hear the crack in my voice. I knew I should have told her about Albert and me sooner. We have kept it a secret far too long. Could my closest friend have developed feelings for the man I am utterly in love with? I know he deserves a young, never-married bride, but I did not expect it to be Margo. I had hoped he would find some foreign woman and spend eternal bliss far from my view.

"I did not plan to court Albert. I believe if those were his intentions, he would have made them clear years ago. Yet, I was so clear at the time that I did not desire a husband.

Maybe that is why he did not declare his intentions. What do you think, Lily?"

I feel the sweat begin to gather on my forehead. Should I confess, tell her of the love that has existed between Albert and me for years? Or should I say nothing and support my friend in her need to find a suitable husband. A need I do not have. My future is set, and I will be comfortable until my dying day. She is just trying to achieve the same.

The conversation continues as I try to determine if she has romantic feelings for Albert, but thankfully, she admits she does not. This plan of hers is simply out of desperation, worried not only for herself but the Landons and the home they raised her in. She is right to worry as if she does marry the wrong man, he will have the title and the power to change her life drastically should he see fit. I will not allow such a fate to fall on her, nor will Albert. Let us just hope there is another option than him marrying her.

After that conversation, I asked Margo to wait in the library before dinner and that I would meet her shortly. I never did get the chance to meet here, as Albert returned home from his time with Edward earlier than expected and we were able to speak privately about Margo's intentions about marrying for friendship.

"My love, please do not let this concern you." My head is tucked under Albert's chin as he holds me close. "You assisted the Landons in raising that very strong young woman. It is a nod to your credit that she has given this serious thought. But that is all it is, darling. Just a thought."

I pull out of his arms to face him. "What if it turns into more of a thought?"

"I have a very good feeling that Margo needing to find a husband will not be a concern much longer. I have shared with you how Edward Riley feels about her...and how he has felt this way for some years now. It is only a matter of time before she catches up to him."

He stalks toward me, his hands exploring my waist, his body pressed close to mine, as he places gentle kisses on my neck. "Soon enough, they will realize what they are missing by keeping their distance from one another."

How could I have questioned this man? His affections fog my mind, but I must try to stay alert. We are still having a conversation. "How can you be so sure they will come to a romantic resolution?" I breathe out as his kisses on my neck become more intentional.

He pulls back just enough to look into my eyes, our lips only a breath away, "Would you like to make a wager, my love?"

And that was when we placed bets on how soon our two friends would realize their love for each other. I guessed sooner than him, but only because I wanted it to happen as soon as possible so I could put any worry of her marrying Albert out of my head.

Now, she is to be a wife with a husband who will never expect her to spend more time in London than she wants. Being so secluded from society may prove problematic when they eventually inherit their titles, but that is a conversation I can have with her another day.

When the carriage turns, Margo asks, "Are we not going to Eton Cottage?"

"You will be preparing for the ceremony with me, Margo," I share.

Albert adds, "And I shall be your escort back to Eton Cottage."

"And where will you be?" she questions Edward.

Edward dramatically leans toward her but does not quiet his voice. "I am about to wed the most demanding woman in all of England. There is still much I need to prepare if she is to agree to this marriage."

Albert and I laugh at his mocking. There is no question that Edward Riley knows exactly who he is about to marry. And with equal certainty, I can say he could not love any woman more than he loves Margo.

With a grand smile, Margo asks, "I suppose, but what about Mrs. Landon? I'm sure she would like to help me prepare for my wedding."

Edward answers, "This itinerary was her idea. She has delivered a selection of dresses to the Calderwood Estate for you. She sends her best and looks forward to seeing you shortly."

A short distance later, we arrive at Calderwood Estate. My excitement overtakes me—it is so good to be home. The gentlemen help us out of the carriage before Albert and I say our goodbyes to Edward and make our way inside to give the bride and groom some privacy before they must part.

Once inside, Claire is waiting to greet us in the larger foyer. She approaches but halts. "Mr. Berry, what is that on your coat?" She looks closer and a shocked expression grows on her face. "Is that blood?"

Albert looks down, surprised. "I suppose it is. Had a bit of a tussle this morning in London, but now we must prepare for this evening's wedding." He shrugs out of his coat and hangs it over his arm.

Claire remains silently stunned until I ask, "Could you have baths run for us, oh and Miss Eton too? She will be inside shortly."

Claire's attention finally returns, and she nods. "Yes, my lady. We have received the dresses from Eton Cottage and placed them in the room Miss Eton typically occupies during her visit."

I thank Claire as Margo enters behind us. With everything arranged, it is time to prepare for the long-anticipated wedding of Miss Margaret Eton. Oh, how the residents of London will be upset they have missed such an occasion.

12

Walking through the halls of Eton Cottage with the nuptials set to take place shortly, I feel a sense of belonging. I always do when I enter this home. It is as if all of the love shared here over the years lives within these walls. From almost infancy, Margo was raised here by Mr. and Mrs. Tom Landon, the estate caretakers. One could not find two better people than the Landon's. Having no children of their own, they raised Margo and loved her more than the Eton's ever cared to.

While nothing can compare to the time Lily and I spend together at her country estate, there is a part of me that longs to share a home similar to Eton Cottage with her. To remove all formality, staff, and concern for consequences of our connection. To fill with laughter, love, and warmth that is all our own.

But for now, I will be sustained with each moment I have in her presence, regardless of location. We parted just moments ago after delivering the soon-to-be Mrs. Riley to the Landons. The only parental figures she will have in attendance when her vows are exchanged. While it was not shocking, it was disappointing that Lord and Lady Eton could not be bothered to interrupt their social calendars for their only child's wedding.

To hell with them. Margo has all she needs here. In addition to the Landons, Lily and I are happy to bear witness to the union that will bring her a lifetime of happiness.

The cottage is quiet, minus the sound of laughter in the garden, where I find the guests who were able to drop everything to attend at a moment's notice. First, there is Mr. Richard Landon—the brother of Mr. Landon—his wife, Alice, and their two boys, Tom and Arthur, who are no longer boys, of course, but distinguished young men. Arthur, who is skilled with the violin, has agreed to play during the ceremony and is currently sharing his music sheets with the vicar.

I leave them to it and walk in the direction of the Riley family.

"Evening, Lord and Lady, Riley," I announce my presence, "And Miss Riley." I bow to all three and they return the gesture quickly, then begin their inquiry.

"Albert, how great to see you," Lord Riley beams. "What a surprise this announcement was, was it not?"

"Not to me, Papa," Evelyn chimes in with a prideful smile. "Isn't that right, Albert."

"Evelyn," her mother chides.

"Mother. We are not in society. We are at Margo's

home. No one here will suspect anything illicit between Albert and I if I use his first name." How brazen this young lady has gotten since her holiday with Margo Eton.

"It is not a good habit to form, Evelyn," Lady Riley pauses to speak to me, "My apologies, Albert."

Before I can assure her there is no need to apologize because I would not dare tell her that I agree with her daughter, Evelyn starts again. "And it is acceptable for you to refer to him by his first name?"

"Yes, because I knew him as a child, I am old enough to be his mother, and I am married, Evelyn." Lady Riley's exasperation is cracking through her typical facade. It reminds me of Margo's younger days when she would push back strongly on Lily's directives. Raising a strong-minded young lady does appear to have its struggles.

As if sent from the heavens, Lily appears and joins our conversation. "Good evening, Lord and Lady Riley." She bows and then addresses their daughter, "Miss Riley, always a pleasure to see you. Could you help me select the flowers for Margo's bouquet?"

"Of course." Before she leaves, she turns back to her mother and emphasizes, "*Lady Calderwood*."

Lady Riley rolls her eyes at her daughter and then turns the conversation back to the wedding. "Did you know about Edward's connection with Miss Eton prior to his announcement this morning, Albert?"

"Yes, Lady Riley. I must admit, I was aware of the

affections both parties held for each other prior to this morning.”

“They could not have held such intentions for long. I do not recall him mentioning Miss Eton other than when Evelyn started a friendship with her.” Lady Riley is still trying to understand how this sudden union came to be.

“And even then, Edward was adamantly against Evelyn befriending her,” Lord Riley adds.

“I can not speak to the precise sequence of their adoration, but as you know, they are both obstinate creatures.” Both of Edward’s parents nod in agreement. “I am, however, quite certain they were always on this path to each other. They just took a few wrong turns along the way.”

Lady Riley is watching me intently—her look is not filled with suspicion but trust.

“Well said, Albert,” Lord Riley says and raises his glass, “To the happy couple.”

It seems they were not able to gain much information from their son, who surprisingly is missing from their group. I shall have to seek him out. “Speaking of, I have wished the bride well, but I have yet to see the groom. Do you know where I can find him?”

“Here he is now.” His father points behind me. I turn and see Edward approaching from the southern side of the cottage, fixing the cuffs of his jacket.

“I shall see to our man. I look forward to conversing

more with you after the ceremony." I take my leave and make my way to my dear friend.

"Well, here we are, Mr. Riley." I pat Edward on the shoulder. "Your bride is with the Landons, Lily is off picking flowers with your sister and I thought to come check on you."

"Albert..." Edward pauses, "Thank you."

"It was my pleasure to serve as her escort on her wedding day."

"Yes, but also for your patience during my stay at Eton Cottage. I was battling myself for the entirety I was fighting with her. And you kept the course—you could have insisted I leave her be or demanded I face my feelings for her, even when I denied them so."

"It would have done no good to force you to admit your feelings for Margo earlier than when you were ready. I am almost certain that if I had, you would have fought them all the more and delayed this inevitable outcome."

He laughs lightly, "Yes, I suppose eight years is a long enough deferment." He turns, with a serious gaze, and asks, "How do you do it, my friend?"

"What is that? You mean deal with your bickering with Miss Eton—I barely survived."

"No, but I apologize about our bickering and I would like to say it will cease, but I do not think that we will ever be in absolute agreement."

"I believe you are correct." I wink at him.

Edward lowers his voice. "How do you manage to not be married to Lily?" I am taken aback by his question. We both look around quickly to confirm that no one is close enough to hear us before he continues. "The moment I was sure of Margo's affections, I needed to make her mine. There was no other option and no time to waste. I know you feel just as strongly about Lily. How do you endure being apart from her?"

I take a deep breath, "This is not the evening for that conversation, but I will give you a brief explanation. While the love we share is the most natural and pure thing I have ever experienced, the circumstances surrounding it are more complex than any problems I have faced in my life." Sadness covers his face, and I try to prevent it. "That being said, the time we do spend together is pure bliss, which allows us to endure the separation and secrecy."

"Yes, of course. I do hope we will see the day when you both can live that bliss without interruption," Edward shares, and I know he means that. He is a different man than before; he still has his gentlemanly qualities about him, but now he seems...whole.

"Thank you, Edward. Now, it is time for you to become a husband. Are there any further preparations we must make?"

We both turn to look at the altar he has made in the garden. Richard Landon is asking everyone to take their seats while his son, Arthur is at the front with the vicar. "How did you convince him to perform the ceremony outside of the church?" I ask. This sort of thing is unheard of.

"He, I mean, the church, has been compensated

handsomely. Also, it seems he has a soft spot for Margo. He was in favor of not forcing her to marry in London where shallow onlookers could attend."

The subtle but romantic notes of the violin fill the air and the vicar waves for Edward.

"It is time, Mr. Riley."

I take my place next to Lily. We share a smile before turning to admire the beautiful bride making her way to her groom. I do not know what it is like to have a child marry, but a tear comes to my eye, nonetheless. Margo is family, and to see her finally getting her happy ending gives me a joy I did not think possible.

Mr. and Mrs. Edward Riley stand before us. A collective sigh of relief is heard from each direction. After years of dealing with the fallout of their perceived unrequited love and simultaneous dislike toward each other, we can all hope the solidification of this union will put an end to all of that...or at least most of it.

With Margo at his side, Edward moves past the crowd of applause and escorts her directly inside. I offer Lily my arm and she takes it without reservation. While they are behaviors we would never exhibit in London, in this small group, an innocent gesture such as this could not be harmful. Yet, it is exhilarating nonetheless.

As we move from the garden and into Eton Cottage, I allow myself a moment of fantasy. Longingly, I look over at Lily. To say she is the love of my life is a vast understatement. She is the force behind my every thought, desire, and need. My mind wonders how I would feel if it had been us just pronounced husband and wife. How I wish to no longer limit our love to stolen moments in crowds or secret rendezvous.

"You look radiant tonight." A proclamation that should have waited until we are alone, but with so little time together, I am losing the ability to withhold these affirmations that consume my mind.

The setting sun behind us gives just enough light to see the flush of Lily's cheeks as she smiles. "Thank you, Albert," she whispers.

Stopping before we cross the entrance, I want to enjoy her in this light a little longer. As I stalk closer to her, she looks around to check for onlookers. I lower my voice, "You should be warned, I plan to dance with you this evening."

Shivers run through her body as she giggles. "Yes, there will be plenty of time for that later, Mr. Berry."

"No, you are mistaken, my lady. I plan to dance with you among our friends during this evening's celebration." I move my hand to her waist and pull her into me as my back hits the wall, just out of sight for everyone inside the house. "Later, when you mentioned we will have plenty of time, I plan to ravish you." Lifting her delicate scarf from her neck, I place soft kisses on her warm skin at first, yet as she molds to my body, my mouth becomes more forceful and desperate for the taste of her.

Just as Lily's panting in my ear threatens to undo me, she brings me back to the present. "The wedding party, Albert."

Carefully releasing her from my hold, I help her find her balance and fix her scarf to cover the evidence of our brief tryst. Then I assess myself, slightly disheveled, but I am not the center of attention; it should go unnoticed.

Looking around the interior of Eton Cottage, it is clear our absence was not noticed. Evelyn Riley is currently drawing almost everyone's attention while she reprimands her older brother. "How could you not wake me, Eddy?" she pleads with him.

"I cannot blame her, she was hoping for this conclusion for weeks now," I say to Lily quietly.

"She is a tough young lady. It's as if she is a mixture of both Margo and Edward," Lily says. "Perhaps she is the preview of what we could expect from any children they may have."

"How very frightening," I say with an exaggerated shiver. "I suppose we should enjoy the peace while we have it."

"Something tells me Evelyn will be keeping us all busy for quite some time," Lily says with a smile on her face. I was wondering if she would feel a sense of loss with Margo no longer needing her as a chaperone at the high-society balls in London. Yet, it is becoming evident she is developing affection for the younger Riley sibling.

As the newlyweds are visiting with Edward's family, Lily and I make our way over to the larger group of the Landon families. Mr. Landon's nephews, Tom and Arthur, are moving a pianoforte into the corner of the sitting room in their uncle's direction. Once in place,

Lily moves toward it, "Margo hated this instrument so much." She glides her hands over the top and shakes her head.

Mrs. Landon laughs, "Yes, so much so we had to move it somewhere she did not have to look at it. She swore she could not bear the sight of it."

"With all the musically inclined guests this evening, I thought perhaps it could get some use after all these years." Mr. Landon pats it.

"I would be happy to play for everyone, but I must rely on Arthur here to relieve me occasionally so that I may have some dances with the lovely Lady Calderwood."

"Of course, Albert. I did not expect you to play the entire evening, but you are so talented, I must confess I was hopeful you would gift us with a song or two," Mr. Landon says.

Young Arthur comes to my side. "I would be happy to play the first round of songs, sir. I do not have any plans of dancing and would be happy to provide music throughout the night."

"Thank you, my boy." I turn to Lily and extend my hand, "May I have this dance?"

Placing her hand into mine, answering cautiously, "You may."

We make our way to the center of the room with the other couples present, as Arthur Landon plays the violin, Evelyn Riley and Tom Landon are the only two left standing near Arthur.

I notice Lady Riley's gaze stopping at Lily and me

for just a moment longer than I would consider innocent, but she quickly returns her attention to her daughter. "Do you think she suspects something?" Lily whispers to me.

"If she does, let her. I promise you, I will behave myself until we take our leave so that Lady Riley has no reason to suspect we are anything more than the closest friends of the bride and groom."

"I rather enjoy it when you forget to behave yourself," she says before I turn her in my arms.

"Just because I know what is going on between you both now does not mean I want to know such details," Margo says as she and Edward move closer to us.

"Be gone with you, Mrs. Riley." I exaggerate her new name.

"If I have my way, you will not see her for days, Albert," Edward mocks.

"Well, you will need nourishments. We hope to see you both at breakfast tomorrow, at the Calderwood Estate, of course. I would like to offer a reprieve for the Landons as well," Lily offers with a directive tone.

"Yes, Lily! That would be great," Margo answers.

"Enough of this distraction. I must remove my wife before you make any other plans for her, Lady Calderwood. I have every intention of monopolizing her schedule for the time being." He smirks and twirls his bride in his arms to the other side of the room.

"I had a suspicion you would want to host when I spoke with Claire early this morning. It is a very generous gesture for you to offer room to all the guests here for the wedding," I tell her.

"Yes, well, as I did not have time to find them a gift, I think privacy for the next few days will be a gift enough." Lily wickedly grins at me.

I spin her once again before bringing her back to me. "Yes, all good for them, but I must make my intentions clear, love. This great number of guests will not deter me from joining you in your bed this evening."

Thankful for the loud conversations happening around us, combined with the violin playing, no one else seems to hear our words. "I would not dream of deterring you, good sir. In fact, I planned to reduce any barriers to your plan. I was able to put most of our guests in the west wing. The only people staying near us in the east wing are our dear friends, Mr. and Mrs. Tom Landon."

"Well, I suppose it would not be the first time they caught me sneaking into your room, so no harm there."

Lily laughs, "Our secret is safe with them."

The music ends and Arthur rises from his seat. Mrs. Landon encourages everyone to eat before we begin playing cards.

The night continues, the drinks flow, and everyone is enjoying the celebration of Margo and Edward. Yet, Lady Riley seems to be particularly watchful over her daughter this evening. I do not see why. Everyone in attendance is family to the bride and groom. It is not as if Harold Grange is at the table.

I would kill him if he were.

When Margo and Evelyn excuse themselves for a moment, Lady Riley turns her attention to Lily. The conversation is innocent and polite at first, but as it continues, it takes a particular turn. "Tell me, Lady Calderwood, have these impromptu nuptials made you consider remarrying?"

Lily is unable to contain her shock at Lady Riley's personal inquiry. "I am sorry, Lady Riley?" No, Lily, you heard the meddlesome woman correctly.

"I asked if you had plans to remarry? Find another husband rather than stay a widow for the rest of your life?"

Find another husband, as if she misplaced the last one.

It is clear this woman has drunk more than she can handle. I wish Margo was here—she would surely put an end to this. As a man, I cannot do the same without it being seen as a great offense.

Even though Lady Riley is being excessively offensive at this moment.

Lily, clearly searching for an acceptable answer finally says, "I have not thought much on the matter, Lady Riley. I am happy with my life as it is."

"You may be content now, but your days will surely become monotonous. Now that Miss Eton is married, and you have no children of your own, surely you will be at a loss to fill your days."

Lily is silent. I clench my fists under the table, forcing them into my legs to stop myself from standing to defend her. It is not a gentleman's place to intervene in ladies' conversations. I look to her husband, but Lord

Riley is deep in conversation with Mr. Landon and Edward.

Unfortunately, Lady Riley takes the opportunity to continue. "Please do not think me unkind, Lady Calderwood. I just worry for you."

Under the table, I move my legs against Lily's slightly so that no one would notice, but it is all I can do to comfort her at this time. Thankfully, Margo and Evelyn return and take Lady Riley's attention away from Lily. She rises from the table and turns to me, "I need some air." I move to join her, but she puts her hand on my shoulder and says, "Alone, please."

I nod and watch her leave the room. Waiting until I hear the grand door close, I sit back in my seat. I never thought too much of Edward's mother, but now I see she is not someone I would ever seek out for company. Of course, she does not know of Lily's insecurities, but surely a woman of her age knows better than to broach such topics at a dinner party.

Years ago, when Lily and I were no more than friends, I was staying at Eton Cottage but visiting her at the Calderwood Estate. I had yet to recognize my romantic feelings for her, but I did feel a connection, a need to support this woman who was left in such a way. Benedict's family had just left and she was distraught and in such a vulnerable state. Margo was too young to comfort her, but I was glad to be a shoulder for her to cry on.

Lily's hands on the mantle support her while she sobs. I stand an arm's length away, not certain if it is appropriate to go to her. "They do not mean to, but they can be exceptionally cruel." She cries as she turns and falls to the floor, with her arms wrapped around herself.

I lower to my knees beside her silently.

She continues, "They know I wanted a child, as did Benedict! We tried and tried, but that is all we could do. We could not create a miracle." Her body heaves with her breaths, "There is nothing I can do to change that now. Yet, they will never forgive me. Never..."

"I am sorry, Lily." It sounds shallow coming from my lips, but I am sorrier in this moment than I ever have been in my life, more than how sorry I am for the disappointment I am to my father, sorrier for never being able to give my mother the happy life she deserves. I am truly sorry that this kind individual is being punished for things that are out of her control.

"Albert, I swear..." She turns to look at me and I shatter at the sight of her. "If I could bring Benedict back, I would. I want him back—I miss him. And if it were my choice, we would have a house full of children." She cries into her hands. "They...his family...his mother and sister, they blame me for all of it."

I place my arm cautiously around her to console her, and she immediately turns into my touch. "Thank you for being here, Albert." She sniffles into my shoulder.

It was that night I knew for certain I would devote all of my days to consoling her if she needed it.

Since that night, I have cursed every woman of London society who reminds Lily she is a childless widow at each opportunity they get. Blaming her for his death and not having children is egregious.

"We have set up smaller tables in the parlor for a few games of cards. Please head in and find your seats. Do not forget your drinks," Mrs. Landon says, always the perfect hostess.

I move to join Lily outside, but she returns to find a seat at one of the card tables. Two seats remain vacant, I look around hoping to fill them before Lady Riley decides to sit with us. Evelyn is lagging behind everyone speaking with Arthur Landon. They are the perfect pair to play with us, I am certain neither would dare to say anything to upset Lily.

"Arthur, Evelyn! Come play with us." Evey's face lights up as she moves in our direction with a reserved Arthur trailing behind her.

After only a few rounds, I begin to notice Evelyn's affection for the young man. She laughs more than needed at his mediocre jokes. I catch Lily's eyes during one of Evelyn's laughing fits and she winks at me. *So, it is not just my imagination.*

"I win," Lily declares, and the rest of us applaud her. "With that, I think I need to refill my drink." She looks around the table. "It seems we could also use more to drink. Evey, would you grab Arthur's glass and we can run to the kitchen quickly?"

"Sure." Evelyn blushes as she takes the empty glass in front of Arthur. He thanks her but does not lift his gaze to meet hers. He did not act like this when I spoke with him earlier. I suspect this could be a mutual pining we have blooming in front of us.

Looking around the room, Edward is infatuated with his bride. Surely, as his best mate, it is my duty to find out this young man's thoughts about Evelyn. *Tough-talk to him a little.*

"So, Arthur...I see you have spent a great deal of your evening speaking with Miss Riley..."

14

Pride fills me as I watch Margo with her new husband. I could not have imagined such a match, but I truly believe there is no one better for her than Edward Riley. There is not a man in London who would deny their attraction to her beauty, but once they were acquainted with her demeanor, I doubt they would be happy in her company. Yet, Edward has indeed witnessed every side of Margo and loves her just the same for it.

A true love match requires each party to display their most honest self without worry of judgment or punishment. That is what I see when I look at the new Mr. and Mrs. Edward Riley.

"My dear," Albert calls as he joins me for a moment of privacy outside of the entrance to Eton Cottage. Just as Margo has shown herself completely to Edward, I have done the same for this astounding man. In these last years, I have been more honest with him than I have sometimes been with myself. And in those moments, bearing every part of my being to him, Albert is constant. Never shying away from my pain but embracing it as a part of me. And in providing that trusting comfort, our love bloomed.

His warm arm slides around my waist, "Darling, are you feeling well?"

"Better now." I lean into his touch.

He purrs, "I suggest we take our leave, get these guests settled, and move to the part of our evening I have been anticipating since I had you pressed against me in the garden."

"Yes, I do believe the celebrations are coming to an end." Reluctantly, I pull out of his embrace.

What would it be like to stay connected to him at all times?

Theo brings the carriage around to take the Riley's to Calderwood Estate for their stay this evening. We were disappointed that Theo did not feel comfortable joining in our celebration this evening due to his lord and lady attending. I made sure to ask Claire that he be included in the dinner she had planned for my staff.

My favorite purple shawl wrapped around my shoulders is not enough to ward off the cold night breeze. Once the Riley's carriage is out of sight, Albert places his jacket around my shoulders before wrapping his arms around me once more. Feeling safe with the remaining company, I lean in and place a kiss on his cheek.

A loud gasp comes from behind us. We both turn

quickly to find Evelyn Riley standing between Tom and Arthur. The young men look unfazed, but Evey's mouth is open, and her finger is pointed at Albert and me as she seems frozen in place. I had assumed she was in her family's carriage with her parents, but thinking back, I did not see her enter with them. I turn to Albert—he is already watching for my reaction. With a slight shrug, I silently communicate that there is not much reason to deny it now.

"Evelyn…" Albert turns to the young woman. With that, she launches toward us, throwing her arms around both of our necks and pulling us into a hug with her.

"Albert. Lily." Her words come out muffled as she squeezes between the two of us. I pull her in tight. Spending so much time worrying about the wrong people finding out about Albert and me and how negative their reactions will be, I never consider the positive reactions when we tell the right people.

She finally pulls away. "Oh, Albert. I am so happy for you, and for Lily." The joy on her face is contagious and so moving. Moisture begins to accumulate in my eyes. I turn away to brush away the quick tear falling on my cheek.

"Thank you, Evey." That is the most I can say.

Albert continues, "Evelyn, dear. We appreciate your kindness, but we must ask you to keep what you now know to yourself." Her face falls as the reality of our situation hits her. "Like many other things that are commonplace at Eton Cottage, we do not share the knowledge of our love with those outside of this small circle."

"Of course, Albert." Evelyn turns to Tom and Arthur standing behind her. Albert and I look back. While I do not believe we ever spoke about this directly with them, we have assumed that their uncle, Mr. Thomas Landon, had.

"Your secret is safe with us," Tom calls as he holds his hand over his heart.

"Our best regards to you both," Arthur follows up with a wave.

"We appreciate your confidentiality." Albert places his hand in mine when the young people resume their conversation as it was before their discovery.

The newlyweds join us outside. Albert and I separate as he moves to speak with Edward, and Margo comes up to my side. So distracted in her bliss, she must not have realized her guests already started taking their leave. "Everyone will be making their way to Calderwood Estate. I have offered to host them for the next few days."

"That is not necessary. I do not want to impose. I would be happy to have everyone here," she insists.

While attempting to hide my grin, I lower my voice, "Trust me, Margo. You will be much happier to have Eton Cottage to yourselves as newlyweds." With a slight blush, Margo watches as Mr. and Mrs. Landon are ushered into the next carriage. They do not have nights away from Eton Cottage often, and throughout the night, they have thanked me more than they need to about the offer to stay at my home.

The second carriage arrives for Mr. Landon's brother and his family. Tom moves in the direction of the carriage, then continues on and disappears from view for a moment before returning with the reins to one of Margo's horses. When he sees the surprise on our faces, he explains, "I enjoy late-night rides and will have the carriage to guide my journey. Good night." I notice his brother is not joining them but do not bring attention to it—*yet*.

After the carriage and its escort are out of sight, Evelyn and Arthur make their presence known to Margo and Edward. Albert and I smile to ourselves. Margo notices and I can see the understanding in her face. When she looks back at Evelyn, the young lady blushes and turns away from us.

After our final goodbyes for the evening and my reminder to Margo that she is welcome at breakfast in the morning, Albert moves to help everyone into the carriage. He holds his hand out for Evelyn first. She thanks him and sits against the far window on the left side. He turns to help me and whispers, "Sit next to her." I nod, fully aware of his masterful plan.

I am surprised when he directs Arthur in next, which allows him the seat across from Evelyn. Albert has always been protective of Margo, but given she never took any interest in young men, they never got too close to her. This is a different side of Albert than I am familiar with, but it does not surprise me either.

The short journey is spent in silence. While Evelyn steals many glimpses of Arthur Landon, he keeps his gaze firmly out the window. Albert is watching the two with an intensity that he may need to jump up and separate them at a moment's notice. I quite enjoy being a spectator myself.

Upon our arrival, Claire meets us at the front entrance. "Welcome home, Lady Calderwood. Nice to see you, Mr. Berry."

"Thank you, Claire. Let me introduce you to Arthur Landon, Mr. Thomas Landon's youngest nephew and Evelyn Riley, the younger sister of Margo's husband, Mr. Riley."

"Welcome. Both of your parents have arrived and have been seen to their rooms," Claire says.

"Did you offer them the opportunity for a nightcap?" I ask.

"Yes, my lady, they all declined. I believe they are all tired from the excitement of the evening. I did inform them of the breakfast tomorrow and the plans you have made for the day."

"Oh yes, thank you." I turn to my final guests. "I shall ask you both, as you seem to be the only ones not yet turned in for the night. Would you two like to sit before retiring?"

They both shake their heads. Albert tilts his head at their matching response.

"Would you like me to show you both to your rooms? Your luggage arrived earlier and is already waiting for you there," Claire offers. I must speak with her later about our suspicions of these two.

Before either can answer, Albert interjects. "I would be happy to show the young Mr. Landon to his room, Claire. Has his brother retired yet?"

Evelyn's cheeks begin to turn a light shade of pink and Arthur's eyes look anywhere but in her direction.

"No, I believe he is still in the stables, speaking with Edmund, our stable hand." Claire seems to be catching on.

"Splendid. Arthur, you and I can fetch your brother, and then I will be happy to show you to your room." He turns in the direction of the stable and, without turning back, yells, "Goodnight, Evelyn."

Arthur risks a look her way but does not dare say anything. He only offers her a shy smile before turning tail after Albert.

"Right this way, Miss Riley." Claire holds an arm in the direction of the west side of the estate.

Evelyn looks back at me, "Good night, Lily," she says before running to catch up to Claire. I hear her say, "You can call me Evey if you do not mind me calling you Claire?"

I hear Claire's soft voice agree before they both fade with the distance.

Standing in the foyer of this great estate, I wonder what my guests thought of it as they entered. It is so rare for me to have so many visitors here at one time. Within society, it is in poor form to not arrive first and welcome them individually. I doubt either of the Landon families would feel affronted by being greeted by Claire, but perhaps Lord and Lady Riley were. Though, no more affronted than they were to share their evening with people below their class in society. I was sure they expected Lord and Lady Eton to join the party. Which shows how little they know the Etons.

I suppose the last time I had a guest that was not the Landons or Margo was Albert. I remember when he visited for the first time after Benedict passed away. It was years after he met Margo at her first ball. I worried it would feel odd to have another man visit me, yet the moment he crossed the threshold, I felt nothing but comfort. All reservations about having another man in my home evaporated in his presence. This may not be his home, but when he is here, it feels whole again—I feel whole again. I remember wanting to run into his arms upon his arrival, but I kept my composure and welcomed him warmly with my words only, fidgeting my hands over my dress to keep them from acting out of line. I suppose even then, when I thought of him as nothing more than a good friend, I felt safe with him, content in his company.

As I am standing, still in my shawl, Theo enters the foyer. "Oh, Lady Calderwood. Mr. Berry asked me to relay this note to you if you were still downstairs."

I take the small note and thank him. "Are you finding your stay here comfortable, Theo?"

"Yes, my lady. Everyone has been very welcoming. Thank you for your generosity."

"No trouble at all, Theo. Goodnight."

He bows and turns back in the direction he came. I open the note.

Please do not wait for me to return.

I shall be seeing the boys to their room once I am sure a particular young lady will be well settled in her room.

Get some rest.

I shall do the same and then check in on you later.

I clutch the note close so as not to drop it and make my way in the direction of the East wing.

~

I WAKE what must be hours later, my body stiff from sleep. I sit up to stretch when I realize Albert has not come to my room. I am slightly disappointed, but I must admit, I was quite exhausted myself and fell asleep the moment my cheek touched the pillows. Hopefully, he is doing the same. He had even less sleep than I did the night before.

Pushing the many blankets off my legs, I feel overheated and decide to venture to the kitchen for a drink, then I can check on Albert. Grabbing my robe, I quietly move from my room and walk through the silent halls.

That is until I am halted by a loud "Ouch!" and the sight of candlelight. No longer bothering with candles during my late-night strolls, having learned these halls many years ago, I am confident in my ability to maneuver them without any light. Though, it seems one of my guests is struggling even with the assistance of candlelight.

Upon closer inspection, I can identify the injured party. "Evelyn, did you hurt yourself?"

She squints in the direction of my voice and holds her candle out. "Lily?"

"Yes, dear."

"Oh, I am fine. Just lost."

"Can I help you find your way?" I am glad it is me who stumbled across her. I have an idea why she may be out of bed, but I certainly hope I am mistaken. It is one thing to flirt a little and have private conversations as a young girl. It is another if she is sneaking around to a man's bedroom in the middle of the night. Sure, that is precisely what I was going to do after I had grabbed a drink, but my situation is *vastly* different from Evelyn Riley's.

"Oh…" She stumbles to think of an answer. It seems I was right in my assumption.

"I am heading to the kitchen for a drink. Would you care to join me?" I ask.

"Uh…"

"Come, Evelyn." Only hours after Margo has become her own woman, I find myself with another obstinate young lady who needs a tough influence. I hold her gaze until she nods. I turn without another word, watching that the candlelight stays close behind me as I make my way to the kitchen.

I place a cup of hot tea in front of Evelyn and slip into the seat next to her.

"Evelyn, I look forward to our friendship expanding. I feel I must start this discussion by reminding you that I had a hand in raising Margaret Eton. You may think you can get things past me, but I assure you. I am ten steps ahead of you."

Her gaze locks on mine and she fidgets her fingers in her lap.

"Why were you out of your room this evening?"

"I… Well…"

I hold up my hand. "Anything you share with me will not be shared with your parents. At least not from my mouth."

She purses her lips. "I could not sleep." She looks

from me to her teacup. "I was walking around to see if anyone else had trouble sleeping."

"Anyone in particular?"

She shakes her head.

"Evelyn."

She hangs her head, focusing strongly on her tea as she admits, "Arthur Landon."

Just as I thought. "And were you successful?"

"No. I knew it was foolish when I went looking for him. He told me not to."

So it was Evey who was leading this perusal, not Arthur. "He is a sensible young man." She slouches in her seat at my words. "That is not to say he would be foolish to pursue you. I just mean this is not the way to go about it." That grabs her attention.

I continue, "As your friend, with many years of experience you have yet to gain, please take my counsel. I can not tell you who to love. I can not tell you how to love. But I will tell you there is a right way and many, many wrong ways to go about achieving that love."

Evelyn listens intently to my words and I notice water pooling in her eyes.

"Start from the beginning, Evey. We have all night."

And she does just that...

15

The sunlight casting through the window slowly wakes me from my heavy slumber. My muscles are stiff from the lack of movement in the night. It feels as though I have slept for days. Disappointment flows when the realization hits that I did not wake up to visit Lily in the evening. *All those sultry promises I made her—now broken. I will just have to double my efforts this evening.*

Saucy images of Lily, writhing beneath my touch, turn my thoughts into a more optimistic mood. Is it early enough that I can sneak to her room without being noticed or her being missed by her guests? We could keep our voices down—both claim to have overslept...

A knock startles me out of my daydream, "Mr. Berry, it is Claire. Are you awake?"

"Ye—" The word comes out brisk, I clear my throat. "Yes, Claire."

"Lady Calderwood is downstairs waiting to receive any guests who wake before breakfast is served. You are welcome to join her when you are ready."

"Thank you, Claire." I hear her footsteps grow softer as she leaves her place on the opposite side of my door.

I take my time dressing for the day, deciding it is better to share Lily with her guests. It is so out of the ordinary for her to have such a large number of visitors in her home. She should enjoy the company.

Until they take their leave and I have her all to myself again.

My feet glide down the steps of the grand staircase. Evidence of my plentiful time spent here. I hear the hum of discussions coming from the dining room. A booming laugh carries over the other voices that belongs to none other than Mr. Landon. Upon entering the room, I ask, "Had I known this breakfast would be so entertaining, I would have rushed."

The two Landon families sit at one end of the table, with the Riley family seated at the opposite and four seats in the middle, one already occupied by Lily. My heart jumps a little when she waves me over to sit beside her. Had she not, I would have selected the seat across from her. I give her a puzzled look as I pull out my chair. She replies with a sly grin, "The newlyweds will surely want to sit together."

"Yes, of course."

She turns to me and lowers her voice to a whisper, "Your presence was missed last night." How brazen of her to make such a comment with so much company surrounding us.

My eyes hold her gaze for a brief moment. "I will be sure to repent this evening."

A blush covers her cheek as she turns back to her guests. The chatter continues as we wait for the guests of honor. With the seating selection, I assumed the conversations would be equally sequestered, yet I was wrong. Lord Riley dropped all social manners and is talking above the other conversations while sharing jokes with the Landons.

The two empty chairs between them do not stop Evelyn from talking with Arthur, and his brother adds to the discussion when possible. I look over at Lily and notice a grand smile on her face. She is not engaged in any particular conversation, but watching with glee at the scene happening at her table.

Seeing the joy this brings her makes me want to find a way to make it happen more often. It is possible with Edward and Margo's union we could entertain this group on a regular basis. Yet, if hosting becomes taxing on Lily's hospitality, I may need to find an alternative. I could not host at my family's estate—my mother would be ecstatic, but my father would ruin the evening for sure. Perhaps I can rent a home in the country, hire a trusted staff, and use it only to host parties like this.

Margo comes running into the room with her husband's hand tightly in hers, pulling him along. "Our greatest apologies, I know we are late."

As Edward pulls the chair next to Evelyn out for his

wife, "I am not sorry we are late. I am quite glad for it." Margo blushes while just about everyone else laughs, myself included.

"Edward!" It would seem Lady Riley did not find his frankness particularly amusing. She looks to Lord Riley for support, but he chuckles and shakes his head.

"Let us change the discussion. We received notification of our wedding gift from Lord and Lady Eton this morning. They have transferred the deed to Eton Cottage to Edward and I." Margo talks directly to the Landons, tears in her eyes. They are mirroring her happiness. Surely, once she decided to marry Edward, they all knew their futures were secured, but this settles any last concern.

"Will it be Riley Cottage now?" Evelyn asks.

The newlyweds turn to each other, "We had not discussed a name change," Margo confesses.

"I do not see any need to change the name. With so much history at Eton Cottage, I think it should keep the name," Edward confirms.

Margo beams at her husband. "Eton Cottage, it will forever be then."

The smell of fresh fruit and toasted bread fills the air as the servers deliver our breakfast to the table. Lily certainly outdid herself with this selection. Everything is available, from fruit to eggs and meats, with bread and pastries of all kinds.

As we are finishing our meal, Lady Riley thanks Lily for hosting her family and tells Edward that they will be leaving shortly.

"So soon?" Edward asks.

"And what do you need us for, son. You are on your honeymoon, after all," his father answers. "Not that I would mind visiting with these wonderful people longer, but your mother insists it is time for us to return to London."

"Another time then, Lord Riley," Mr. Thomas Landon addresses him directly.

"Yes, I am sure with this union, we will be seeing each other often throughout the year," Lord Riley assures him.

"Well, I suppose we should go see to our bags." Lady Riley begins to stand.

"Mother, can't we stay at least one more night?" Evelyn begs.

"No, Evelyn. You will understand one day why your brother and his bride need privacy," Lady Riley denies her daughter.

Margo opens her mouth, but Edward clears his throat and leans in to whisper in his wife's ear. She blushes and then turns with a disappointed look at her young friend. I cannot blame Edward. I am thinking just the same when Lily begins to speak. Although, unlike my friend, I cannot whisper promises of scandalous nights that will be so wild it would be inappropriate for Evelyn to share a roof with us.

"Miss Riley, it was a pleasure to have you and I want you to know you are always welcome to holiday here at the Calderwood Estate. You name the date and I shall arrange it," Lily reassures the young lady while squeezing my thigh under the table. My body responds to her sultry touch as I attempt to keep my face to appear unaffected. It would seem her mind is aligned with mine. I repress a groan that tries so desperately to escape my mouth.

Evelyn Riley reluctantly rises from the table to follow her parents from the room. As they pass through the grand doors in front of her, she steals a glance back to whom I can only assume is Arthur Landon. I follow her longing look to his face. It is blank of all expressions. Not a cruel, uncaring look, just completely schooled. As if he is too afraid to return her look or, worse, show sadness. Perhaps this infatuation is not as two-sided as I imagine.

The door closes behind her and Mr. Landon announces that he and his wife will be leaving later today. They have been asked to stay with his brother, Mr. Richard Landon's family, in town for a fortnight.

"Please do not feel pushed out of your own home, Mr. Landon," Margo pleads.

"Not at all, my dear. You enjoy your honeymoon. We will spend time in town and then see you when we return," he reassures her.

"When you return, we can discuss permanent residences for Margo and myself," Edward says. "With everything happening so quickly, we have not had a chance to discuss how to move forward while we await the two estates."

"Of course, and you have plenty of time to do so," Mrs. Landon says.

As my friends discuss their future and the changes that will come from their union, I wrongly let my mind wander to an idea I try to avoid. It does no good to dwell on a dream that may never come. Yet, it lives on, as it has every day since that night Lily confessed her feelings for me were more than friendship.

The small area of the library is only lit by the fire burning in front of us. I watch it in silence as every piece of my soul aches to touch her. But I cannot. When my friendship evolved into longing and love for Lily Calderwood, I do not know, but if I could go back and stop it, I would. This admiration does her no good and clouds my judgment.

I am beginning to slip up more and more around her, acting in ways that go beyond the general niceties of friends. Brushing our arms as I pass by her, leaning in too close while showing her a particular phrase in my book, and conceding to her request, we call each other by our given names.

Now, I sit beside her on the floor in front of our chairs with maps stretched out in front of us.

"Where will you travel to next, Albert?" In truth, I have no desire to travel any longer. I know in my heart that I have found what I spent so many years looking for. Yet, I must travel to reset my mind. To clear it of these impossible wishes for Lily and me.

"I have not decided yet. Do you have any suggestions, Lily?" Her name leaves my lips, and I wonder if she can hear the desperation in my voice.

When she turns her face to mine, something has changed. My breathing stops, her eyes move from my eyes to my lips, lingering for a moment, then slowly back up to meet my gaze as her body leans in closer. We are a breath away, and she inhales, "What would you say if I suggested you stay, to not travel..."

My restraint teeters, holding on by a thread, I only have enough strength to stop myself from kissing her, so my words leave my lips unfiltered. "I would say I will do anything you ever ask of me. If you say to stay, I will never leave your side until you wish for it."

Her breath catches, "Albert..." Did she not expect my answer? Does she truly not notice that I have fallen for her?

"Tell me what you need, Lily. I will see to your every desire until my last breath." These words should have never been spoken, but I have lost the ability to stop them. Let them come, let her hear them, but I can do no more. If we are to kiss, it must be her wish. I can live with the consequences of declaring an unrequited love, but I know I will never be able to heal from her rejection if I kiss her.

"I want something I know I cannot have. I want so much more for you. You deserve better, more than I can ever give you." Could it be? Is she confessing she feels as I do? I must know.

"Lily, tell me... I beg of you, tell me you want this too..."

"I did not recognize it at first. I thought it was just our friendship, but the more it grew, the less I could deny it."

"Lily... Please," I plead.

"You, Albert." I search her eyes for the truth I am struggling to believe. "I am in love with you, Albe—"

All that restraint and good intention to allow her to be the one to initiate our kiss dissipated the moment she said she loved me. Of course, she prefaced it with the declaration that this is not something either of us can truly have. I will ponder that meaning and its consequences later. Now, I will give my love every moment of my attention.

The battle between wanting to consume her completely and ravish her the way I have dreamt of so many times wages against the sense in my mind telling me to be gentle. Our lips make contact, at first softly, before growing rough with her urgency. I follow Lilly's lead, bringing my hands to hold her neck, softly stroking the skin of her cheek as our kiss deepens. Her tongue breaks through my lips. I welcome the intrusion as I am consumed by her taste. Sweet, just as everything else about her. The warmth of her palms reaches my chest before they travel over my body, moving to my back, giving her the anchor she needs to pull me closer to her. Our bodies flush against one another, our rushed breaths syncing together.

She pulls out of the kiss, but not far, touching her forehead to mine. I search her eyes for any signs of regret but see no signs of it.

"Albert..." she breathes.

"Lily..." I answer.

Since then, I have promised to face what Lily and I have with discretion, letting her set the rules. I know the dream of marrying her may never come true, but I cannot seem to shake the desire that lives in my mind.

I find her hand under the table and squeeze it gently. I do not need to be married to her. I only need to be with her in any way I can.

16

The fire crackles next to me and the smell of burning wood is accented by something sweeter that I just cannot place. I sit in the library with my hands covering my eyes, just as Albert instructed. While I wait for him, I reminisce about the past few days. After seeing my closest friend get married and hosting the newlyweds' families in my home, even if for too brief, I have spent the time since enjoying Albert's company all to myself.

The evening after the wedding, we gave the staff time off as thanks for the hard work they put in for the last-minute ceremony. Which left Albert and I to have the entirety of the Calderwood Estate to ourselves. Even after returning, the staff are so discreet we barely know they are here.

A lesson I have learned time and time again is you cannot have it all. Yet, in these days with Albert, he is all I could ever ask for. If only our love was something that would not disappoint everyone around us. *No, there will be plenty of time to dwell once we are separated.* While Albert is with me, I need to push those thoughts away and give him my every attention.

"Are you ready yet?" I ask.

"Not yet, my love," Albert whispers.

"How much longer will I need to cover my eyes?" It feels as though I have been sitting like this for ages.

"Just a moment more, darling." In truth, I will wait as long as he asks as the anticipation bubbles from within. This is not the first time Albert has prepared a romantic surprise for me. He is such a thoughtful man. "Ready, my dear." He runs his hands up my arms until they circle my wrists. His strength pulls me up to him as I open my eyes.

Forgetting his plans, I lose myself in his rich brown eyes, so full of his adoration for me. I wrap my arms around his neck and close the distance between us. Albert does not hesitate as he claims my mouth. His lips are gentle, but his force is not. My body melts in his arms yet stays in place as his hold tightens around my waist.

He steps away and I sigh with disappointment. A short laugh leaves his lips. "All in good time, love." Once at my side, he holds his hand out for mine. "Let us move our evening out to the terrace."

The moon is not very bright tonight, but Albert accounted for that. He placed small candles around the entirety of the terrace, up the stairs, and along the railings. In the center is a cluster of blankets with an overflowing basket.

"An evening picnic for you, my beautiful." Pride feels his voice, as it should.

"This is perfect, Albert. Thank you!"

After we are settled beside one another, Albert opens the basket. He begins placing the fruits and cheeses out for us. Next, his large hand grabs the wine bottle, tipping it to fill each of our glasses. Our fingers brush and my body warms with excitement as he hands me the glass. He raises his glass, "To you, Lily." The toast we share is a secret tradition to all but us. Just like most things with Albert, they are all my secrets to treasure.

"To you, Albert," I reply.

"To us," we say together.

What an impeccable evening Albert has given us, but as it often happens, thoughts of parting with him start to rise again. It is selfish of me to have these moments with Albert, moments he should be sharing with a young bride.

"What is bothering you, my dear?"

"Nothing at all. I am perfectly joyful at this moment," I lie. "When did you have time to plan all of this?"

"Lily..." My deflection does not work—I should have known. I have not been able to keep much from Albert lately. We are getting so close, he knows when I am hiding things from him. "Tell me, love, what troubles you so that I can vanquish it this instant."

He likely already knows what is bothering me. We have had this discussion so many times, but he never sees reason. And I never have the strength to push him toward that reason. That does not mean it bothers me any less.

"Do you not want what Edward has found, a marriage with a nice young woman, just like your parents are expecting of you? What society is expecting of you."

Albert answers, "To say I want what Edward has is a bit of a stretch. That marriage will be unlike any other I have witnessed and I am not sure it is something I would covet."

"You know my meaning..."

"Of course I do. As I have told you many times, I would be elated to be your husband. You need only ask."

He knows it is not as simple as he makes it sound. For we both have obstacles that will stand in our way if we try to pursue this. I attempt to voice these concerns, but he speaks before I can start.

"Lily, there is no other woman walking this Earth that I can love as I love you. I am sure others will think they know better and that we should not be together, but I can say with absolute certainty that they are wrong. And even underneath your rebuttals, you are certain of it too."

"Albert..."

"I will never be happy with another woman, just as I will never be happy if we are parted. What we have now, while inconsistent, is a gift I could never have imagined for myself. If you so choose one day to take me as your husband, I will make it so. But know, too, if you shall never decide to take me as your husband, I will love you no less. Each and every moment with you is paradise, marriage or not."

Not strong enough to question him while I am wrapped in his embrace, I stand. "And what of your father?"

He stands to meet me. "Damn him. He matters not, for I do not have any interest in his opinions for my wife."

"Albert, are you sure you are not just spending your time with me as a distraction for the life you will inevitably lead when you assume your father's duties? You need an heir." I do not want it to be true, I cannot bear the thought of Albert no longer being with me, but I must face the truth in front of us.

"I could not care less if I have an heir." He leans over placing his hands on his legs, as if he is preparing to pounce. Lust fills his eyes as he stalks toward me, pausing only to shed his jacket. "I will give you anything you desire, my love. If you still question that, I must do my best to prove my devotion."

Setting my wine down first, I reclaim my seat, sitting tall at his advances. The combination of the candles and moonlight reflects off his eyes as if I can see the fire within him. He stops with his lips a breath from mine, I sense it—he's going to tease me. Not this time. I lean forward to connect us, I feel his smile on his lips as he wraps one arm around my waist but continues moving on me. With his hand on my back for support, he forces me to lean backward until I am laid out beneath him.

"Exquisite," Albert murmurs. His tongue presses against my neck as it makes its way to just under my ear. One of his hands works to push my skirt up to free my legs for him.

I wrap my arms around his neck, groaning as his tongue slips between my lips. While somehow keeping most of his weight off me, he presses his hips into mine. His masterful fingers begin to graze up and down my legs to my core, slowly at first but growing faster as my body rises to meet his touch.

"Albert." Without being able to remember any words, I call to him between our passionate kisses.

"Yes? My love."

I feel his hand move between us, his knuckles graze my most sensitive space while he works to untie his britches.

"Hurry." The anticipation makes me demanding.

"I shall never rush such intimate times that I am honored to share with you, Lily." I feel his bareness touch my waiting body. I squirm beneath him. If he does not claim me soon, I shall take matters into my own hands.

Thankfully, it does not come to that as in the next breath, he plunges himself inside me. A deep groan escapes his lips as I relax under his efforts. Switching between rough thrusts and careful pulses in and out of me.

This is bliss.

My body tingles from head to toe.

My mind is blank in an amorous fog.

My heart beats rapidly, feeling the full extent of his love.

All altruistic thoughts burn away as my greed for this good man overtakes all else. Since the first touch of his lips all those years ago, I know deep down I would never truly be able to walk away from him. Our movements are erratic and our moans grow louder. As we approach our ecstasy, I make a wish to the stars above us that I will get to selfishly keep this man for the rest of our lives. To be able to experience this toe-curling pleasure, only Albert Berry can give me for the rest of time.

Sleep comes and goes, only interrupted for brief moments, to remind me that Lily lies nestled next to me and this reality is far better than any dream I could have. I kiss her forehead and fall back into a peaceful slumber.

A faint thumping noise pulls me from my sleep—perhaps a bird is at the window. I pull Lily's back closer to my chest, nuzzling into her neck and attempting to ignore it. But it grows louder and louder.

"Is someone knocking?" Lily asks, her voice heavy from sleep. The knocking turns to banging. Lily sits up with alarm.

As we both slowly rise from the bed, still unsure of the source of that sound, Claire's voice comes through the door. "Lady Calderwood!" She is partially yelling Lily's name, then lowers her voice to call for me, "Mr. Berry!"

I rush to the door and open it. "What is the matter?"

She looks between us and I recognize that look. "Lady Augusta Calderwood has just arrived. I ran here as soon as I saw her carriage approaching. I believe her daughters may be with her. There was far too much luggage on top of the carriage for just her." Lily rises from the bed. Thankfully, we are dressed in our night clothes. I begin changing into my dress clothes immediately. Claire faces away briefly to provide me a moment of privacy.

Lily does not speak but nods her head in understanding.

Turning to me, Claire warns. "We will welcome them with breakfast in the main sitting room. You should be clear to leave through your usual route. If anything changes, we will notify you immediately." She pauses, "I am always sorry to deliver such news."

"Thank you, Claire."

Once the door is closed, I turn to Lily. Tears are welling up in her eyes. She runs into my arms, "Albert, I thought we would have more time... I am sorry."

"You have no reason to apologize."

"That does not make me any less sorry to see you go."

"I hate to part from you." With her engulfed in my embrace, I kiss her one last time before I must go. Her lips press into mine, and I can only hope they leave a deep enough impression to hold me over until I can see her again.

We break apart too quickly, but know we must

make haste. She has guests awaiting her company and I must take my leave before any of Lady Augusta's staff can notice me. I steal one more glance at Lily before I close the door softly behind me.

It is not uncommon for widows to take lovers, Lily is not doing anything wrong by society's standards, but I understand her wish to keep this from Benedict's family and how they may take it personally, especially since we are more than just lovers.

Our relationship can be seen as me taking Benedict's place, but that is not how I ever want this to be perceived. I do not wish to erase his memory. Even if Lily and I were to be married, I would never want him forgotten. It was thanks to him that I met Lily.

This is not the first time we have been taken by surprise at the unexpected arrival of Lady Augusta Calderwood. Thankfully, over the years, it has only happened a handful of times, but that first time was quite a shock.

Lily and I lay under the covers, naked, limbs tangled together, even in sleep, unable to keep our bodies apart. "Lily, Albert!" Claire shouts as she stands at the foot of the bed and we both startle and sit up. I notice the sheet slipping down Lily's chest but catch it before she exposes herself to Claire. It is bad enough Claire has to see us in this state. "My apologies, I tried knocking at first, but you did not answer and then I called you, but you continued to sleep. I would not have disturbed you had it not been such an urgent matter."

I can only assume the exhaustion from the previous

night's vigorous activities settled us into such a deep sleep that we did not notice Claire's knocking.

"What is the matter, Claire?" No trace of anger in Lily's tone, only concern.

"It is Lady Augusta Calderwood. Her carriage has just arrived."

"She's here?" Lily jumps out of bed, taking the sheet with her. I quickly grab a pillow to cover myself from Claire.

"Yes, my lady. We have her settled in the sitting room. I informed her you were not feeling well last night and that I would check to see if your condition has improved. I did tell her to anticipate some delay in your company."

Lily freezes at Claire's words. We knew she approved of our connection and she herself informed us that the rest of the staff at the Calderwood Estate felt the same, but ultimately, they are employed by the Calderwood family. It is at great risk that Claire and the others have decided to deceive the matriarch of this family to keep our secret safe. Lily moves to Claire and hugs her tightly, "Thank you, Claire."

Claire reciprocates, "Of course."

Relaying my appreciation to Claire must wait until I can reach my clothes. She releases Lily and delivers her instructions. "You must dress, but nothing too formal. Remember, you are sick." Lily nods. "And you, Mr. Berry, I shall wait in the hall for you to dress and then I will escort you. I have a plan to get you out unnoticed. However, I do not believe we will be able to have your horse ready without the notice of Lady Augusta's staff."

"I can go to Eton Cottage and borrow one of theirs if needed."

"Excellent plan, sir."

She checks Lily once more and then moves to wait outside the bedroom door.

"I am sorry, Albert." Lily runs to me. "I will write to you after speaking with Lady Augusta. If I can convince her I may be contagious, she may leave directly. If not, I will inform you how long she plans to stay."

Claire knocks at the door to rush us along. I almost trip as I rush to dress. Once my boots are on, I quickly kiss Lily. "I look forward to your letter." Then open the door to meet Claire and make my discreet exit.

It seems I still have some luck left. After descending the staircase located in the back corner of the East Wing, mostly used by the staff, I check to be sure no one is around. I leave the Calderwood Estate through the staff quarters at the back of the home and begin my walk toward Eton Cottage. The Landons are more than used to my sudden appearances and the reason for them. Yet, the Landons will not have returned to Eton Cottage yet, still visiting with their family in town. Now, only Edward and Margo are occupying the residence to enjoy time to themselves during their honeymoon.

I say a prayer that my luck will improve and that I will not be intruding on my friends during their amorous activities.

I decide to enter Eton Cottage through the back entrance near the kitchen. Knocking loudly, I call out, hoping they can hear me. "Hello there. It is your dear friend, Albert Berry. Hello. Hello."

"Albert?" Margo calls.

"Yes." I open the door but close my eyes. Using my hands to guide me into the home. I continue to shout so there is no room for error. "I am entering the kitchen. Please stop me if you are not in a suitable state to entertain."

Edward laughs, "Open your eyes, Albert. You are going to walk into the table."

"Are you sure?"

"Yes, open them," Margo says.

I follow her direction with caution, opening only one eye first and very slowly. Relief floods through me when I see my friends seated at the table, fully clothed with their breakfast plates before them. I could not be happier that I did not interrupt them, but I still needed to tease them. "Well, this certainly appears to be a very boring honeymoon."

"One does need to eat, Albert," Margo shares as she stands.

"Yes, to regain the energy spent last night." Edward shrugs his shoulders confidently.

"Please take a seat. Can I make you a plate?"

"Yes, that would be great. Thank you, Margo."

"What do we owe the surprise visit? Is Lily outside waiting to be sure we are dressed as well?" Edward asks.

"No, Lily will not be joining us. She has received a

very unexpected visit from Lady Augusta Calderwood and her daughters this morning."

Margo runs back to the table. "They came unexpectedly? What did you say? Is Lily all right? Should I go to her?"

"No, dear Margo. All is well. I was able to leave without any of their notice."

"Awfully sly of you, Albert. I am impressed." Edward raises his mug to me.

"I must admit this is not the first time they have arrived without warning and I have needed to make a hasty exit."

"Is it not?" Margo asks.

"No, and this is where I escape to each time. The Landons were always kind enough to take me in and it has always happened so early, you were either sleeping or too tired to realize I had no horse of my own."

She rejoins us at the table, plopping down in her chair. "I am so sorry I was so obtuse for so long, Albert. You must think I am an awful friend."

"Not at all, Margo."

"Well, let me make it up to you now. How can I help today? Would you like me to deliver a note to Lily for you?"

"I may ask that of you later. Claire will see that a letter from Lily will be delivered soon once she knows the duration of her relatives' stay. If I should need to respond, you can deliver it without suspicion."

"Yes, of course. I would be happy to."

Edward leans in, "I am sorry, Albert." He reaches for

his wife's hand and squeezes. "Anything we can do to help, you have our full support."

I know it is difficult for them to understand my current position. The times Lily and I are together are worth the tough times like today. I will endure this separation, counting down until I can be with her again. I am just not sure when that will be...

Claire accompanies me to the grand parlor to meet with the women of the Calderwood family. As I enter the room, the only one to stand is the young gentleman. Robert Harris, soon-to-be Robert Calderwood. While his gentlemanly welcome would seem proper, it is his attempt to show dominance over me. I nod respectfully at them all and take my seat in a chair closest to the window.

"How are you feeling, Lily?" Edith asks with genuine concern on her face.

"Better than last night, thank you. But still not at my best."

"Well, be assured, your beauty masks it all." How thankful I am for Edith. Though I never went as far to trust her as a confidant, her pleasant demeanor has always helped to balance the icy way her sister has treated me.

Amelia was never particularly friendly but was not

as cruel before her brother's death. She was intrusive about us not having children immediately after marriage, but since she began having her own children, they have kept her distracted enough.

I refrain from asking for the reason for their sudden arrival since, on previous occasions, it has been taken as the utmost insult. "Beautiful weather for your travels, Lady Calderwood." I address Benedict's mother directly with hopes that it will lead her to the subject of disclosing her intentions.

"Yes, yes. It was." She has her grandson seated between her and his mother, both fussing over his jacket, which seems perfectly in place from where I am seated. He delights at the attention they bestow upon him. At the age of fifteen, he still has much maturing to do. I can only hope once he is sent away for schooling he will excel in their absence.

For now, we must endure an overindulgent young man who forces all his young mates to refer to him as Lord Calderwood. I would not be surprised to find the number of his mates dwindling quite quickly. When he last visited the country estate, he was thirteen and insisted on taking inventory of his assets. He spent an entire day outside counting our livestock. I may have told him we have a great number of geese, *of which we have none,* but encouraged him to keep at it when he could not find them. His mother does nothing to curb his demands, so I felt I had no choice but to take matters into my own hands.

Though, I suppose I should be thankful this visit

only consists of the four of them. With a large number of children between Amelia and Edith, when the entirety of their families visit, it takes some preparation. Edith has much younger children and I look forward to their visits, I like to have gifts and particular foods they enjoy ready for them.

Yet, Lady Calderwood does not typically like to travel with so many children. Frustrating as it is, they are not the grandchildren she wanted. She mourns not only the loss of her husband and son but also the loss of having grandchildren from Benedict and me. If only she would embrace the many grandchildren she has been blessed with. Just as she did with her own children, favoring her son over her daughters, she barely interacts with her granddaughters.

Even with the girls outnumbering the boys, they are still receiving the same second-rate treatment. While each of the eldest sons will inherit their own titles, it is the Calderwood title and its legacy that she holds above all else. She only began to show Robert such attention once it was determined he would take Benedict's title. She even treats him as if he were Benedict at times.

It would be simple for me to find endless reasons to hate Lady Augusta. When we lost Benedict, I first sought her for comfort, but she immediately pushed me away with accusations that I should have done something, should have been able to stop this from happening—that his death was somehow preventable. At first, I was devastated by her cruelty, but over time, I have been able to accept I was not at fault and she was simply acting out. I cannot claim to know the experience of losing a child, so I do not try.

This journey of grief is hers and hers alone. I can spend every night praying for her to find peace, but she believes peace is acknowledging his death, a fact she still struggles to accept.

Amelia's abrupt turn in my direction pulls my attention from my thoughts of her mother. "It is all the talk around London that your obstinate little friend, Miss Eton, has finally decided to marry."

Amelia, more than the others has always had negative opinions of my friendship with Margo. I suppose she, like her mother, prefers I stay in mourning permanently rather than give my life some purpose. "Yes, Margaret, now Mrs. Riley, has recently married."

"The details of the courtship are still very ambiguous. She was known for denouncing marriage and mocking all women who became wives with children." *Margo never voiced such things.* Yet, I know Amelia is one to indulge in the rumor mill. "Do you know what caused the sudden change of heart? And why did she select Mr. Edward Riley? We all assumed it would certainly be Mr. Albert Berry."

"Why would you have assumed that?" I ask, forgetting myself. I should school my reactions to mentions of Albert's name in their company.

"Well, as she seemed to never be interested in marriage and he did not appear to be interested in any woman, it would make sense for them to have a marriage by law only."

If only they knew just how very interested Albert is in women…well, at least one woman. I look over Amelia's shoulder and out onto the terrace, letting the memories of our remarkable lovemaking from just last night play in my mind.

"Your cheeks are blushing!" Amelia calls out. "I am correct about one of those assumptions. Does Mr. Riley fall into the same predicament, not having any interest in women and acting as an out for Miss Eton?"

"I can assure you, Mr. Riley and the new Mrs. Riley are very much in love. They simply decided to court outside of the watchful eyes of London."

Amelia shrugs, no longer interested if there is not any scandal to be shared. She turns back to her son, as a tale of love is not enough to keep her interest.

"Yes, well, I am glad all that nonsense has settled and you can return your attention to this family." Lady Augusta clears her throat. "As you know, Benedict's birthday is coming soon."

It is in two months.

"As always, we need to celebrate him."

Yes, of course.

Each year, I host a family dinner. Some years, we hold them in the city, others here in the country to celebrate Benedict on his birthday. Yet, she has never come so early to plan a dinner before.

"This is the year he would have turned five and forty."

Yes, I know.

"I believe we should throw a ball in his honor." A

ball is not what she wants. A ball includes dancing, laughter, and happiness. Lady Augusta wants a larger audience to mourn with her.

"We could hold a grand dinner if you would prefer. I can have multiple tables set in the ballroom. That may be a more forlorn setting for remembering Benedict," I suggest.

Immediately, my suggestion is refused. "Benedict loved such grand celebrations!" She pauses to squint her eyes in anger at me. "We will have a ball. It was not a suggestion. If he were alive, we would be holding the ball to celebrate. So, we will proceed. It will be held here, in our family estate and it will be on his birthday." Her face softens just the slightest and I see tears in the bottom of her eyes.

This is how she holds on to her late son.

"Yes, Lady Augusta. Of course," I answer.

"Amelia and Edith, I would like you here as much as you can be to help with the preparations. I shall stay for the duration to make sure everything is just as it should be." My stomach knots. I will be spending the remaining weeks until Benedict's birthday sharing a roof with Lady Augusta, which also means there will be no chance to see Albert in the next two months.

"It will be a celebration of his life. I do not want it to come across that we are celebrating his death, but more a show of how much he is missed. I expect you all to be dressed in black. A bright color would be offensive. See to it that your dresses are ordered soon so that they can be ready in time." Lady Augusta seems to have most of this event already planned out.

I CURL myself under a blanket as I sit next to the fireplace in the library. Lady Augusta and her daughters are surely settling into their rooms by now.

There is a soft knock at the door. Claire does not bother to announce herself but slips in and quickly closes the door behind her.

"I knew this is where I would find you," she says.

"And how did you know that?" I ask.

"The library is yours. It is the only room in the house you seek out when you are upset."

"You know me so well. This is the only room in the house I can claim feels truly like home," I tell her, and she gives me a look that tells me to go on. "Benedict never cared for the library. I do not think I ever saw him in this room once. He enjoyed being outside and interacting with nature far more. So it became mine." I sigh, "And in time, it became mine and Albert's room."

"Oh yes, my lady. I can remember that day," she says with a kind but soft laugh.

"What day?"

"The day it became a room you shared with Albert... if that even was the first time..." She eyes me knowingly. Oh, yes. She is recalling the day she discovered Albert and me in the library when we were certain no one knew of our amorous endeavors.

My limbs spread out from my body in different directions. Albert lifts one of my legs over his shoulder to deepen his connection with me. My body tingles as his hands travel over my body, lingering when I squirm beneath his touch. "You are exquisite, my love.

"Albert..." Words escape me.

"Tell me, Lily. What do you need?" His voice is low and commanding.

"You."

His hands move to my waist, grabbing tightly to steady me against his force. "Then you shall have all of me."

My breath catches as he goes feral beneath me, his movements wild, his gaze locked onto mine. I feel my muscles tensing as he begins to lose his rhythm, the moment overtaking him.

BOOM BOOM BOOM!

We freeze immediately. The loud knocking stops, "Lady Calderwood, are you in there? This door is locked," Claire calls loudly from the other side of the door.

"Yes, Claire!" I turn to Albert—disappointment is in his eyes, but he quickly schools himself and backs up to allow me to stand. "I did not realize it was locked. I must have fallen asleep," I say as I fix my dress and he pulls his trousers back on. Silently, he points to the book stacks and then tiptoes back toward them. I nod and make my way to the door to unlock it for her.

She enters and gives me an assessing look. "Miss Eton has arrived to visit with you." Oh, Margo. What horrible timing you have. Yet, if I was honest about Albert and me with her, I am sure she would be more than respectful. That is a matter for another time.

"You are flushed and breathing quickly, Lady Calderwood... You said you were napping?" Something in Claire's voice tells me she does not believe me but is waiting to see if I will be honest with her. I hold my tongue.

She looks at me as my governess would when I was caught being naughty as a child. "Is Mr. Berry just as flushed? I can hear his heavy breathing from here."

My mouth falls open.

"You may come out, Mr. Berry!" she yells over my shoulder.

He walks to my side and places his hand in mine before pulling it to his lips for a quick kiss. His eyes meet mine as he nods. Strong, steady Albert. Always ready to take on the world by my side.

"Claire..." I begin talking, but truly, I do not know where to start. Should I beg her to keep our secret? Or lie and tell her this is the first time it has happened?

It's not.

She holds her hand up to stop me. "We are all well into adulthood, Lady Calderwood. There is no need for the guilty looks on your faces." Albert squeezes my hand once more, but I cannot look away from Claire. "To be honest, I am happy for you, for both of you." She looks between us. "And I am not the only one. I am sorry to say, but you are not very good at keeping this a secret, at least not here." I gasp. Claire is one thing, but if the entire staff knows, surely they will tell Lady Augusta. It would break her heart.

Claire must notice my panic because she quickly

reassures me. "Everyone employed at this estate is pleased you have found love again. They have all sworn to keep your secret as long as it continues to bring you such happiness."

The shock has silenced me, so Albert answers for us. "Thank you, Claire. We owe you a great deal for your discretion, as the same goes for the entire staff here."

I drop his hand and run into Claire's arms. "Thank you." She wraps her arms around me and holds me close as tears fall from my eyes.

"You deserve to be loved by a man as good as Albert. You have our full support," she whispers back.

When we release our embrace, she reminds me. "You do have a guest waiting for you, I will let her know you will both be with her shortly." And she takes her leave.

"I miss him already," I say to Claire.

"Of course you do. At his side is where you belong." Claire sits beside me on the arm of the chair. "Until then, I will be here to help you endure the next two months."

I pull my hand out from under the blanket to hold hers. "Thank you, Claire."

This sun is still high in the afternoon sky when John, a footman from the Calderwood Estate, hands me a letter with Lily's unofficial seal. She uses the seal stamp of branches with leaves rather than the one with her "C" initial to provide another level of secrecy. "Would you like me to wait for your reply?" he asks, standing in the doorway of Eton Cottage. I had anticipated Lily to write and decided to wait in the sitting room for someone to deliver it since finishing breakfast with Margo and Edward.

"Yes, John. Just give me a moment. Please feel free to come in and have a seat." I wave him into the house while I move in the opposite direction to gain privacy while reading my letter.

Dearest Albert,

I had not anticipated our time together would end so quickly.

Please know I already miss you terribly.

After speaking with Lady Augusta, her daughters, and her grandson, they have informed me the reason for this visit is to begin preparations for Benedict's birthday celebration. Although, this year, Lady Augusta would like a much grander celebration as it would have been a monumental birthday of five and forty. She plans to throw a ball at the Calderwood Estate.

While the majority of the guests do not plan to stay for more than a few days, Lady Augusta is adamant that she will reside in the country for the duration of the preparations through the night of the ball.

It has been years since we have been without one another for such a long period of time. I must remind myself that we have endured a much longer separation than this. Yet, I do not anticipate that fact making your absence any more bearable.

I must assure you, I will be thinking of you every moment until we can be reunited.

-Lily

I close the letter and tuck it into my jacket pocket that hovers over my heart. Only her letters belong there. I return to John, "I will just be a moment. I am going to pen my reply."

"Certainly, sir." John is familiar with Eton Cottage and moves toward the kitchen, I imagine for a drink while he waits.

Eton Cottage does not have many visitors, but the few they get are treated as family. Lily and I each have rooms at Eton Cottage. I was not sure if I would be spending the night here, but it does look that way. It is unsure when Lily's staff will be able to sneak my belongings out of the grand estate without notice of her visitors or their staff. The secret of our love has always been difficult but never felt like a burden to me. I can only hope the staff at the Calderwood Estate continue to feel the same.

While Lily was able to send out my letter without concern, I am careful how I write to her. If it were to be intercepted, there could be great consequences. Keeping it with me always, I reach inside the pocket of my jacket, pulling out the stamp of a tree without any branches. As these stamps are only used when we are apart, I felt the significance of the two was quite fitting. I begin to write in code to inform her of my plans without making an indication of the author or recipient's identities.

My Enchanting Blossom,

My family has called on me to return home to assist with urgent matters. Please send your family my best. I am sorry I was not able to visit with them this evening.

With the weather changing, I do not know when I will see you again, but rest assured, it will be as soon as I can return to your side.

I shall not find a single night of restful sleep during our time apart. My heart will long for you, my body will crave the touch of yours, and my soul will be restless until it can be reunited with its match.

-The man who loves you more than life itself

Edward is passing in the hall when I emerge from my room, letter in hand. "Have you heard from Lily?"

"Yes, it seems the Calderwoods have planned an extended stay without informing Lily."

He places his hand on my shoulder, "I am sorry, my friend."

My instinct is to shrug off his concern and tell him this is something we are more than accustomed to, but instead, I answer honestly. "Thank you, Edward. It never gets easier."

He squeezes my shoulder, then offers, "Would you like Margo and I to deliver that" He points to the letter in my hand.

"No need, John is downstairs. He delivered Lily's letter and is waiting for my reply. I would, however, ask if you would not mind my intrusion on your honeymoon for a little longer. I have to wait until the staff have the clearance to bring my things from the Calderwood Estate before I can take my leave back to London."

"Stay as long as you like." He smiles and begins to walk in the opposite direction I am headed. "Your presence will not slow down my plans." He laughs and continues on his way.

"Please keep your lascivious plans out of the common areas, for my sake," I beg.

"I shall do my best, but no guarantees!" he yells as he turns the corner.

"Thank you for waiting. Here is the letter for Lady Calderwood." John takes it in hand. "Can you please have my luggage sent here at your earliest convenience?"

"Of course, Mr. Berry. We will wait until the transportation of your belongings can go unnoticed."

"Take as long as you need. I will not return to London until they arrive." I nod as he bows and takes his leave.

Moving to the kitchen, I make myself a cucumber sandwich and sit to contemplate how I will survive the next two months without Lily.

An hour or two later, I return to my room. It is as I left it. Mrs. Landon insisted I leave extra clothes here permanently as a precaution for times such as these. I change after washing up, mourning every moment, knowing I was washing away any remnants of Lily's perfume off my body.

Trying to pass the time, I go to the window but find no joy or distraction in the view of the road below. After pacing around the room and still finding no relief, I finally sit, but not even the books placed next to my bed are able to distract me from my pain.

I am anxious to get to London. It is a particular torture to be so close geographically to Lily without any way of getting to her. In the city, I will at least be too far away to ruin both of our lives on an impulse by storming in the front entrance of the Calderwood Estate and declaring my undying love to her—consequences be damned.

The thought of wrapping her in my arms and ending all this secrecy of our love fills my mind. I would not be able to speak, but I would show her the depths of my devotion.

For now, though, while she is out of reach, I can use words.

Leaving the bed, I sit at the desk that occupies the area beneath a window that faces her estate. With a quill in hand, I write to her.

The first letter includes instructions, for the remaining letters I will write.

I am restless in this room, longing for the sight of your smile. Contemplating destroying everything we keep private to just get one more kiss from your soft lips. Nothing can distract my thoughts of you, and I have no desire to fight them.

So to keep our secret safe, I have decided to write to you. I do not know the length of these letters or how many there will be by the time I finish. I imagine I will write until my hand can no longer hold a quill because I will never lack the ability to find ways to declare my love for you.

When you are feeling particularly lonely, open a letter. I hope this will suffice until we can be in each other's embrace once again.

I am yours.

I fold the letter and seal it with the naked tree seal.

Letting it dry while I write the next letter. The process repeats over and over. Some letters are pages long, others a few sentences. When I move the blank parchment in front of me, I let the first thought I have of her guide the letter's contents.

I write her a letter about how I love waking up before her in the morning. There is no better view than watching her move from blissful sleep into hope for the new day in front of her. The way the sun's rays bring out the different shades within her blonde hair.

I write a letter confessing I am a sick man who spends hours contemplating how her body fits perfectly with mine. How I will long for her touch during this seclusion we are forced to endure.

I write a letter telling her how I never truly feel at home unless we are together. No residence gives me comfort as her presence provides.

I write a letter telling her how I prefer to make love near the fireplace because it quickens the blush on her chest and cheeks.

I write a letter telling her how when we are apart, I seek out flowers. They comfort me, being the closest thing I can find to her beauty. They also remind me of our time in the country, as her estate is surrounded by them.

I write a letter reminding her that she is my reason for living. My heart beats only for her.

Then I write many, many more letters.

I swore I would save the letters, not opening them too soon. I wanted to reserve them for the nights after I had been separated from Albert for weeks. This stack of letters was delivered just two days ago. I opened his first letter as soon as they arrived.

Albert knows I am not patient—that is why he sent so many. Surely, I can just open one now and that will keep me content for at least a week.

When you lay your head on your pillow at night,
lonely in that large bed by yourself, please do not
forget how treasured you are, my love.

I cherish the light you bring to my life, making
the most unbearable times peaceful.

I delight in the feel of your hand, your elegant
fingers interlaced with mine, as we walk through
fields of flowers behind your estate while the sun
caresses the horizon.

I admire you for the person you are. Your
strength is only equal to your kindness.

I relish in the way your body was made for mine.
Even the most innocent of touches ignites my lust
for you.

If given my way, I would spend an eternity
worshiping you.

Lady Calderwood,

Thank you for hosting me during my travels in the English countryside. It was a great pleasure to rest between destinations and share in your company. As I have now moved on, I must confess I still think of the tulips in your garden each and every day since my departure.

All the best,

Albert Berry

I let a quiet giggle escape my lips. The distance between us is irrelevant—Albert's words alone have the power to make me flush with need.

I move the unopened letters to the satchel they were delivered in and return them to the back corner of my closet.

I read the latest letter over and over again, giving into my desire for the man I love to be lying next to me at this moment. This letter is not enough, though. I need more of him. I look over to the closet.

No, I need to save those.

But I do have an entire box of the letters he has sent

to me over the years. I kneel down to reach under my bed and pull out the small lock box beneath it. It is modest, as its purpose is to hide away letters I would never want discovered. The plain olive paint that covers the exterior is starting to peel around the corners, but most importantly, the lock is just as secure as the first time I used it.

Dust has formed on top of the box, evidence of how little Albert and I have been apart lately. I smile at that thought. The coming weeks would surely prove difficult. I move to my jewelry box and peel back the fabric at the bottom to reveal the key.

Locking my bedroom door for privacy. I would not have taken this precaution had I not been hosting my guests. After it clicks in place, I pick the box up from the floor and place it on the bed in front of me. As soon as the box is unlocked, the top bursts backward and letters fall out onto the bed. I suppose I will need another soon. I do not think this will be able to close at all if I put any more letters in it.

The thought of having a second box of letters is bittersweet. I do not ever wish to stop receiving love letters from Albert, but the need for the letters is something I am not sure I want to continue. They are proof of the fragmented life we live.

What would life be like if I were to marry Albert? Surely, I would keep the letters, but there would be no need for the locked box and the hidden key.

No use in dwelling on such things.

I lift a letter from my bed and lay back as I begin to read.

The air does not sustain me as it should.

My lungs resist when I attempt a full breath. There is a mutiny in my chest.

Nothing is working properly while my heart aches for you.

I swear I will get to you soon. And when I do, I will not hold back.

I will show you how much I have missed you.

I will show you how I have longed for your touch.

I will make up for every moment lost between us.

This is one of the first letters he sent. I recall he would write as himself, but in a code only I could decipher. In that particular letter, he was referencing when we walked hand and hand each morning through the garden. It was his way of telling me he was thinking of me.

I search through the box to find more from that time. They are easy to spot because that was when he was still using his B wax seal stamp. Before he purchased our code seals for us.

Lady Calderwood,

I hope you are well and please send my best to your young friend, Miss Eton. It was a pleasure to see you both in town this month.

I am writing with a request. I am furnishing my apartment and I must beg for the maker of the settee in your private sitting room. I found the piece's comfort and durability unmatched to any I have ever occupied before. You must share the maker of such a fine piece.

Eagerly awaiting your reply.

Mr. Albert Berry

Alone in my room, I blush at this letter. Surely, he

had no intention of purchasing furniture. He simply meant to remind me of the ravenous night we spent mauling each other on said settee.

Lady Calderwood,

I have traveled far and wide, and I must relay to you that I have found no library I prefer more than the one that resides within your country estate.
I cannot find one specific reason, but perhaps the atmosphere you have created in that room is what makes it unmatched. How it inspires such passion within me. A blistering hot need for literature, if you will.

I hope you and your library are quite well.

Mr. Berry

Albert is very vocal that the library is one of his favorite rooms to make love, and I must admit, it is one of mine too. Although, I do not believe it has much to do with the room as it has to do with the lover.

He must have fireplaces at the Berry family residences that he enjoys. I smirk to myself, as if I can hear his reply. I have never been to his family's residences, and furthermore, we have never made love in front of those fireplaces.

Albert has invited me to visit his family estates with vague discussions, but I have never pushed the matter. He does not enjoy spending time with his family in London and particularly avoids his family's country estate. His avoidance is driven by the strained relationship Albert has with his father. I struggle to understand at times. I had a kind yet mostly distant father and mother, but with so many daughters, they never put such expectations on any of us. Once the last of us were married, they moved to Wales with my eldest sister, who made the most prosperous match.

What if the Berry family estate were to become ours if we wed?

Would we make love in front of those fireplaces? Could I make a place Albert dislikes so much a home for us? Could he ever truly be happy in a place like that? Would I be happy to leave my home and move there?

To make it our own would take much effort, but it does have potential. A place where we do not have to hide our relationship, even when unexpected guests arrive. A place where we can run the household and a partnership. A place where I do not have to lock away the love letters he writes to me. One day...we may live those lives...*but not yet.*

I close my eyes and place my hand into the box, mixing the letters around before selecting another to read. I notice the dead tree seal on the parchment. I smile at the memory of when Albert presented them to me.

"Rather than leaving our letters unsealed, I procured these for us to use." Albert lifts the fabric in his hand to reveal two wax seal stamps.

He picks the first up and hands it to me. I take it and examine the seal. "Branches with leaves," he explains. "You are the beauty in our union."

"And yours?" I ask.

He lifts his to show me. It is a grand tree, taking up the entity of the seal, but upon further inspection, I can see the tree's branches are bare. "Where are the leaves?" I ask.

"You have them, love." My breath catches as he speaks. "I am the steady foundation for our love. Without you, I am a dead tree. When we reunite, it is as if spring has arrived and I can bloom back to life."

A tear falls down my cheek as I allow the pain of missing him to overtake me.

"Where is she?" Lady Augusta's shrill voice carries from the hallway outside my bedroom door. I suppose it fitting that she be the reason for the abrupt end to me pitying myself for being away from Albert. Now that her daughters have taken their leave, I have become her only option for company.

I rush to push the letters back into the small box. It takes all my force to get it closed and locked. It does not look secure, though. "Please stay closed," I whisper to it. I place it on the floor and use my foot to push it under the bed.

Running to the door, I unlock it before Lady Augusta

can discover it was locked in the first place. She hates locked doors.

I back up to my bed as she pushes the door open. "Where have you been? We need to finalize the guest list!"

As if she would actually value my input.

"I apologize, Lady Augusta. I had a headache, I was resting."

"Well, you seem in perfect health to me. Come, the lists are in the dining room." Without checking to see if I am following her she exits the room.

Each step I take is one further away from Lily. My body strains against the distance, unwilling to act at full capacity without my other half. I returned to London last night, deciding to stay in my apartment for the evening, but it did not matter. Sleep escaped me. Now, my eyes are dry and my mind foggy as I slowly climb the steps to my family's townhouse.

I knock twice and am soon greeted by Griffin, "Good morning to you, sir." He moves aside to grant me entry. "Lord and Lady Berry are not in residence at this time. They are currently in the country."

My spirit lifts a little at the good news. Being without Lily and in the overbearing presence of my father can be a very difficult time to manage, but if his constant beratement is removed, survival becomes a little more achievable.

"Can I get you something to eat, sir?"

"Yes, thank you." I move toward the sitting room.

"Your father has left some letters and papers for your review should you arrive in his absence." *Of course, he did.* "They are in the study. I can prepare it while you eat." He bows and takes his leave.

I settle into the settee and smile. The resemblance to the one at the Calderwood Estate is almost exact. Yet, this one does not hold the memories of its twin.

I am pulled from my erotic thoughts when Griffin enters carrying the tray of tea and small pastries. I thank him and ask, "When are my parents scheduled to return?"

"In one week's time, sir."

I lean back, making myself more comfortable. "Very good." He leaves me to bask in the good news he just delivered. I grab a handful of biscuits and make my way to the study.

The first thing I check is the mail. I look through each letter, but none of them are from Lily. I did not expect her to write so soon. When the women of the Calderwood family are in residence, they usually keep her quite busy. I smile at the thought of her reading my letters late at night before she falls asleep.

Reclining in the large high-back chair, I allow myself a moment to wonder what life will be like when I become Lord Berry. I do not care for my father, but I understand enough to know these heavy responsibilities are a large contributor to his disagreeable countenance. I wish him to live a very long life and continue to hold his title as long as possible...if only far away from me.

It would be nice to improve our relationship, but that is a dream I have held onto since my childhood. One I have long stopped believing would come to pass. As the years progress, I care less and less for his approval. When such standards are beyond reason, it can drive a man to madness, trying to achieve the impossible.

After hours of staring at ledgers and letters from the tenants, I take the opportunity to leave the house. For certain matters, my father requests I meet with the accountants in town. After organizing the desk, I step out into the cool early midday air of the city.

THE SUN HAS SET by the time I have finally completed my tasks for the day. Still undecided about where I will sleep tonight, I head to my gentlemen's club for a quick drink and light dinner while I decide. It will be good to be seen at such a place. Keeping up appearances for men is just as important as being seen at balls for women.

This club's memberships are bestowed to only the highest and most prestigious families in London. Unfortunately, the club does not revoke memberships as new generations come of age, which has proven problematic over the years. Some men are able to uphold their father's good reputations, others not so much.

Upon entering the building, I am met with the smell of smoke and whiskey. The room, while well-lit, still has a fog building in particular corners. At night, they open the windows to let it out, which is why I typically prefer to come earlier in the day before it gets too overwhelming.

"Albert!" I scan the tables to see the man calling my name. "Albert Berry." William Armstrong is waving his arms like a young boy calling for his mother. I smile at my overexcited friend.

I make my way to his small table, with the only other chair still unoccupied. "William, old chap." I shake his hand. "How long has it been?"

"I believe the last I saw you was when our paths crossed years ago in Greece." William and I met as young men during university. We bonded quickly over our desire to travel. He gestures for me to sit with him.

"Yes, I think you are correct."

The waiter arrives, "I will have another." William raises his empty glass. "And one for my friend?" He watches me for approval.

"Of course, thank you." When the waiter leaves, I ask, "What are you doing back in England? I remember a time when you swore you would never step foot back in this country. I was certain it was a matter of time before I heard tales of you becoming a pirate."

William laughs. "What a life that would be to live." I see the happiness leave his face. "My father is ill. It seems I may be inheriting my title before I can get myself killed at sea."

"I am sorry to hear that. Your father is a good man." Heavy is the burden of men who are only sons but have dreams of a life beyond English high society.

Our glasses are placed on the table in front of us and he takes a drink. "Tell me, how are you? What has been happening in London?" His eyes pop open wide. "Is it true your friend, Edward Riley, was the one to marry the unobtainable Miss Eton?"

"Yes, they are both close friends of mine and I can confirm they are married. I acted as a witness myself." I can feel myself smiling as I share the good news with him.

A throat clears loudly and obnoxiously behind William. He turns and I follow his gaze to the dark corner behind him. Upon closer inspection, sitting in a poorly lit corner, is Harold Grange. It does not escape me that he sits sideways so that only one side of his face is visible to most in the room. Edward hits with his right hand—most of the damage he inflicted was located on Harold's left side, the side he is trying to hide now. A wicked smile curls my lips as I bask in the knowledge that he still has not healed from the beating we delivered.

William may know of Grange's reputation, but there is no need to involve him. I can handle him.

William turns back to me as I rise. "Please excuse me while I handle this."

William nods, "I will be here if you need assistance."

Harold Grange should be thankful this interaction is happening in an establishment such as this. Even so, I am quite disappointed that I cannot beat the life out of him once again. My hands fist at my sides as I approach him.

I take the seat across from him, placing my hands on the table and interlacing my fingers. "What are you doing here, Harold?"

"Enough with the civility, Albert. I heard what you told that other gentleman. You think I am going to buy that story that Riley has already wed Miss Eton—not a chance. That woman is completely set against marriage and I am to believe she jumped into it not a day after I announced our engagement. This is a stall tactic. As soon as Lord Eton returns to town, I will be notified and secure a meeting with him. Then this matter will be resolved."

His confidence is comical. I suppose he is right to be suspicious of the timing. I would have legally married her just to keep her from the awful fate of becoming his wife. I certainly would have lied and said she was already married to delay it as well. Yet, none of that was necessary in the end.

With a laugh, I shake my head, "Suit yourself, but Lord Eton will confirm his daughter is married."

"I will not be made a fool, Albert. That fortune will be mine." Harold loses control of his temper.

"It is meant to be Margaret Eton's fortune, never yours." His temper is baiting mine, but I must remember our surroundings. "You have made quite the fool of yourself, even more than everyone in London already thought of you. Best to move your fortune-hunting endeavors somewhere else." I stand to walk away, having nothing more to say to this delusional git.

Harold brushes past me and then William, who I now realize is standing behind me in solidarity. Good friends are hard to find, but when you have them, they are easy to spot.

Harold slams the doors upon his exit.

LATER THAT EVENING, after returning to my parents' townhome, I pull out a quill and parchment to write to Edward about the meeting I had with Harold. I share all the details of Grange's dramatic claims. Ending the letter with assurance that I will seek out Lord Eton the moment he returns to town so this matter can be settled once and for all.

After sealing that letter, I write another, and address it to the new Mrs. Margaret Riley. It only contains a single line. "Please deliver this for me." Margo will know when she opens it. I have sent many letters through Mrs. Landon and even Claire in this manner, but I wanted to send it through Margo this time. With the Calderwood's visiting, Lily will need to see her friend and this will be the perfect excuse.

I enclose the letter for Lily with my tree seal inside of the letter I addressed to Margo and I seal that with my "B" crest.

When I post these in the morning, I will stop by the florist to have flowers sent to Margo and an extra bouquet of lilies. She will know where to deliver them.

22

Only three more weeks.

The responses to our invitations have been incoming for days. They are spread out, covering the table in the dining room. Lady Augusta sits at the head of the table with pages of her guest list as I open and read off each name to her.

"The Hardcastle family will be attending."

"Wonderful, Catherine is such a dear friend." She dramatically places a checkmark on her page.

I open another, "The Wiese family will be attending."

"Theodore and Bradley are such sweet children, yet I suppose they are no longer children. It has been some ten years since we have seen them." Another grand checkmark.

"The Weaver family will be unable to attend."

Good for them.

"And why not?"

Probably because they would rather spend their evening enjoying their lives and the love they have for each other.

I find when couples are forced to attend these events, they look at me with such pity and then hold each other closer. A reminder that they could lose each other in the blink of an eye. I act as a reminder people do not typically seek out.

"It seems they are traveling abroad. I believe someone from their staff sent the response on their behalf."

A likely excuse.

"Continue." She is still shaking her head at the offense.

"Lord and Lady Riley have sent their reply for themselves and their daughter." Directly underneath, I find another, "The newlyweds, Mr. and Mrs. Riley have also confirmed." I smile to myself, knowing Margo would not decline, but seeing her name among the others makes this moment a little more pleasant.

"The Arnolds and the Pattechats will also be attending." Opening multiple at a time, I hope to expedite this process.

"Good."

The next I open is sealed with the all too familiar "B." I turn it over to be sure it is the response and not a letter for me. No, it is addressed to Lady Augusta.

Lady Augusta,

I respond on behalf of my parents, Lord and
Lady Berry and I.

We will be in attendance.

Thank you for honoring us with an invitation to
such a significant event.

Mr. Albert Berry

My fingers graze his signature. I am elated at the
thought of seeing him again, but it will not be the
reunion either of us would want.

"Well?" Lady Augusta shouts to me, making me
jump slightly in my seat.

"Yes, sorry. The writing was poor. Lord and Lady
Berry will be attending with their son, Mr. Albert
Berry."

"My dear friend, Teresa! I knew she would not let
anything stop her from joining our celebration of
Benedict." She smiles brightly and adds another
checkmark. I place Albert's reply aside from the others

that will be disposed of. It is not a love letter, but it is the most recent contact I have had from him and I will treasure it just as I do the others.

As we are finishing up, Claire comes to collect the responses we no longer need now that Lady Augusta's guest list is finalized. "A letter for you, my lady." She hands me a letter and I panic slightly. If it is from Albert, I should wait to open it. She must notice the concern on my face and continues. "It just came from Eton Cottage, Mrs. Riley, I believe."

I open it while Lady Augusta slowly rises from the table with the help of her footman.

My Dearest Friend,

I cannot express how much I miss your company. While I appreciate the time you allotted for me to enjoy my honeymoon, we are ready to receive guests and I must insist you be the first.

Please join us for dinner this evening at Eton Cottage.

Yours,
Margo

This is not the first letter I have received from Margo. I know the Landons have long since returned to Eton Cottage. Looking up, Claire smiles at me. This was meant to be read with this very audience in the hope I could have a night away from the Calderwood Estate.

"Lady Augusta, could you spare me at dinner this evening?" I ask.

"Why on Earth would I do that? Are you asking to eat in a separate room than me?"

"Not at all. I just received this letter from my closest friend, Miss Eton, now Mrs. Riley." I hold the letter out toward her in an offer of proof. "She is now accepting guests and I would like to see her. It has been weeks since she wed."

Her eyes move to the note, squinting at it but never reaching for it. "I suppose so."

"Thank you, Lady Augusta."

I turn with Claire and leave the room before she can change her mind.

"May I speak freely?" Claire asks once we are alone in my room.

"Of course. You never need to ask."

"It really riles me when she speaks to you as a child." Claire's hands are in fists before she crosses them in front of herself.

"I suppose I should take it as her way of treating me like a part of her family." After spending so many years attempting to please the woman, I stopped wasting my time.

"It still is not right. You are a grown woman. You

should be able to visit your friend without requiring her permission."

What would I do without Claire? She is very much just as much a friend of mine as Margo. Once again, the thought of becoming Albert's wife would mean walking away from the staff here. These people who have cared for me all these years. The least I can do is care for them and remain as the lady of the house to see they are happy in their employment.

"Claire, would you join me for dinner this evening?" Claire has been to Eton Cottage a number of times but never to share a meal. Not because she was not invited but because she always declined. I think she felt guilty that we could not invite the entire staff for dinner. While they would all be welcome at Eton Cottage, there simply isn't enough room for everyone.

"Yes, I think I will this evening, Lady Calderwood." She smiles and stands taller. "Thank you."

"Thank you for finally accepting, and you will need to call me Lily going forward after sharing a meal."

"Certainly, once Lady Augusta takes her leave." Claire makes a stern face, her smile a straight line as her eyes widen, which makes me think she is trying to impersonate the woman.

"Well, you need to get ready as well. I will meet you at the carriage." I shoo her out the door. "Do not forget to dress warmly!"

⌁

"Welcome, Lily!" Mr. Landon shouts from the doorway and we take our exit from the carriage. "Claire, do we finally have the pleasure of your company this evening?" His voice booms so loud I worry Lady Augusta will hear him.

"I was more than happy for some fresh air," she says with a smile on her face.

"And fresh company, I am sure." He elbows her as he raises his eyebrows.

"Mr. Landon, let the ladies come in from the cold!" Mrs. Landon calls from behind her husband, who takes up the entirety of the doorframe.

Mr. Landon moves out toward the carriage, allowing us to enter while he gives instructions to John and Leonard telling them where to take the horses and to join us for dinner. As soon as I enter my friend's home, I feel like a weight has lifted.

"Lily!" Margo throws her arms around me before I have a chance to remove my shawl. "I am so very happy to see you."

"As am I, Margo." I pull out of her embrace. "Mrs. Riley, you are absolutely radiant." She smiles and holds out her hand to take my shawl. She greets Claire who is currently arm in arm with Mrs. Landon, moving further into the house.

"Yes, married life is far better than I could have dreamt. Why did you not tell me how grand it would be?" Margo says with a smirk.

"I believe I told you plenty about the joys of marriage. I just left out the more intimate details for you to discover for yourself. And you had your books. You were more prepared than most young ladies, including myself, when the wedding night arrived."

"Yes, but reading about it and living the experience is much different," she says in a hushed voice as we pass by the Landons and move into the large sitting room. She walks me directly to a small table that has a large vase filled with lilies and a letter below it with a bare tree wax seal.

"I shall leave you to enjoy your letter." She pulls her arm from mine and turns back in the direction of the kitchen.

The air does not sustain me as it should.

My lungs resist when I attempt a full breath.
There is a mutiny in my chest.

Nothing is working properly while my heart
aches for you.

I swear I will get to you soon. And when I do,
I will not hold back.

I will show you how much I have missed you.

I will show you how I have longed for your
touch.

I will make up for every moment lost between
us.

I hold the letter to my chest in the hope of soothing the ache in my heart. The flowers are beautiful—I will place them in my bedroom. If anyone should see us carrying them in, I can say they are a gift from Margo.

Lifting the vase, I slide my letter underneath for me to retrieve after dinner. Everyone under this roof is aware of our relationship. I have no need to hide it.

The pressing thought returns to the front of my mind again, of a world where I do not have to hide my love for Albert. Here at Eton Cottage, I can pretend to live in that world, even just for the evening.

When I enter the dining room, everyone is already seated and I notice Margo has made a plate for me. She pats the empty chair between her and Claire for me to join them.

The Landons finish telling stories from their travels during Margo and Edward's honeymoon. Edward is coy when answering questions about how he and his new bride spent the past weeks. Then, he changes the subject by turning the conversation to me.

"Lily and Claire, what have you been up to since we last saw you?" Edward asks.

Claire gives me a sorrowful look. I am sure she anticipated a night we could forget about the upcoming ball, but I do not mind speaking of it with these people. The pressure is completely removed here. I pat her knee under the table before answering him.

"Well, we have had some visitors from my late husband's family. His mother, in particular, arrived just days after we last saw you."

"And she has remained," Claire adds.

"Yes, she plans to stay for the duration of the preparations for a ball we will be hosting in a few weeks' time. I believe you responded you will be attending."

Margo and Edward nod as he reaches for her hand closest to him while she uses the other to hold mine.

"This ball is a celebration of my late husband, Lord

Calderwood's birthday. He would have been five and forty this year."

It is Edward's reaction that I am not expecting. Everyone else in this room is more than familiar with the situation I find myself in. Edward and I have the newest friendship in our circle. The good man that he is struggles to contain the emotions on his face. At first, his eyebrows shoot up in surprise, only for them to furrow as sorrow fills his eyes. He clearly does not know how to sympathize with me over my late husband's birthday while being perfectly aware of my love for his closest friend. He looks to his wife for direction, but she just squeezes his hand and lets me continue.

"Yes, I miss Benedict very much. The Calderwood family typically gathers for an intimate dinner on his birthday each year. This year, however, Lady Augusta is looking to host a grand event in his name."

I reach for a drink, my throat suddenly feeling so dry. Frankly, I enjoy celebrating his birthday each year. I enjoy any chance I get to remember that wonderful man I married. Thinking of him every day, as I do with bittersweet memories, will not bring him back. A fact I accepted years ago, yet his mother has not reached that acceptance yet.

Edward speaks first. "We will be there, Lily. We will come early and stay late. Anything you need that evening or leading up to it, Margo and I will be there."

I smile at him, I think with time, we shall become very close friends. "Thank you, Edward."

"We are happy to host Edward's family and Albert

here at Eton Cottage to make more rooms available at the Calderwood Estate," Mrs. Landon offers.

"Yes, and if you still run out of rooms, you can always offer yours to your guests and come stay with us," Margo adds.

"Let us hope it does not come to that," I say, laughing at the thought of telling Lady Augusta I was staying elsewhere that evening.

"Evelyn is very happy to have a reason to drag our parents back to the country." Edward beams while speaking of his younger sister. "I must admit, I have missed her myself. She has written to us each week asking when she can return to Eton Cottage."

"It will be lovely to see her again," I add.

The rest of the night passes filled with a delicious meal, great company, and endless laughter.

23

"How can you claim to know what goes on within this estate if you are never present to deal with these matters?" Lord Berry slams his hand down on his desk. Since my parents returned from the country, my father has taken every moment to remind me of his disappointment that I have not been there in over a year. Eating before having such discussions would have been a much better way to begin our day.

"You left the ledgers for me to look over. I did as you asked. It does not require current knowledge about the happenings in each household to review the numbers. I do not need to be privy to the disposition of the chickens on each farm." I should not raise my voice, knowing it upsets my mother, who is surely standing on the other side of the door listening.

"I am not getting any younger, Albert. With each

day that passes, you get closer to taking the role of Lord Berry." He is not elderly either. "You are not a young man anymore. The excuse that you are off sowing your oats, traveling the world is growing tiresome. These people are asking for you. It is time you take on a more present role in this family."

I suppose there is truth in what he says. It is not the tenants' fault that I do not enjoy spending time with my father. The celebration in honor of Benedict Calderwood is still weeks away. I may as well keep myself busy while I wait. Once Lily and I have served these familial obligations, we will be able to enjoy time together without interruption.

"Shall we leave today, then?" My father freezes at my question. I already sent the letter to the Calderwoods that we would attend, which is the motivation behind my offer, as it guarantees a time limit.

He takes a moment to consider his reply. Straightening his back as if he won a battle. His brows furrow, suspicious of his easy win. "Tomorrow. First thing."

"Are we finished here?" I may have given him exactly what he wanted, but I will not make it pleasant for him. He is not the reason I agreed. I did so selfishly to occupy my mind until I could be with Lily again.

"Yes. Go find your mother. Let her know of our plans." I nod. "I assume she will want to accompany us."

I cross the room in two steps, my hand tight on the

doorknob. Not realizing how tense I am, the door swings open with great force, nearly hitting Griffin. His hand lifted in a fist as if he was about to knock.

"Mr. Berry, a guest has just arrived for you."

"For Albert?" my father asks, surprised that anyone could possibly want to spend time with me.

"Yes, sir." He turns back to me. "She is waiting in the parlor for you." Before he moves past me and into my father's office.

She is waiting... Could it be Lily? My body warms with joy at the thought of seeing her until reality sweeps in to remind me she would not visit unless it was necessary. What if something has happened and she traveled here to seek my help?

I do not bother another look back in my father's direction. I am torn between running to her but also not wanting to raise so much suspicion that my father follows me. Steadying my pace as I go, I hear my father's voice grow quieter as he remains in discussion with Griffin. My heart is pounding against my chest as if it is trying to burst free of my slow pace to get to Lily.

I enter the room and release the breath I am holding. Sitting alone on the settee is a nervous looking Miss Evelyn Riley, her fingers twisting around each other. Disappointment floods through my body, but I do not let it reach my face. It is not Evelyn's fault that I incorrectly assumed it was Lily. I would never want her to think her company is unwanted. Although, it is unexpected.

"Mr. Berry." Her voice is shaky as she rises and bows in greeting.

"Evelyn, within the privacy of my home, please call me Albert." However, if either of my parents heard such informality between us, they would certainly leap to assumptions there is something much more to our friendship. Speaking of parents and knowing how formal the Rileys are, I look around for her maid. "Evelyn, did you come unchaperoned?"

She falls back into the seat and relaxes, but just slightly. "Thank you, Albert. My parents are out for the day, I was able to convince Theo to bring me. Maria is outside with him."

Shaking my head, I should not be surprised she was able to leave without notice. I take a seat in the high back chair across from the very determined young lady in front of me. "What do I owe this unexpected visit?"

"The celebration for the late Lord Calderwood, Edward said you received an invitation as well as our family?"

"Yes, that is correct." She recently discovered Lily and I in an embrace at Eton Cottage. Could she be here to seek if I need comfort over the upcoming event?

"Perfect." Her smile grows larger than it has since her arrival. "I was wondering if you are planning to head to the country earlier than the ball? You see, as much as I beg, my parents refuse to go any sooner than they are required. I thought that perhaps you were planning to use this occasion to spend additional time at Eton Cottage to visit with its residents." What a calculating young lady. *I wonder...could this request have to do with seeing a young man who is related to said residents?*

"If you are planning to travel there earlier, can I possibly accompany you?" She worries her lip. Her hands begin dancing in her lap again.

If only the young Miss Riley could have arrived an hour earlier this morning, but now I have promised my father we would leave together first thing tomorrow morning. Though, the thought of spending time at Eton Cottage fills me with a rush of anticipation.

I could see Lily.

My father will not allow me to rescind my offer completely. He most likely will not spare me even for one night. But maybe an afternoon could be possible. It is not an outlandish request. I would travel separately, arriving just a few hours later in the evening than they will. It is not directly on the way to my family's estate, but not so much out of the way that it would cause more than a slight delay.

"Albert, please." Evey must have taken my silence as deliberation. I know she loves her brother and Margo, but this feels like more than wanting to see them. She is an adult. It is high time I start to treat her as one.

I lean forward, lowering my voice. "I am going to ask you one question. I only want a yes or no answer." Her eyes grow wide. "Am I correct to assume your insistence on spending more time at Eton Cottage is beyond just seeing your brother and his wife?"

Her head pulls back in surprise. She lowers her gaze

and takes a moment before she answers. When she looks back at me, I see a look I am fairly familiar with, "Yes."

Arthur Landon is a sturdy young man, coming from a good family, but that family does not exist in the same sphere as the Riley family. If they decide to pursue this, they will face many difficulties in their way, but who am I to advise against pursuing such a difficult match?

Not sure if Evelyn was expecting such a hasty voyage so soon after her request, but it is the only offer I can make. "Can you be ready to leave first thing tomorrow?"

Her squeal is the only warning I have before she jumps up from her seat and throws her arms around me. "Thank you, Albert! Yes, I will be ready before the sun rises if you would like."

I release her. "Wait just a moment. Will your parents approve of your sudden travel plans?"

She reclaims her seat across from me. "At this point, I have become such a bother to them. I believe they will be relieved to have a break from my company."

"If I do not hear from you this evening, I will be waiting outside your home at eight sharp tomorrow morning to escort you to Eton Cottage." She squeals again. "Evelyn, before you go, can I give you a bit of advice?"

She nods.

"Love is not an easy beast to tame. Even the purest and destined by the stars type of love can become unmanageable when the world does not understand it. Be sure this is what you both truly want before you begin to walk this almost impossible road." She remains quiet, which tells me she understands completely.

That is enough lecturing for one day. I stand and hold my hand out in the direction of the entrance. "You have packing to see to, Miss Riley."

"Thank you, Mr. Berry." As we are now standing in the corridor, she bows and then takes her leave.

I turn and begin to search for my father. He is in the dining room with my mother. "Who was your guest, darling?" she asks.

"Miss Evelyn Riley, the younger sister of my dear friend, Mr. Edward Riley."

"The Rileys, that is a good family," my father adds.

I jump at the chance to use his good opinion of their family to my advantage. "Yes, she did come with a request." They both turn their gaze toward me. I grab the back of the chair in front of me, but that is the only evidence I am concerned about the request I will be making. "She asked if I were traveling to Eton Cottage soon. She misses her brother terribly and has not seen him since the wedding months ago. With the honeymoon concluded, she asked if I would escort her to Eton Cottage to visit with him."

"Her parents will not be visiting their son?" he asks. As if he would visit me at such a rate.

"They are unable to make the trip until closer to the event at the Calderwood Estate that we will be attending. Edward, my friend, has requested I act in his place as her male escort on this short journey."

"We have plans to visit the country," Father says, his tone growing deeper.

"Yes, Father, of course. I was wondering if you would allow me to deliver Miss Riley to her brother tomorrow while you and Mother head directly to the Berry Estate. I will see Miss Riley safely to her destination, perhaps stop for a luncheon, and then continue my travels to our country estate. Arriving only a couple hours after the two of you."

He sits back in his seat as my mother answers, "Well, that is perfectly reasonable, Albert. I am sure your friend will greatly appreciate the gesture."

With her approval, it will be difficult for my father to deny the request. "Yes, well, I suppose it will not be an issue," he says harshly. "With Miss Eton recently married, I was worried you were left without any prospects, but perhaps this journey with Miss Riley will be a chance for you to see if she would make a good wife for you."

His suggestion is preposterous. If he took the time to know me better as a man, he would know the honor I hold for my friends and their families, both of which I am growing to consider Miss Evelyn Riley. It is his own doing he has never bothered to learn about the people I care for, though, deep down, I know it is for the best. He would surely sour them with his off-putting personality.

I nod and remove myself from the room at once. No

need to acknowledge the mention of Evelyn becoming my bride. The less I discuss marriage with my father, the better. I head directly to my bedroom to pen a note to the newlywed Rileys.

Margo & Edward,

Please excuse the informality, but I am in a rush to get this message to you. I just had the pleasure of an unexpected visit from Miss Evelyn Riley, who is desperate to visit you both in the country. I have agreed to escort her to Eton Cottage first thing tomorrow morning. You can expect us there in the early midday.

If you can, please inform a particular neighbor of yours. I would very much like the chance to see her.

I will not be able to stay more than a few hours as my father will be expecting me at the Berry Estate later that evening.

-Albert

24

Lily

Days pass, but at a much slower pace than I would like, and still, three weeks remain until Benedict's birthday celebration. Each consists of the same daily tasks. Breakfast with Lady Augusta is followed by an update from her housekeeper and acting lady's maid while she is here, who is assisting her with the endless preparations and any changes that must be made or new issues popping up.

I planned a beautiful ball within a day's time just a few months ago, which proves there is no need for such prolonged deliberation.

Followed by a quick luncheon where we discuss how the weather may be on the day of the ball, including how cross Lady Augusta is that Benedict's birthday does not occur in a warmer month.

Thankfully, that is one topic of discontentment that she cannot possibly blame me for.

Without many opportunities for a quiet moment to

myself, I try to steal away before dinner but am unsuccessful. It is beginning to feel as though I have been sitting at this table with her for weeks. The only variety is the food—the discussion always remains the same.

This evening we begin assigning the guests rooms. "The Rileys have notified us they will not need a guest room."

"And why not? They sent their attendance confirmation weeks ago?"

If you would let me finish before interrupting, I would have explained.

"They will be in attendance but offered to stay at Eton Cottage with their son and his new wife to free up extra space here."

"Oh." She purses her lips but eventually determines this is acceptable. "Fine then, but do be sure they know I am expecting them to return here in the morning before their departure."

"Of course." I take a deep breath and hope I can deliver this next bit without suspicion. "Lord and Lady Berry will be staying with us, but their son, Mr. Albert Berry, is a very close friend of Edward Riley. He has also elected to stay at Eton Cottage."

"Has he married yet?" she asks, not knowing the weight of her question.

"I—" My voice comes out strained. I cough discreetly to clear it. "I do not believe so."

"Hmm." She does not continue and I could not be more thankful for her indifference.

"Has Amelia confirmed when she will be joining us?" I ask to solidify the change of conversation.

"Yes, I believe she will arrive in a week's time." Lady Augusta barely lifts her head to answer me. That is when I notice Claire waving at me from the hallway. The door is only half open, I suppose to avoid any other attention. I check to make sure Lady Augusta is not looking when I tilt my head to the side to question what Claire is doing.

She beckons me with both hands.

Now? I mouth in question.

She nods with such enthusiasm her entire body moves.

"Please excuse me, Lady Augusta. I just need a moment." I stand before she can argue and walk casually past the footmen stationed behind her.

Claire disappears from view as I walk in her direction. I make my way through the door and close it behind me. I need not look far as she grabs my hand and begins to pull me away from the dining room.

To my surprise, she takes me to the study and pushes me in before closing and locking the door.

"What is the matter, Claire?" Worry is starting to build.

She pulls me into a hug and, in a low voice, tells me, "Edward Riley just arrived from Eton Cottage. He came to the servants' entrance and asked to go for a walk."

I pull back slightly to look at her. "A walk?"

Assuming Lady Augusta's staff was nearby and he did not want an audience. "He announced that his wife's birthday was coming up and he needed my assistance on how to celebrate."

Now, I separate fully from her. "Margo's birthday is not until February."

"It was a ruse!" She is clearly getting exasperated with my inability to guess what this is all about. "He wanted to inform me immediately that your presence is requested—well, he demanded—at Eton Cottage tomorrow. They are to receive his sister, Miss Riley, and her escort, Mr. Albert Berry, at midday!"

A joyful scream escapes my lips before I quickly move my hand to cover my mouth.

Albert is coming.

"Now, Miss Riley will be staying for the duration and leaving with her parents after Lord Calderwood's birthday celebration, but Albert Berry, unfortunately, can only stay for mere hours tomorrow. It is imperative that you are there during the day."

"Yes, I will go now and wait for him." I turn to go to my room and pack immediately.

Claire grabs my arm and pulls me back. "Do not forget Lady Augusta. You can not possibly disappear for two days."

"Oh yes, but I will leave first thing tomorrow morning before I see her so that I cannot risk her argument." *I need to think of a reason.* "Do you think the arrival of Miss Eton will be enough of an excuse to visit Eton Cottage?"

"Yes, I think so. Perhaps inform her right before bed that you will be visiting tomorrow and to not expect you at breakfast. Once you are gone, she can endure your absence for the remainder of the day."

Kicking my legs beneath the covers, I cannot contain my excitement.

Is Albert feeling the same eagerness in his bed this evening?

Does he find it impossible to sleep as I do?

This time apart has been agony for me. I want to declare I will never allow such time to pass without him again, but I know that is not a guarantee I can make.

If I were to be his wife, separation would never be a concern again.

I should not be thinking such things, especially as Benedict's birthday approaches. However, I know that in my heart, Benedict would want me to continue living in his absence. It is his mother that would never wish for me to lose the name of Calderwood. As much as she seems to dislike me, I believe she only holds me close because I am the last evidence of Benedict's life.

Yet, is it fair to put her needs before my own...and Albert's?

No, enough worrying for Lady Augusta.

Tomorrow is for Albert and me. One clandestine afternoon will not have any effect on her.

And I plan to enjoy it to the fullest.

Since Albert re-entered my life at Margo's first ball, I have felt a raw pull toward him. Seeing him that night changed everything in me. At the time, I never expected it to become romantic, but I knew I longed for his presence in my life. When we parted that night, I could not sleep, thinking of him and how I could see him again.

Without children, I could have never anticipated the fight Margo would have put up in regard to attending her first ball. She is a lovely young lady whom I deeply care for, but tonight, I detest her stubborn behaviors.

With a quick introduction between Albert and Margo, he asks for a dance and whisks her away to the dance floor. Then the most unexpected thing happens, jealousy rings throughout my body. When I offered to serve as Margo's chaperone, it was because I missed London society, but not a single thought of re-entering as an eligible woman myself crossed my mind.

Looking around at the other gentlemen in the room, none of them, dancing or otherwise, sparks any emotion from me. It is as if everyone in this room looks foggy, yet when I look back at Albert, he is clear as a bright sunny day.

She smiles in his arms and he smirks at her. Perhaps that is the reason for my emotions, that this man might be the perfect match for Margo. He is slightly older, but not so much that it would be considered scandalous.

The music ends and he returns Margo to my side with a head nod, and then he is gone. The night continues and Margo's mood seems to have improved after her dance with Albert. It is torture to hold my tongue, but I must wait until we leave to ask what they discussed.

"Miss Eton." A young man, Edward Riley, approaches.

"Lady Calderwood." He bows to us both. He is a friend of Margo's. Their fathers are business partners, and I recall meeting him once or twice before either came of age.

"Mr. Riley," she beams with excitement. Though she has never mentioned romantic feelings, it seems she may hold the young man in high esteem.

"Would you do me the great honor of dancing the next song with me?" His voice has a bit of a shake. The handsome young man appears nervous as he holds out his hand to her.

"Certainly." She takes it and does not bother to look in my direction as they make their way to the dance floor.

"They could make for a good match." The husky voice comes from behind me. Albert. He steps to my side.

"You know the young man, Mr. Berry?" I ask, trying to ignore the warm feeling covering my body. If it were any other man, I would find it unsettling, but it is just the opposite. With him standing next to me, it is as if all of my worries and frustrations from the evening are melting off of me.

"Yes, Mr. Edward Riley is a close friend and a good man."

"Such as yourself?"

He laughs, "I am not sure how others consider me."

"I think you are one of the very best men." The truth breaks free from my lips before I can think better of it. Although, it has been years since having the good fortune to share his company. I have a sense that he has only increased in his goodness during our years apart.

A slight blush colors his cheeks above his heavy beard. He swallows and shakes his head slightly, turning his attention to Margo dancing with his friend—who I am glad to hear he believes is a better match for her than himself. Although I have no right to feel in such a way.

"Is Miss Eton a relative of yours?" he asks, still not turning to face me.

"No, her country estate is close to the Calderwood Estate. I have known her since she was a small child." I stop myself from talking too much about my affection for my friend. "Her parents, Lord and Lady Eton, allow me to act as her escort in society."

He looks at me and says, "That is very kind of you to take on that role. From our dance, it was clear she is very unsure of her entrance. I am sure she is grateful for your support."

"It is my honor." Our conversation pauses as we watch Margo and Mr. Riley. They are not smiling or laughing, though they are talking.

"Are you in London for long, Mr. Berry? Or is this a brief pause from your traveling?" I ask and hate myself for hoping he will say he is staying in town.

"I have not decided that yet, Lady Calderwood, but I do have a feeling I need a break from travel." I try to hide my smile.

"Perhaps we shall see each other again then?" I cannot help but be hopeful.

He holds my gaze, his smile so warm and welcoming. "If that is what you wish, I will be happy to arrange it."

The music ends and we both look toward the dance floor. Margo looks indifferent, but Mr. Riley looks to be *attempting, but failing, to control his emotions. He turns briskly away from her and storms off.*

"I think I should go check on my friend," Albert says as Margo reaches us. "I must bid you both a farewell. It was an honor to dance with you, Miss Eton." He bows to her. "It was a pleasure to see you again, Lady Calderwood." He bows to me but does not break eye contact. Then he rushes off in the direction his friend went moments earlier.

That night, I could not sleep, feeling the loss of Albert Berry's comforting presence. I once considered him a friend, and I suppose I still do. Yet, when I saw him previously, I was a married woman who was utterly infatuated with her husband. I had the protection and comfort at that time and did not seek it in others. Not that I realized I had been lacking it until Albert approached me.

When would I be able to see him next? I will have to check the date of the next ball and hope he is in attendance too.

Morning comes and Margo is up and dressed early in anticipation of her first morning of accepting gentleman callers.

As we wait in the sitting room, Darcy appears to announce the first caller. "A Mr. Albert Berry."

We both stand and I feel my cheeks flush as they strain from the large smile on my face.

"Good morning, ladies." He bows to us both. Margo seems confused and I must match her expression.

He quickly explains. "It was not until later last night that I realized with Lady Calderwood acting as your chaperone, there is not a gentleman of the house to act as a male chaperone this morning. I had nothing else on my schedule and wanted to offer my services."

"Thank you, Mr. Berry. That is very kind of you."

"Well, you mentioned wanting to see me again, so here I am." He moves to take the seat beside me. Our chairs are set back from the main entertaining area to leave that for Margo's callers. "If there is anything else you ever need, Lady Calderwood. You only need to ask and I will see it done."

A promise he has kept every day since that very morning.

25

Once I admit sleep will not come for me tonight, I think of an idea. Something I can do for Albert to show him how much I love and miss him during our time apart.

Just as he did for me, I begin to write him letters. Enough that will allow one for each of the remaining days we are apart. With a large stack of parchment, I light the candles on my desk and pull the wax and my seal with the branches and leaves from the drawer.

My letters do not compare to what Albert writes to me, but I try my best. The endless effort he has put into expressing the depth of his devotion is not lost on me. Hopefully, I can show my reciprocation, even if it is done so with poorly written love letters.

When I miss you most, I find myself among endless volumes of love stories.

Brushing my hands over their spines, I both envy and pity them.

Envying that their main characters shall remain bound together, never to be separated beyond the hardcovers. That their love is safe within these walls, never to be disturbed.

Pitying that as grand as their love stories may be, they will never be as great as ours.

After completing a stack that professes my love, I try my hand at writing something that will ignite a fire within him. One that will leave him wanting without consolation.

Even in your absence, my body longs for you. The memory of your touch lingers on my skin, hovering over me like the brush of a feather but never strong enough to satisfy this perpetual yearning.

When we reunite, do not take your time; do not linger.

Simply make your presence known.

I shiver as I think of Albert reading such a note. I fold it quickly, drip the wax over the fold, and secure it with my secret seal.

I write enough to last until we can reunite privately once our family obligations are behind us. When all of the wax is dry, I pull the satchel that Albert's letters were delivered inside of out from under my bed. I move the few remaining unopened letters from Albert to the new lockbox that Claire was able to secure for me. The satchel will be ideal for delivering the letters I wrote to him tomorrow without stirring any attention. I place the bag next to the dress Claire has laid out for me.

Sleep finally comes for me, but it is brief and I soon rise to greet the sun. I dress quickly, smiling as I do. Unable to contain my eagerness. The dress I wear is closer to the country dresses Margo has custom-made for her. The skirt is far more flowy—ideal for horseback riding, which is how I plan to arrive at Eton Cottage. I do not need the grand fair of a carriage. Preferring to leave the Calderwood Estate with as little notice as possible.

THE COOL MORNING air brushes against my cheeks as the details of Eton Cottage's structure come into view. As soon as I am close enough to notice a large man waiting outside by the stables, I wave to greet Mr. Landon.

When I finally reach my destination, he is there waiting to assist my dismount from the horse. "What a pleasure it is to see you again, Lily." It is always comforting when he calls me Lily rather than my title by marriage.

"And you, Mr. Landon." Yet, I will refuse to be so informal with him—he is my senior and a parental figure to Margo. I prefer to show him my respect in that way.

"They are waiting for you inside. I will join you in a moment."

I hand him the reins and make my way through the back entrance to the kitchen. Delicious smells overtake my senses, and a pain in my stomach reminds me that I forgot to eat in my haste to begin my travels.

"Lily!" Margo squeals and jumps into my embrace. "Mrs. Landon has been baking since last night. You must try these cakes." She releases me to pull out a chair next to her. I sit and look around the room. None of the surroundings have changed, but in a very brief time, the lives of its occupants are completely different.

Edward is seated across from me. "I want to thank you for stopping by to go on a walk with Claire yesterday, Edward."

His mischievous smile grows. "It was my idea and if I may say so, I thought it was quite bright of me."

"Yes, you are so very intelligent, darling," Margo praises her husband.

He continues, "I was not expecting so many suspicious eyes when I arrived, though."

Not wanting to dwell on the situation at the Calderwood Estate, I try to change the topic of conversation. "Yes, well, your efforts are very much appreciated. Have you any idea when your guests will be arriving?"

Mrs. Landon answers as she carries a large pot of hot water for tea to the table. "It will surely be a few hours, dear." She hands me a small blue mug with a smile and squeezes my shoulder. "We are glad to have your company to ourselves while we wait."

The morning hours are relaxing, I did not realize

how tense I had become in the last months, but the ease I feel in my muscles is proof that I should more regularly seek the company of my friends. Yet, even with the comfort of Eton Cottage, anticipation continues to build with each passing minute, knowing Albert gets closer and closer.

Margo stands at my side, holding her hand out for me. "I have a new book to show you. I left it in the library, walk with me?"

I take her hand and hope this short excursion will help the time pass more quickly. Once we can no longer hear the laughter from the kitchen, she leans and asks, "Are you unwell, Lily?" I look at her, but she continues. "You were practically buzzing at the table, fidgeting with your hands, unable to sit still."

"Oh goodness, I apologize. I did not notice I was doing any of that." With a look back at the kitchen, I wonder if anyone else noticed my odd behavior.

"I just thought a walk might be good to work out some of your nerves. I must confess, I do not ever recall seeing you like this before. Is it anticipation for Albert's arrival, or have things at the Calderwood Estate become too much of a burden?"

My sweet Margo. Albert and I kept this secret from her for so long—too long. But I cannot go back and change that. I can, however, be thankful I can speak honestly with her now. "It has been a very stressful time with Lady Augusta and her expectations for Benedict's grand celebration this year."

"Is that tough, thinking and talking about him so

much?" Sadness covers her face. "I know you loved him and miss him terribly. I worry that this is forcing you to relive his loss."

I squeeze the arm that is linked with mine. "Your concern warms my heart, Margo. I must admit, it does prove to be difficult at times, especially the talk of this being his birthday. Although, over the years, I have lived with my grief and learned to accept that it is something I will carry with me for the rest of my days. But that does not mean I should not continue living."

Margo listens closely as we approach the door to her library but stops short of entering. She stands and waits for me to continue.

"It is Lady Augusta who still lives in those days right after we lost him. I wish she would find acceptance and a new purpose in her life. She has so many grandchildren from her daughters, but she is too ingratiated in her sorrow to enjoy their company."

With a deep exhale, I release all of my concerns for the happenings at the Calderwood Estate. "My anxious behaviors are all for the anticipation of Albert's arrival." I watch her smile grow. "I miss him so very much."

"That is good to hear because I have a plan for his arrival."

"A plan?" I ask her.

She backs against the library door and opens it behind her. "I do not have a new book to show you," she confesses, "but being that the library gives a perfect view of the drive, we can watch for his arrival here." She pats the large windowsill where she places pillows and blankets for us.

"Thank you." I immediately sit with my back to the left panel giving me a direct view of the front entrance of Eton Cottage. "This is just what I needed."

Margo sits across from me, her feet curling next to mine, our blankets overlapping each other. "Tell me, how are you truly enjoying your marriage? Now that you have some time to adjust. Is it every horror you anticipated?"

"Just the opposite, actually." She laughs. "Although, I am quite certain that a marriage with any other man would not compare."

"I must agree with you there. I truly believe Edward Riley is the only man who can handle you."

Quiet moments pass as we enjoy the view outside her cottage. It is an unusually sunny day for this time of year as the trees begin to lose their leaves. I smile at how they remind me of Albert and my secret seals.

Margo perks upright and I turn to look. There it is, Albert's carriage! I jump up, releasing myself from the blankets. Margo follows but grabs my arm as I move toward the door. "Wait."

Shock fills my system. How can she expect me to wait? I need to go to him.

"I have a plan, remember?"

"I thought watching for the carriage from the library window was your plan."

"No—well, that was just the first part." I am losing my patience. "You stay here."

"I will not." I pull away from her just as she holds her grasp firmly.

"Yes, rather than you two having to pretend to be nothing more than acquaintances in front of his coachmen, you should stay here. When he exits the carriage, Mr. Landon will occupy the coachmen and I will instruct Albert to find you here. Also, we have plans to take Evelyn to the lake for a picnic." Her eyes narrow at me and she lowers her voice. "So you will have the house to yourselves."

I stop fighting her. I do not want to waste a moment of my brief time with Albert, but her plot has a reason. We will not be able to show our feelings in front of his staff. I move back to the window. They are just about to the entrance of Eton Cottage. I nod at Margo and sit back down at the window.

She smiles in victory.

"Well, do not just stand there. He is about to exit the carriage. Make haste! Send him up here immediately," I shout at her. Her face blushes and she does a little dance before leaving and closing the door behind her.

The carriage comes to a stop.

My heart begins to race.

As the carriage door opens, my hands grow clammy. I run them over the blanket, watching intently. A coachman holds out his hand. The dark brown, almost black hair with a white bow tied at the top is the first thing I see as Evelyn Riley disembarks. Even from this distance, I can see her excitement.

The coachman moves back a step to allow for the

carriage's other occupant to make his exit. I rise to my feet, letting the curtains fall in front of the window, standing at an angle that I can still see through a minimal opening.

Albert looks around at his audience. He looks over them again.

He is looking for me.

My mouth goes dry. While Evelyn still has an arm around her brother and Margo. Albert shakes Mr. Landon's hand and offers Mrs. Landon a hug.

When Evelyn is at his side to greet the Landons, he turns to Edward and Margo. Albert pulls Margo into a hug and I can see his lips moving to her ear. I can not see from this angle if she replies, but it seems she does. He pulls back with a smile on his face. Edward pats him on the shoulder and tips his head in the direction of the library.

Mr. Landon makes a big show of instructing the coachmen and guides them to the stables in the opposite direction. Once they are out of sight, Albert almost runs into the house.

I rest my back against the wall next to the window, finding my legs growing weaker as I hear footsteps, loud and quickly approaching the library door.

26

Remain calm, remain calm...*you cannot make the carriage move any quicker. We will arrive when the horses deliver us to Eton Cottage and no sooner.*

My gaze is locked on the view of the English countryside, but I am so distracted the sun could set and I would not realize the change.

What if Margo was unable to reach her?

There is a chance, slight at that, but still possible, that she was not made aware of my brief visit. Or worse, she was made aware but is unable to separate herself from Lady Augusta.

A silent prayer fills my mind, please let her be there when I arrive.

I need to see her.

I can feel myself wasting away with each passing day I am separated from her. Without Lily, nothing drives me, nothing soothes me, nothing sustains me.

"Albert." Evelyn pulls me out of my trepidation. I look up to see her eyes wide with worry. "Are you unwell?"

Serious conversation about her interest in Arthur Landon occupied the first hour of our journey. I do not want to overstep my closest friend, but I did feel I could act in an older brother capacity for the time, sharing my personal experiences, such that Edward has never endured. If she and Arthur choose to pursue this life, I want her to know of the hardships she may face.

While what I know of him, he is a good young man, certainly from a good family, there is no use denying that he lives in a circle far from the privileged upbringing she experienced being a member of such a high-ranking family. By the end of our conversation, she did promise that she would share all of this with Edward and Margo during her stay at Eton Cottage.

"Yes, I am fine." Her eyes narrow at my response. She clearly does not believe me. "Why—are you unwell?"

"No, I am fine. It is your leg causing the cabin to shake more than the uneven road." I still my leg, not realizing it was moving to begin with. "Look at your hands, they are red from how tight you are clenching your fists." Now that she points it out, my hands are sore. I release the grip, turning my palms up. I can see marks from where my fingernails were digging into my skin.

I suppose while trying to suppress my thoughts and nerves, they found an outlet physically. If Lily is waiting for me at Eton Cottage, I cannot let her see me in such a state. Not because I want to hide these feelings but because I do not want them to overtake the moment. We can talk about such things when we have more time. I want this afternoon to be filled exclusively with joy.

Still owing my passenger an explanation, I look up at a young girl who very likely will find herself in a similar situation in the near future. So, I must be honest with her.

"I want so desperately to see Lily." After another deep breath, I express my fears out loud for the first time. "What if she was not able to leave the Calderwood Estate...what if she will not be at Eton Cottage when we arrive?"

Evelyn moves to sit beside me, placing her hand in mine and resting her head on my shoulder. At this moment, I am reminded of how lucky I am to be surrounded by such supportive women in my life. Evelyn is Edward's sister, but I have watched this girl grow from a young child. Now, she sits next to me, maturing more and more each day. I care for her as I do Margo and will protect her just as fiercely. Letting my head lean on hers as I squeeze her hand.

We sit in silence like that until Evelyn picks her head up and announces she can see Eton Cottage. She tightens her grasp on my hand one last time then returns to her original seat across from me.

The carriage comes to a final stop and one of the coachmen moves to open the door for us. As Evey takes her exit, our hosts all pour out of the main entrance to Eton Cottage. Evelyn blocks my view, but as soon as she is fully out, I take my chance to exit the carriage. I immediately search the faces of our welcoming party. While they are each important people in my life, none are the one I am looking for. I check again, but do not see her. I can feel my insides crushing.

I try to push down my emotions as I greet the Landons and then move to Margo and Edward when Evelyn lets them out of her hug. I hold out my hand to Margo and pull her into an embrace. I whisper in her ear. "She was not able to come?"

Thankfully, without a moment to waste, Margo replies, "She is waiting for you in the library." I begin to pull out of Margo's arms, anxious to get to my love, but she pulls me back in. "We will be taking Evelyn on a picnic by the lake. You will have the house to yourselves." Then she releases me.

Edward, surely knowing what his wife just shared with me, pats me on the back. I do not waste another moment and all but run into the house until I am outside of the library.

She is on the other side.

I knock once, then call to her, "Lily, I wish to enter this library and ravish you madly. If you are directly on the other side of this door, I need you to step back. Once my hand touches this handle, my desire for you will take over."

I listen for her response. It never comes, but the handle starts to turn as the door creaks open. With the sun shining in from the window behind her, she looks every bit the angel I believe her to be.

There are no words, only actions. I lift her from the doorway and walk her back into the library, kicking the door closed behind me.

Her familiar scent fills my nose and overtakes my senses. Her arms and legs wrap around me, touching her forehead to mine. "I have missed you," she whispers.

"I am here now." My words are not enough. I need to demonstrate my longing in a way she cannot deny. Her hands weave through my hair as I decide where to take her first.

When I have my destination in mind, I command, "Kiss me." Lily does not hesitate—her soft lips collide with mine. My tongue forces entry between them, pulling a low moan from her throat.

I begin to walk, never releasing her from my hold. Trying to not use too much force, I back her up against the sturdiest bookshelf in Eton Cottage's library. Her hands pull from my head to scrunch up the loose fabric of her skirts and the bottom of her chemise. She moves to release me from my trousers, but I stop her. "Not yet, love."

Her head tilts in question as she tries to control her heavy breathing. I hate to disappoint, but I am sure my next move will make up for it.

I move my arms under each of her thighs and lift her up until her legs hang over my shoulder, displaying her core at eye level for me, an exquisite feast indeed. "Hold on to the top."

Lily's arms move lightning-fast over her head, grasping the top lip of the large bookshelf.

Of course, I usually prefer to take my time with this particular endeavor, but my lady is wanting and I can not deny her any longer. I tighten my grip on her thighs as I focus my attention on her apex. My lips push forward, quickly followed by my tongue, forcefully tracing every inch of her. I place the most pressure on the area I know is her favorite and am rewarded when her legs begin to shake on either side of my face. Then I pull back, not ready to end this quite so soon. Moving lower, I work my tongue in and out of her, eliciting a moan with each thrust.

With her thighs pressing in on my ears, I can barely make out her muffled words. I pause to look up at the beauty above me. Her face is flushed the bright red of an apple, sweat glistening over her skin and her hair tousled already.

Her breath is heavy as she releases each word individually. "I. Need. You."

"You have me, darling, all of me."

She shakes her head. "On. The. Floor."

"Right away." I pull one hand out from under her thighs to wrap around her waist. She lets go of the shelf, placing her hands on my shoulders as I lower her to stand before me.

A wicked smile covers her face before she pulls on the hem of my shirt and lifts it over my head. As she kisses me, her hands graze over my bare chest until they reach my waist and she undoes my trousers. "Lie down." Her voice is low and sultry. I nearly melt onto the floor.

Once there, she kneels and crawls up my body, stopping when she is seated on top of me. Her heat covering my strained body is bliss. I grab onto her waist and begin to rock back-and-forth over her soft flesh. She moans, securing herself by placing her hands firmly on my chest. When she looks down at me, desire fills her eyes. She lifts her hips slightly to allow me to ease into her.

Lily pulses above me, and I match her rhythm the best I can. My body begins to take control and my thoughts become less and less focused.

What have I done to deserve such a passionate, beautiful, exquisite woman....and her insatiable desires?

27

Lily's head is tucked between my neck and shoulder, and her hand lazily moves across my chest as we lay intertwined on the large settee in the Eton Cottage Library. The fog of our euphoric lovemaking begins to clear. It is then I realize we have not spoken a single word to one another since our lovemaking ended.

"Do you feel that, my darling?" I ask as I run my hand through her disheveled blonde strands.

She lifts her head enough to look at me, "What are you feeling?"

"Our souls, at peace." She smiles at my words, "Since we parted, a battle has waged within me. Only now settled that we are reunited."

"Yes, I do feel it too." Her body covers mine, yet she moves in as if it is not close enough.

We lie in silence, enjoying this moment just a little longer. I must be sure to thank our hosts, who have orchestrated this opportunity for Lily and me to be alone. Given they vacated their own home for us, they most likely assumed we would find our way to one of our rooms. I look around at the books stacked around us, lining the walls. Little did they know we have a proclivity for libraries.

Lily leans up, placing her chin on her hand as it rests over my heart. "These weeks without you have been difficult, but I know it is my fault we must be separated."

"We each have family obligations to see to. Let us hope our services now will gain us a great debt of privacy in the hereafter."

"And how would you like to spend that great amount of privacy, Mr. Berry?" Her look becomes mischievous.

"Very much like I am at this moment." I reach down and grasp her backside, pulling it up on my body before hooking my hands to the back of her thighs, bending them to sit her up on top of me. "Yes, I believe this will do just fine."

She begins to rock her hips back-and-forth, reigniting the flame within me. I grab onto her delicate skin as her hands fall to my chest.

She freezes and turns to the door.

"What is it?"

She does not answer but remains silent. That is when I hear them. Voices below us, laughter growing louder throughout the cottage. It seems the picnic has ended and our friends have returned.

Bending, her bare chest is flush against mine, moving her lips a breath from mine. "I suppose this will need to be postponed."

She moves her leg to step off the settee, but I catch her around the waist, holding her in place. "I think not."

WHAT MUST BE AT LEAST an hour later, we join our hosts. The Landons have set out sandwiches for us. Both Lily and I make a plate for ourselves., as it seems we are quite famished from our vigorous activities.

Everyone is gathering in the sitting room, Evelyn looking absolutely at home among the residents of Eton Cottage. That reminds me, this has become her brother's home recently too.

"Edward, my friend. I have not had the chance to ask you, how are you enjoying living in the country?"

He pulls his wife closer to his side. "The Riley family has a country estate, but Eton Cottage, I truly consider to be my home." He places a kiss on her cheek.

I notice Evelyn longingly looking at the pair of them. "And you, Evelyn? It seems you have grown quite fond of being here as well."

She perks up. "I certainly do. Not only do I greatly enjoy the company, but it is also a respite from the exhausting demands of London society and my mother's insistence that I find a husband as soon as possible."

I hold my tongue—now is not the time to insist she

share her additional reason for wanting to be close to a certain young man. I trust she will share that soon enough—in privacy—I am sure of it.

"Thank you again for detouring your trip today to deliver her safely, Albert." Edward seems very pleased to have his sister here.

"It was my pleasure." I realize the innuendo as soon as it leaves my mouth. Margo chuckles under her breath and shakes her head at Lily. I narrow my eyes at my friend as her husband nudges her with his elbow. The Landons begin laughing at us while Evelyn looks only slightly confused.

The Landons have never been one to keep members of someone's staff excluded from their home, yet in this case, they directed the coachmen of the Berry Estate to pass the afternoon in the visitor's hall. A small sitting room somewhat removed from the house that has not been used in years. Mrs. Landon assured me they would be provided with an excellent afternoon. She saw to prepare meals for them and left plenty of refreshments, books, and decks of cards for entertainment to pass the time. If they had been invited in, Lily and I would have needed to be far more mindful of our interactions. With such little time together this afternoon, the Landons made sure we did not have to worry about such things.

Hours of enjoyable conversation pass, but my visit is coming to an end. As the sun falls closer to the horizon, I prepare to take my leave. "I suppose it is time for my departure," I announce as I squeeze Lily's hand and begin to rise.

Mrs. Landon stands first, "Give them a moment. Mr. Landon will gather the coachmen to prepare the carriage. We will wait outside to say our goodbyes."

"I suppose your coachmen are not aware of my presence. It may be best if we part now," Lily suggests.

"Damn them. I want to see you as I drive away, taking every chance to admire your beauty until I am out of view." I bring her in closely, but she pulls away.

"Oh! Wait right here, I have something for you." She turns and runs out of the room.

"Should I accompany you?"

Her voice is already growing louder and she is back through the door. "No need." She smiles, holding the satchel I sent her letters in. Handing it to me, I can feel letters inside. Could she be returning them?

"Your letters have kept me company through the prolonged ordeal I must endure at the Calderwood Estate. I know your next destination will not be ideal. I wanted to repay the favor and send you off with a letter for each remaining day we will be apart." Mesmerized by her enthusiasm, I try to engrain this view in my memory.

I lift the satchel strap over my head and secure it across my chest. My hands find her neck and my thumbs graze her cheeks. I pull her close to me, our foreheads touching, "Thank you, Lily. I will treasure them."

Our kiss is not as urgent as it was in the library, it is gentle, neither one wanting to break away first. The sound of the horses bringing the carriage around startles us and we both turn toward the noise.

We walk hand and hand to the door, where the rest of our party awaits. They each exit before us, and I keep my fingers interlocked with Lily's until the last possible moment. When we are the only ones left, I release her hand. As our connection breaks, I feel a sharp pain in my chest. And so the battle within me begins yet again.

The Landons are first. Mr. Landon holds out his hand and, with a firm shake, says, "It was great to see you, old friend. Safe Travels." Mrs. Landon pulls me into a hug, "Be well, Albert."

Next are the newlyweds. Margo leaps into my arms as she always has. "I look forward to your return. Come sooner if you can." I nod at her.

If only that were an option.

Edward shakes my hand and slaps my shoulder with the other. I do the same in return. "Not to be improper, but if you should find yourself in need of a distraction in the form of unexpected company while at the Berry Estate, write to us. We would be happy to come visit." Edward knows very well of the tension between my father and me. That is a kind offer for him to make.

"Let us hope it does not come to that and I can simply return to Eton Cottage in a little more than a fortnight as planned."

Evelyn hugs me, much like Margo does, "Thank you for escorting me here this morning, Albert," she whispers into my ear. "And thank you for the valuable advice you shared with me during the journey."

"I hope you have an enjoyable visit, Evelyn." I pull out of her embrace to face the most difficult goodbye.

Lily tilts her head and smiles at me. Opening her arms, I suppose it would not appear odd to the coachmen who just saw me hug the rest of the women in this party. "Safe travels, Albert."

I let her face fall toward them so I can whisper to her ear without their notice. "I love you with each breath I take. I will think of you every moment we are apart."

"Albert..." The breathily way she says my name is more than enough. I pull away, not wanting to linger too long in our embrace.

I turn back to them all once more before entering the carriage. "I shall see you all soon." Waves are exchanged as the latch on the door locks into place. Then I am pulled away from Eton Cottage, watching Lily for as long as I can.

THE MOON IS bright in the sky as I exit the carriage and make my way up the stairs to the grand entrance of the Berry Estate. Behind me, I hear the removal of my luggage, but I do not bother to look back. *If this were my home, I would stay and offer to carry some in myself.* However, my father would never stand for such informal behaviors. I squeeze the leather strap across my chest, the satchel in the same place since Lily gave it to me.

Once inside, I move toward the sitting room.

"Good evening, Mother." A cough sounds from the far right of the room, where my father is seated, propped in the direction of the window. "Good evening, Father."

I select the seat next to my mother. She asks, "Are you hungry, my dear?"

"You should have been here for dinner," Father states.

"Yes, I would like something, but I can call for it to be sent to my room." Her face falls hearing that I am not planning to visit with her.

"Before you go, tell us how your day went. Was your friend happy to see his sister?" she asks.

"Indeed, he was," I answer.

"And how was your time with the young lady?" My father's inquiry is not very discreet, although I am sure he did not mean it to be. "After your friend swooped in to marry Miss Eton, perhaps his sister can act as a suitable replacement to be the next Lady Berry."

"Spending the journey with her was a delightful experience." My father sits up in his seat, foolish man. "Her company is what I would imagine it would have been like to have a younger sister myself."

Lord Berry pushes back in his seat, looking out the window as he scoffs.

My mother senses the tension and tries to take back

control of the conversation. "And she will be staying at Eton Cottage?" I nod. "For how long?"

Perfect way to transition, Mother. "Through the ball at the Calderwood Estate, the one being held in honor of the late Lord Calderwood's birthday."

"Oh, yes. Did you send along our plans to attend, Albert?"

"Yes, Mother. It is taken care of," I answer. "I have also taken the liberty to notify the Calderwood family that you and Father will be staying at their estate, but I have decided to stay at Eton Cottage."

"Why would you do that?" my father asks.

"As I told you, father, Eton Cottage is now the property of Mr. Edward Riley and his bride, Margaret, formally Eton. That is where I delivered the young Miss Riley today. The property sits beside the Calderwood Estate."

"How convenient," Lord Berry snarks.

"As I have an open invitation to stay at Eton Cottage, I believe it would be a great kindness to the Calderwoods to open another room for what I can only imagine is an extensive guest list."

"That was very kind of you, Albert." My mother smiles at me. "I am glad to hear you have such great friends."

"Yes, thank you, Mother."

"While you are at Eton Cottage, I hope you will seriously consider the young Miss Riley." I roll my eyes at his insistence. "Until then, I expect your full attention to be on the matters of our family and the estate."

Unable to think of a civil response, I decide that it is the perfect time for me to excuse myself for the night.

"Right, Father. I will see you in the morning." I lean down to my mother, "Goodnight, Mother. Sleep well."

Once in my room, I finally remove the satchel and instantly mourn the warmth the leather strap provided. Placing it gently on my bed, I remove my jacket and sit at my desk to pick at the tray of food that was just delivered. I sample the meats and cheeses but soon grow bored with them.

I place a glass of wine on the table beside my bed as I open the satchel and pull out the stack of letters tied together with a string. Without untying the string, I pull the letter on top away from the binding.

My heart warms as I see the seal with branches covered in leaves.

I wanted you to know just how much I cherished the letters you gave me, but I knew thanking you was not enough to show my appreciation.

So, I have decided to return the gesture. I have written a letter for each day we will be apart until your expected return to Eton Cottage in a fortnight. I do not claim to share your great talent with words, but I hope they will be enough to make our time apart a little more manageable.

Always,
Yours

28

Fifteen days.

Fifteen days have passed since I was in Albert's arms at Eton Cottage. Yet, this time, the longer we are apart is a reminder of how close I am to seeing him again. We did not discuss our plans, but I assume he will stay back at Eton Cottage until the last of the Calderwood Estate guests take their leave. Then, he will join me under this roof and we can resume the solitary bliss we shared after Margo's wedding.

There is a knock at my bedroom door, followed by James, one of the younger members of my staff, calling to me. "Lady Calderwood, your dress was just delivered. Claire asked me to bring it up to you."

I open the door immediately and move aside as he carries the large box across the room and places it on a small table I have in the corner. I thank him as he leaves me alone to inspect the dress.

It is so rare that I feel anything but utter excitement

at the arrival of a new dress. This box, however, contains a dress I never wish to wear. The black bow holding the lid securely in place reminds me of the endless mourning dresses that were delivered after Benedict's death. Now, over a decade later, I am struggling to find the courage to unravel the bow to reveal the newest black mourning dress.

When Lady Augusta insisted we request custom attire for the celebration, my request for us to wear something other than black was met with an absolute refusal.

"It will be a celebration of his life. I do not want it to come across that we are celebrating his death, but more a show of how much he is missed. I expect you all to be dressed in black. A bright color would be offensive. See to it that your dresses are ordered soon so that they can be ready in time." Lady Augusta's stare moves toward her two daughters and me.

"Of course, Mother." Amelia and her mother are in such a similar mindset.

"Do you have any specifications in mind?" Edith inquires.

"The only specification is that they need to be black." All three of us lift our heads and turn to face the matriarch of the Calderwood family.

"Black, mother?" Edith asks.

"Yes, this entire evening is in honor of your late brother. What other color would you wear?" Lady Augusta is clearly surprised by her daughter's suggestion. Amelia squirms in

her seat, even though she disagrees, but clearly has no plans to voice them.

I shall then. "What if we choose other colors, Lady Augusta?" Her mouth falls open, but I continue before she can interject. "Black is typically for those who recently lost someone. Perhaps we can stick to other dark shades for such an event. We are meant to be celebrating his life, not death. The black might lead guests to the wrong interpretations. I was thinking maybe we each take a different color and have a dress made in its darkest shade. I would like a deep maroon."

Lady Augusta remains silent, scowling as if she is deciding if my suggestion even deserves an answer. Amelia and Edith look between their mother and me. Lady Augusta finally looks away from me, "We will all be in black."

Amelia follows her mother's lead and lowers her gaze to the tea in her lap. Edith meets my eyes and offers a sympathetic look.

I decide to leave the box unopened since I have other matters to distract me. Our guests will begin arriving tomorrow. With the main event two days away, we encouraged them to come earlier if they were able, to enjoy the country with us and allow for time to rest before the festivities rather than a day of travel. Most took us up on our offer.

While I do not expect to enjoy the upcoming days as much as hosting Margo's wedding party, I am looking forward to having the halls of the Calderwood Estate filled. I have always enjoyed hosting, just as Benedict did. Even in his absences, I feel I have become quite an extraordinary host, with parties large and small.

Unfortunately, due to the reason these guests were invited, they will not see me as an accommodating hostess but more so as a widow, who deserves their pity. Not a woman who has learned to face the world alone and orchestrated constant entertainment, and endless meals for them to enjoy while staying in my home.

Then, of course, I must prepare for Amelia's son, Robert, to be strutting around, acting as if he is to be thanked for this event. Introducing himself as Lord Calderwood to anyone who will listen. I am expected to wear a black dress, which will guarantee that every conversation I have will surely consist of condolences.

But it does not have to be like this. If I were to marry Albert...I would never need to worry about such things again. Never be forced back into mourning for my husband, who died years ago.

Remembering a time when I was not so confident in my feelings for Albert, I fought against them so hard at first, thinking I was hurting Benedict by caring for another man. Lady Augusta would most certainly agree. With time, I have learned to be more kind to myself and allow this love for him to grow just as I maintain the love I held for Benedict.

I do mourn his loss, every day. But I also still live my life. Why is it that people do not believe that both can coexist within a person?

It has taken years, but I finally came to the

resolution that I can have love for my long-passed husband and allow my love for Albert to grow. I can be a wife again, be loved again, fully.

FINALLY, we arrive at the day before the ball. The first of our guests arrives, and I am forced to welcome the awful Harold Grange. Watching him enter the foyer of my home makes me feel sick. He accompanies his mother. Hopefully, her presence will keep him well-behaved. Mrs. Grange, also a widow, spends her days with her second son. The eldest Grange son married an heiress in Northern England and left London not long after his father passed.

Lady Augusta fusses over Mrs. Grange, leading her into the sitting room. "Lady Calderwood, be so kind as to show Mr. Grange to the sitting room with us," she instructs over her shoulder. Little does she know how much she is asking of me. I had not planned to speak a single word to this man. The last I saw him, I was swinging an umbrella at his head.

When I finally turn toward him, he has a smug look and holds out his arm for me to take.

Absolutely not.

"This way, Mr. Grange," I say with my hands firmly interlaced in front of me and begin walking, not waiting for him.

"I suppose you are anticipating a great number of guests, Lady Calderwood. I am looking forward to sharing the company of so many great families of London." I am sure he is, given that without his mother's escort, he is aware he would not be so welcome.

I nod in response. Then I realize he may be wondering if Margo will be here with Edward. Grange could be looking to confirm their marriage. Could he have spoken with Lord Eton yet? Regardless, he best not cause any commotion upon their arrival. I must be sure to keep him far away from Margo and Edward, if possible.

"Will Mr. Berry be in attendance this weekend?" Harold asks. "I noticed him whispering to the young Miss Riley before they stepped into a carriage and left the city some weeks ago. Can I assume he has finally set his sights on his friend's younger sister?"

"I do not think their personal business is any of your concern, Mr. Grange. Mr. Berry will be attending the ball. You may ask him intimate details of his personal life directly if you would like."

"Is he not arriving before?" Harold asks.

I freeze. Perhaps I should not have disclosed that Albert will not be here soon. Although, what could he possibly do to me alone? I am no prize he would be interested in marrying.

"No, he is visiting with Edward Riley and his new bride before arriving here." Hopefully, that will remind Harold Grange of the last time the five of us were together.

"Interesting," Harold says and takes a seat.

I turn and exit the room, Amelia is in the foyer. *Perfect.* "Amelia, your mother asked if you would join her in entertaining the guests in the sitting room."

"Who will be here to welcome them?"

"It is my residence, so I feel I should be better suited to greet everyone. I shall escort them directly to you in the sitting room."

Her eyes narrow at me, and I swear I hear her mutter "for now" under her breath as she walks away.

More and more guests arrive as the day lingers on. My thoughts travel to Eton Cottage. Lord and Lady Riley are not expected to be in the country until tomorrow morning. Albert then, too. *How I wish I was among those lodging at Eton Cottage.*

29

The weather is slightly warmer than is expected for this time of year, but the inside of the carriage feels sweltering. I should have offered to ride alongside on horseback. My mother seems happy enough to have the three of us together, so I suppose I can endure. As she has since my earliest memory, she sits beside me, giving my father a bench to himself. I wonder if they sat opposite when it was only the two of them.

It was obvious to me at a very young age that my parents did not have a love match between them. Noticing the look of disappointment when my father would dismiss her kindness or when her requests would go completely ignored. She is the singular reason I feel guilty for leaving when I disappear to the Calderwood Estate for weeks at a time. I could be spending time with her, giving her a break from the cold man who sits across from us now.

"Are you sure you must stay with Edward Riley?" my mother asks. Another pang of guilt sweeps through me.

"I would not want to change my plans with such short notice to the Calderwoods. I will only be sleeping there and plan to accompany you in every activity that is on the itinerary," I promise her, hoping it will suffice. If not for my father, and with Margo's permission, I would invite my mother to Eton Cottage. I cannot help but think she would greatly enjoy it there.

"Leave him to it, Teresa. He has plans to woo the young Miss Riley." He turns to me. "Take full advantage of the opportunity."

"Father, as I have explained before, my intentions with Miss Riley are no different than that of her own brother." I am getting so tired of wasting my words on this subject.

"Do not be foolish, Albert. You socialize so very little, to begin with. Where do you expect to find a wife if not for the sisters of your friends?"

My mother must feel my body tensing as she decides to intercede. "Nicholas, need I remind you we are traveling to a memorial ball for a man who would have been alive to celebrate with us had he not passed away far too soon. This event is being hosted by his widow, who has been left on her own for more than a decade. This evening is not for matchmaking."

Hearing my mother voice her respect for Lily fills my heart. I squeeze her hand in thanks, yet she may never know how much I appreciate her kind words.

"Oh, well yes, I suppose." My father huffs and returns to the book in his hand.

Our first stop will be the Calderwood Estate. If only this carriage could move quicker. I prepare myself for the great restraint it will take to remain in the carriage while my parents take their exit. To not run into the house I am so familiar with, to seek her out. Will she be in the library? My daydreams fill with finding and taking her into my arms, then refuse to ever release her.

No, I will stay hidden in the carriage, as I would have if this ball had been hosted by any other family in London.

Through the years, when Benedict's birthday arrived and his family came to see Lily, I tried to give her privacy. Without being strong enough to be too far from her, I usually stay at Eton Cottage. Far away enough to let her spend this time privately but close enough to be with her in a moment if she needs me. I have made my intentions clear to Lily—I never wish to replace Benedict or for her to forget him.

My mother nudges my side gently to bring me back to the present. Too distracted in my daydreams of Lily, I do not recognize the familiar scenery as we approach her estate.

"We are about to arrive, Albert."

"Oh, yes."

"We will see you this evening." His directive is given with a stern tone. My father must think it is possible I will not attend. Little does he know, nothing could keep me from the Calderwood Estate this evening.

The carriage comes to a stop and I say my goodbyes as they exit at the base of the main entrance. I cannot help but look out as I slide closer to the door. I look around at the welcoming party and other guests who are idling on the front terrace. Some familiar faces among them, but not the one I am longing to see. After their luggage has been removed from the back of the carriage, it jolts beneath me as we set off in the direction of Eton Cottage.

It does not take long for me to reach my destination. I assist the coachmen with my luggage and dismiss them to return to the Calderwood Estate, where they will be able to rest themselves.

As the carriage pulls away, Edward and Mr. Landon emerge from the front doors of Eton Cottage.

"Welcome, Albert!" Mr. Landon calls and bends to pick up one of my bags.

Edward leans down to retrieve the other. "Glad you made it safely."

I reach out in both of their directions. "I can carry those."

"Nonsense," Mr. Landon says.

"You just traveled for hours—stretch your limbs," Edward insists.

The moment I walk into the house, delicious smells overtake me. My legs override my mind and lead me straight to the kitchen, where Mrs. Landon stands over the stove with a pan of meat sizzling in front of her.

"Albert! I was hoping you would arrive early enough for breakfast," she calls to me over her shoulder.

"Awfully glad I did. Everything smells delicious." Sausage is not the only smell filling the kitchen. Fresh bread must be rising in the oven, and a sweetness coming from the jams she has already placed out on the table.

"Is there anything I can help with? I would rather not sit just yet." I roll my shoulders. Sitting in a carriage for hours is one of my least favorite activities.

"I think I have everything handled here."

I look around and notice, "Are we not missing two ladies?"

"Oh, I have been up to wake them twice already." Mrs. Landon sounds frustrated.

"Want to have a little fun, Albert?" Edward's mischievous grin and raised eyebrows tell me he has an idea that is certainly going to cause a bit of trouble.

"What do you have in mind, old chap?" I ask.

He looks to the jam and then to Mrs. Landon, who still has her back toward us. Mr. Landon, however, is already following Edward's train of thought but remains silent.

"Albert needs to stretch his legs, we will see to waking them, Mrs. Landon."

"Thank you, boys!" she calls over her shoulder.

Mr. Landon smiles but keeps his lips tightly closed. His shoulders dancing is the only evidence of his laugh.

Edward quietly grabs a jar of jam and a spoon before turning toward the staircase. I follow along. I do not know which I anticipate more, watching what he plans to do with that jam or seeing the girls seek retribution for the malicious act.

We slowly walk through the hallway, attempting to make very little noise. Edward places his ear next to Evelyn's door. Silence fills the dark space. He looks back at me and nods toward the door handle. I position myself flush against the door as I begin to twist the handle. Surely, this is more than improper, sneaking into a lady's room without announcing ourselves.

As soon as the door opens wide enough, he sneaks in, even more soft with his steps than before. Edward's look of victory tells me she is still sleeping and he can commence with his plan. I follow his lead.

Evelyn Riley looks so much younger than she is, with her limbs sprawled out in every direction, her mouth half open and the blankets tucked right under her chin. In this last year, seeing her dressed in formal gowns with her hair done up, I began to think the child I knew so well was long gone. Yet, seeing her at such peace, she looks more like that little girl than she has in a long time. I must remember, at some point, to thank Edward for allowing me to be a part of his younger sister's life. Giving me experiences I did not expect to have as an only child.

Yet, as I watch her older brother scoop some jam onto his spoon and begin to move it toward her face, I know the innocent-looking young lady is about to disappear. I take a few steps back, with hopes that distance will give me the appearance of innocence in this matter.

He allows a drop to fall onto her cheek, and she begins to stir. Her hand lazily comes to her face, unconsciously aware of the unknown sensation, but she misses brushing it off and resumes her deep slumber.

He looks back at me and blinks. I take two more steps back, closer to the open door, in case I need to make a hasty exit.

I watch as the second dollop of jam lands on Evey's cheek. I swear I can almost hear the splat. This time, her hand comes up quicker to brush off the substance that has disturbed her sleep.

The moment she makes contact with the jam, she wakes instantly. I step into the doorframe, ready to pretend I am coming out of concern and deny being Edward's accomplice in this endeavor. Her arms move slower as she tries to sit up to inspect the sticky substance that now covers her hand.

Edward's laughter is what draws her attention from her own hand to see him standing next to her bed, clutching the jar of jam as his chuckles overcome him.

"Edward!" She does not hesitate to move from the bed and wipe the jam on her hand through his hair. "What were you thinking? I was asleep."

"And you should have been awake." His laughter has become giggles, which continue as he runs out of her reach. "And now you are, thanks to the genius plan we derived."

"We?" She looks up, eyes locking on me. "Albert?

You helped him?" She grabs the jar from Edward's hands and begins to stalk toward me.

She wouldn't...

Oh, no. She really is coming for me.

I turn and run down the hall away from her.

"Do not run. You helped my brother with this—you shall find jam in your hair too." Her hair is a mess, the jam still covering her cheek. She runs after me, covering her hand with fresh jam from the jar.

Just as we pass by the next bedroom door, it opens with a sleepy Margo still wrapped in her dressing gown, rubbing her eyes. "Why is there so much yelling?"

I pull Margo out to use her as a shield. Surely, Evelyn would not risk covering Margo in jam to get to me. Edward stumbles out of Evelyn's room, still laughing.

"I am sure they were coming for you next, Margo. They decided to wake us by putting jam on our faces." Evelyn turns to show her red cheek. "I have already put it in Edward's hair, but since Albert helped him, I need to repay him as well."

It becomes more and more difficult to hold in my laughter, but I know that will not bode well for me. It is then I notice Edward sneaking up behind his sister, still with jam on his spoon. She has no idea and Margo is trying to turn in my grip to face me.

Just as Edward drops the spoon down the back of Evelyn's nightdress, Margo smears jam over my face and beard. She must have grabbed it while I was focused on Edward.

"Breakfast will be ready shortly!" Mr. Landon bellows from the far end of the hallway.

We all drop our hold on each other and turn toward him. Regardless of our ages, this very much feels like we have all just been caught being naughty children.

He stands firm in his spot, waiting for what, I am not sure. An apology, perhaps?

Margo answers, "We will be cleaned up and downstairs shortly."

He crosses his arms over his chest.

Edward replies, "We will be cleaned up and downstairs very, very soon."

Mr. Landon nods and turns to leave, but right before he completely turns away, he shakes his head.

The jam debacle is not mentioned at breakfast, but truly, there is not much conversation at all. Just as usual, Mrs. Landon has cooked an exceptional breakfast and everyone is far too busy eating to stop and engage in conversation.

After the meal ends, Evey and Margo offer to clear the table since they had been unavailable to help with the preparations. Edward walks with me to my room.

"Your parents are not here yet?" I ask.

"No, we are expecting them to arrive much closer to the start of the ball. They may just go directly there."

"Do they not enjoy Eton Cottage?" Since Evelyn came and asked me to escort her to the country, I have wondered why her parents were not interested in visiting.

"I believe my father very much likes being here, but

the unconventional setting does play on my mother's nerves. It is not that I believe she does not agree with it, but more she does not know how to act, which makes her uneasy."

Having known Edward's mother for years, she is certainly the most...uptight of the mothers I am acquainted with from my youth. I nod at him in understanding.

Edward opens the door to my room and asks, "How was your time spent at the Berry Estate?"

"Just as they should be. My father does a great job managing the estate." I sigh, thinking back to the last two weeks. "In fact, I quite enjoyed my time, seeing to the business there when he was not hovering over me."

"That is good to hear. I was worried."

"Thank you, friend, but I am capable of managing my father and his temper. The country estate is grand. There is plenty of space for me to hide when I need a break from him."

He nods, "And how do you think you will manage tonight? Will this be difficult for you?"

After placing my bags in the room, we both move to sit on my bed. "Being apart from her is the most difficult thing by far. Tonight, I shall be in her company, even if not an ideal situation, it will still be good to see her, be near her."

"You are a brave man, Albert. I have always known that, but now I admire you more. It was torture to restrain my feelings for Margo. If I had known she returned them but could not reciprocate them, that is a feat I am not sure I could endure. " I smile weakly at his compliment. "I shall leave you to rest."

He stands and exits my room, closing the door behind him. I move to one of my bags and begin to lay out my attire for the evening when a knock fills the room.

"Did you forget something, my friend?" I open the door and it is not Edward on the other side, but Margo. She smiles and holds out a letter to me.

"This just arrived."

Before I can thank her, she turns on her heels, making her way back toward the main part of the house. I close the door and flip the letter over to see the all too familiar seal, two branches with leaves.

30

I roll over on my back, looking up at the sun-kissed ceiling of my bedroom. While this is not the bedroom we shared as husband and wife, I still think of him the moment my eyes open. "Happy birthday, Benedict," I whisper into the great abyss. The weeks of preparation and frustrations with his family seem to disappear from my memory. I am happy so many people came here today to celebrate him and I will do everything I can to ensure this evening is a joyous occasion...for Benedict.

Tying the belt of my dressing gown, I make my way to the large window across from my bed. Between the open curtains, I lean in to look down at the terrace. It is already busy with staff bringing plates of pastries to the guests, who must be very early risers.

I decide to take a moment and enjoy the beautiful fall morning from my seat on the windowsill. The sun sits atop the horizon, full in its fall glory.

Benedict loved fall mornings, partially because he did so enjoy celebrating his birthday, but also because he loved apples. He always intended to bring apple trees to the property but never got around to seeing it through. The table below is surrounded by people sampling the many apple pastries prepared by my staff. I can see Claire made sure to include whole apples in the offering as well.

In recent years, when Benedict's birthday was celebrated with a small family gathering, I would enjoy the peace and quiet I was allotted during the daytime hours. I never feel particularly talkative on his birthday. I prefer to keep to myself, recalling the memories and the life Benedict and I shared together. Our private life his family was never privy to.

A soft knock pulls my attention back to the day's busy itinerary. I knew today would not allow for much private reflection, but I had hoped for a little more time this morning. Slowly, I move to open the door, surprised to find Edith waiting on the other side.

"Good morning, Lily." Her voice is gentle.

"Good morning, Edith," I move back from the door, "Please come in."

"Thank you." She is also in her dressing gown. Thankfully, her room is not too far from mine. With the many guests, I would be worried she would be seen. "I just wanted to check on you this morning. This day is always particularly difficult for me. I miss him so very much." She shakes her head as if to stop the thought she had. "I just cannot imagine how very tough today must be for you."

I smile softly to comfort her. Her mother tends to make a point of proving she misses him most and judging everyone's actions to determine how much they miss Benedict. It is not a game or a race. We all mourn.

"He is your brother, Edith. We can miss him just as much as one another, each in our own way." I reach for her hand and squeeze it before walking her to my bed.

We both sit and a tear falls down her cheek. I pull her into my arms and hold her. "There have been days when my grief does not allow me to get out of bed. Over the years, his absence has not gotten easier to accept, but I have become wiser in how I grieve. Today is a day he would want us to celebrate him. He would love being the center of attention." She laughs in my arms as I release her.

"You are stronger than all of us, Lily."

"It is not a competition, Edith, but a journey we all must endure."

She wipes her fingers under her eyes and takes a deep breath. "I also came by this morning to inquire about your dress for the evening."

I turn to look at the box with the black bow, still sitting untouched on the table in the corner of the room. Edith follows my gaze.

"I have not opened it yet," I admit. "Trying to prolong the inevitable."

"You spoke of wanting to wear something in a deep red, did you have something in mind?" she asks.

"Indeed." I bound from my bed. "It was one of Benedict's favorite colors. He said it reminded him of apples and fall. I had many dresses made in this color for him after we were wed."

She laughs into her hand as I dig deep within my closet to find it. When I finally have it, I pull it out and hold it in front of my body.

"Oh, Lily, what a beautiful gown!" Walking toward me she runs her hands down the fabric of the skirt.

Amelia does not show any resemblance to her brother, but Edith shares Benedict's smile. It is unfortunate that when we do meet, it is never for occasions that call for the wide smile she wears at this moment. It is as if he is smiling at the dress. That is when I make my decision.

"I think I shall wear this one tonight."

Her eyes widen with excitement and her smile grows even bigger. "That is an excellent idea." She leans in closer and lowers her voice. "I shall wear my navy gown. We can be rebellious together."

I place the maroon gown on top of the box for the black dress and throw my hands around Edith. "Thank you." My eyes begin to water. Her gesture means more than she can know.

Another knock comes through the door, this one more powerful than Edith's. We break apart and I open the door. Claire walks in with a tray of tea and biscuits and an apple.

"I should leave you to dress for the afternoon." Edith moves to the door, "I enjoyed spending time together this morning, Lily."

"As did I."

Claire raises a brow in my direction as she closes and locks the door behind Edith.

"It was a nice surprise," I say and sit while taking a bite of the cut apple. "She seemed to be struggling this morning, missing Benedict. I think it was good for the two of us to be together."

"I always did prefer her to her sister."

"I quite agree with you, Claire."

"Oh, before I forget, your letter has been delivered directly to Miss Margaret Riley at Eton Cottage and she has reassured me she was going straight up to hand it to its recipient."

I blush, thinking about the contents of that letter. I wonder if he is reading it this very minute. Although we will not be able to act as more than acquaintances this evening, that does not dampen my excitement for seeing him.

"Has there been a change in attire for this evening?" Claire says with a pointed look at the deep red dress that is splayed over the box of the dress that was intended for this evening.

I lift my chin. "Yes, there has indeed," I state, practicing my conviction for when I face Lady Augusta this evening in the color-rich dress.

"Good for you!" Claire's support shines through her

smiling face. "Now, let us get you dressed to greet your guests for the afternoon's activities."

I stand and select a light pink dress for the daytime, the perfect precursor for the evening dress.

ALLOWING Lady Augusta to play the role of hostess for the ball, I have elected to arrive much later than her and without an escort. With one final check of my dress, I twirl in front of the mirror. Red stones accent my hair that is pulled back from my face. I typically choose to pin it all above my neck, but tonight, I have decided to leave it draped over one shoulder. Every strand is in place, but as the night progresses, I can guarantee a few strands will break free.

Moving through the hallway to the grand staircase, I already hear the music that fills the entire estate. The band is composed of various string instruments, with the violin being my favorite. Its soft notes bring me comfort as I descend the grand staircase. Exchanging pleasantries with the guests who linger outside the grand ballroom as I pass them.

Having supervised all the preparations the previous days, I should not be surprised at the sight of my ballroom, but its beauty stops me in my place. White flowers in view any direction you turn, garland running up the length of the beams, large pots with massive petal flowers exploding out of them at every doorway and placed at each corner of the dance floor. If I had more of a voice in the planning, I would have incorporated more color, but I do not let that take away from the beauty around me.

No one is dancing yet. I wonder if they are all too afraid to show any enjoyment in Lady Augusta's presence. Tables of food and drink line the right and left walls, with the musicians positioned in the center of the back wall, opposite the main entrance. I twirl once again, taking in the beauty. Benedict would love this— he would love that I loved it. And he would want me to enjoy myself, not just tonight, but every night for the rest of my life. Though I did not see it at the time, hosting this ball was the right thing to do. To remind everyone how loving and caring Benedict was, and how he would want everyone to enjoy every moment they have in this world.

Looking around, I do not spot my guests yet. I suppose it is a little earlier than I encouraged them to arrive. Most of the guests staying were eager to begin. I move toward one of the dessert tables. Having been too nervous earlier, I was unable to eat much. Now, with my nerves at ease, I make a plate for myself, filling it with plenty of apple slices and a few small pastries. With an open spot near the corner where I can indulge without much attention, I quietly enjoy the sweetness of the fruit that is just a shade lighter than my dress.

One guest in particular catches my attention. Monitoring Mr. Grange as he moves toward Albert's father, I listen to him speak. "Lord Berry, what a pleasure to see you."

Albert's father holds out his hand for Mr. Grange, but it is clear he does not recall this man's name. I turn myself toward the wall to hide my laughter. Without looking back, I continue to listen in on their conversation, while I pretend to be fascinated by the flower arrangement before me.

"I am Mr. Harold Grange, sir." Harold stumbles over his words.

"Oh yes, Grange. I believe I knew your father." Another reminder he does not hold any status compared to his father or brother.

"Yes, he was a great man," Harold says with disdain. "I am acquainted with your son. Albert."

I nearly choke on my bite of apple. How dare he mention Albert. Without turning to face the gentlemen I am eavesdropping on, I look over the faces in the ballroom. How I wish Albert were here to interject.

Grange continues, "He has been so close to Miss Margaret Eton for years, I must admit I was shocked to see she married his friend, Mr. Riley." When Lord Berry does not state any opinion, Grange continues, "Were you not surprised?"

Lord Berry answers with disinterest, "It is not my business to worry about the marriage of my son's friends."

"Right, of course," Grange persists. "I did notice Albert taking a particular interest in Mr. Riley's younger sister when they were in town sharing a carriage... appearing to be alone...unchaperoned. Do you believe his intentions lay with Miss Riley?"

"Oh yes, I am very hopeful to see Albert married soon and what better girl than...her." Another name Lord Berry has so quickly forgotten.

Harold must seem happy with the information he believes he has gained from this conversation. "Right then, I shall need to check on my mother. Enjoy your evening, Lord Berry."

"You as well..." Again, Albert's father does not remember Harold's name. This may be the highlight of my evening.

But why was he so concerned with the idea of Albert being interested in Evelyn?

I must share this information with Albert as soon as I can; he still has not arrived and I have yet to be discovered by Lady Augusta. Immediately, I devise a plan. I rapidly move from the ballroom and back up the stairs. It is just my luck that Claire is leaving my room when I approach the door. She looks surprisingly up at me.

I pull her back into the room, not wanting to be overheard, "I need you to do me a favor, Claire."

31

With one last straightening of my cravat, I watch the lovely ladies of our party exit Eton Cottage. Edward Riley stands beside me, marveling at the beauty of both his sister and wife. The Landons follow behind, carrying lanterns to light the walk as they wish us well on our evening. Ahead, the Rileys, who arrived not too terribly long ago, had just enough time to change their attire before they left for the Calderwood Estate. Evelyn requested to ride with us but assured her mother she would find her the moment we arrived. Lily voiced repeatedly how she hates that she was unable to invite the Landons to this evening's ball. They completely understand, but it still feels foolish, nonetheless.

Once inside, the ride is quiet. None of us are sure what to expect from an event held in honor of a man who died over ten years ago. As our carriage approaches, I see the Rileys exiting theirs ahead of us.

The front of the Calderwood Estate is decorated with what seems to be an endless number of candles and garlands made of flowers strung along each railing.

Evelyn is called to her mother's side and enters the grand home. The three of us take our time, enjoying the elaborate decorations before proceeding inside.

The foyer looks beautiful, but does share some similarities to that of a funeral. The music that glides through the air has a somber undertone. Guests gather in small circles, others making their way to the ballroom.

Before we can approach the main entrance to the ballroom, I feel a gentle tap on my shoulder. I turn back to find Claire standing behind me. The movement catches Edward and Margo's attention. She does not say anything but turns toward a hallway just beyond the grand staircase and we follow near behind.

Once we are far enough away from the crowd of guests, Claire whispers, "Lily is upstairs making final preparations. I believe she would welcome some friendly faces."

"Of course." Margo turns back in the direction of the grand staircase.

"Not that way." Claire stops her and looks at me.

"We will take the back stairs," I instruct them and continue down the hall. Surely, they each may assume the reasoning for my knowledge of this discreet route. Margo is most likely aware of it due to the extended time she has spent with Lily here, but it is glaringly obvious why I am aware of it. I am the other man, the lover who must stay hidden.

That does not matter now, what matters is Lily must be in distress. I must reach her.

We approach her door and I knock softly, not waiting for a reply, before I rush into the room with Margo and Edward close behind me.

Lily is like a statue—made for the gods—as she faces the window, only the back of her dress is in my view. Then she turns slowly, slower than time will allow. As her eyes connect with mine, I do not look away but know she is smiling with how the skin crinkles at the corner of her eyes.

I realize the color wrapped around her delicate body is not black but a flawless red—*deep* red. Weeks spent at the Berry Estate without her now seem worth it.

She moves toward me, throwing her arms around my neck. I wrap mine around her waist and hold her tight. I place a kiss on her cheek and we allow moments to pass before we release each other. She then moves to our friends. "Thank you all for coming up here."

"Is everything all right, my love?" I lace my fingers with hers and walk her toward the bed to sit. Momentarily forgetting that we are not alone, I pull her into my lap. The thud of the chair Edward places beside the bed for his wife reminds me to keep my affections appropriate. He leans on the back of the chair behind Margo, waiting for Lily to answer.

"Yes." She brings her hand to her chest. "Oh, I hope you were not worried. All is well. It was just that earlier,

I overheard a conversation and I wanted to make you all aware of it so that we can all be mindful this evening." She looks around. "Where is Evelyn?"

"Downstairs with my parents," Edward answers, "Why do you ask?"

"I am sure she is fine under your mother's watchful eye." She looks around. "I went down to the ballroom earlier, I was at the dessert table, but very much out of the way." She turns to me. "Your father was close by." My free hand begins to squeeze into a fist. If he said anything inappropriate to her, I will be sure to remove him.

"He was approached by Harold Grange."

"Grange is here?" Margo asks.

"Yes, his mother is a close friend of Lady Augusta," Lily answers with an apologetic look at her friend. Margo sits back in her chair and Edward moves to sit on the arm of the chair, pulling his wife close to him.

"You have nothing to worry about, Margo," Edward reminds her. She nods unconvincingly.

"Wait a moment, he was talking with my father?" I ask.

"Yes, he did not recognize Grange, which was greatly pleasurable. Then Grange inquired how you felt about Margo, whom you spent a particular amount of time with, marrying your close friend. Your father was completely indifferent to Edward's marrying Margo."

"That seems consistent with my conversations about their marriage to my father."

"Well, he then asked if the reason you seemingly

approved of the match is because you have set your sights on Edward's sister, Miss Riley." She pauses as we all lean into her as if we all believed to hear her incorrectly. "I was surprised too. He told your father that he witnessed you two entering a carriage in London."

"When I was escorting her to Eton Cottage?" I ask.

"I suppose he would have no way of knowing your destination," Margo states.

"For all Grange knows, it could have been by my request he was acting in my place, as her escort, as a chaperone. How could he have misconstrued something so innocent," Edward contemplates.

"Your father was encouraging of the possible match." Lily's eyes are directed at her hands, fidgeting in her lap. "Although he did not seem to even remember Evelyn's name." She pauses with a deep breath and looks back up to face us. "It struck me as odd how interested Harold was in the possibility of Albert marrying Evelyn. I think we need to watch him throughout the night and keep Evelyn close if she is not with her mother," she instructs.

Margo and Edward rise, Lily and I follow, each ready to run downstairs this instance to protect Evey. But before we go, I need to clarify something, "Lily, I have no desire to marry Evelyn."

"Of course, I know that Albert. I only worry if this will cause problems with your father if he becomes insistent on the marriage."

I can assume everyone in this room is aware of how

little I care for my father's opinion on my choice of bride, but just to be sure, I make my intentions known.

Wrapping an arm around Lily's waist, I hold her flush against my body. My other hand moves to her neck, pulling her into me. I kiss her, knowing we have an audience but not caring any longer. Lily is clearly in need of a reminder that there will never be another woman I love as much as I do her. Her breath catches as her lips part. I use the opportunity to claim her mouth as she has claimed my heart.

Not allowing the kiss to linger too long, but just long enough to ensure my intentions are understood, I pull away. Lily is blushing from her chest up to the tips of her ears. I look back at our friends, "Apologies." That marks the first time we have kissed with witnesses.

They turn back to face us. "Not needed." Edward brings his hand up.

"Shall we return to the ballroom?" Lily asks as she attempts to fan herself with her hand.

"We will go first and meet you down there," Margo instructs as she opens the door. Edward is right behind her, and I follow.

Before closing the door, I wink at her. *Oh the things I will do to her once we are alone.* Hopefully, it will not take more than a day for everyone to vacate this grand estate and then I can have her all to myself once again.

Entering the ballroom with my married friends beside me, there is no doubt everyone in attendance is now aware of our presence. Familiar faces all around, I spot Grange but do not linger. He is not important enough to hold my attention. I then find Evelyn Riley standing between her parents on the opposite side of the room from Grange.

Good.

Not ten steps into the room, my father grabs onto my arm. "I would like a word with you." I can only assume it is in regard to Mr. Grange's meddlesome gossip.

"You go on ahead, I will catch up to you shortly," I instruct Margo and Edward, then follow my father to a bare spot near the entrance of the ballroom.

He turns on me, his face slightly redder than it should be, yet this is becoming a natural occurrence for him.

"Do you mind telling me what you are playing at courting a young lady and not asking for her father's permission first?" He pulls in a deep breath as I remain silent to determine his meaning. "I have on good authority that you are courting your friend Edward's younger sister."

"Father, I must insist your authority is not good, it is certainly bad, completely false."

"Do not play with me. You told me yourself that you escorted her to the country." He takes another deep breath as his face grows more and more red. "Now, I see why you were so insistent to do so."

"I was acting purely on the request of her brother." That is false, but in essence, it is true.

"You were unchaperoned with that young lady. When I saw her father this evening, I inquired to be certain you did the gentlemanly thing and asked his permission, only to find Lord Riley completely perplexed at the question." His breathing accelerates, his face now a similar shade as Lily's dress.

"Father, you are mistaken!" I insist.

"I raised you to be a gentleman, and part of that is fulfilling your duty to marry and produce an heir. But in doing that you must approach marriage in the proper way. I insist you declare your intentions to marry Miss Riley at this very moment. In this room, in front of all these witnesses."

In an attempt to slow the attention we are gaining, I lower my voice. "I will do no such thing as I have no such intention to Miss Riley, nor does she intend to marry me."

"Pardon me?" Father shouts, shaking at this point.

My anger gets the best of me and I yell back, "There is no love match and we will not wed. I will declare nothing this evening."

32

Albert left moments ago, but my skin cannot seem to contain the heat he left behind. I stand in the mirror, watching my chest, willing the blush to rescind low enough behind the fabric of my dress so I can join him in the ballroom.

I move over to the window, opening it slightly, hoping the chill of the autumn evening will shock my body in the opposite direction it is so clearly craving. I never expected to feel Albert's embrace this evening, and certainly not the passion of Albert's kiss.

Yet, it will make the evening so much more enjoyable. Hopefully, my body will be able to remain indifferent when I see Albert downstairs. It will be nothing but pleasant conversations and rushed longing looks across the room.

We have spent years not being able to show our affection in a room full of people. Although, Albert does seem to take it as a challenge. The first time he sent a smoldering look my way, I nearly fainted.

"How much longer must we stay?" Margo prattles on next to me. I had hoped as the years continued, she would find less to complain about while attending balls, but I was not so lucky. Here we are, in her fifth year in society and she still complains just as often as she did her first year. "I have danced with five gentlemen. Can we please leave?"

"You know your parents' rule. You must stay for at least two hours. It will not be much longer now." If only she would dance with more suitors, it would make the time go by much faster and give me a break from her constant complaints.

That is when my attention is drawn to the opposite side of the room. Albert Berry stands in a darkened corner between the refreshments table and the musicians' stage. His eyes lock on me. I look around to see if anyone has noticed, but not a single person is looking in his direction.

I look back to the dimly lit corner, his stare growing darker by the moment. Then he lowers his glass from his face, his lips pull up just the slightest to one side as his eyes burn while he looks the length of my entire body. When he reconnects with my gaze, his lips part as his chest moves. Then, his tongue slides out to lick his lips.

I struggle to contain the shiver that my body so desperately wants to release. I knew he would be in attendance tonight, so I was sure to bring my fan. Waving it over my face, I can only hope it is keeping my blush at bay.

He brings his drink back to his lips. How jealous I am of that glass. I recall the feel of his lips on mine, my breath skips at the memory. As if he can read my thoughts, he winks at me. Lifting the fan to cover my face, his seductive smirk looks back at me.

"What if we leave a little early? I will say I became ill if anyone asks." Margo breaks the intense moment I was sharing with Albert. I turn to her—she does not notice, as she never does.

When I look back at the corner, he is gone.

I move back to the mirror to make a final inspection of my exposed skin. All redness from blushing has receded. As I am pulling my shawl off the chair next to my mirror, I hear it.

I freeze to listen. Shouting coming from both directions, I can hear it through the open window and from the hallway outside the door. I rush to the window and look down at the terrace below. Those standing outside are all facing into the ballroom. I turn and run out of my bedroom, not bothering to lock it behind me.

Lifting my skirt to not trip on it, I make haste down the grand staircase. I reach the bottom and the yelling is getting closer, clearly coming from the ballroom. I rush in to see a crowd of people in a circle to the right of the entrance. Standing at the center, I recognize the back of Edward and Margo's heads.

Thank goodness they are so tall.

"Margaret!" I yell to her, but before I can see if she hears me, a hand latches on to my arm and pulls me back to face away from the crowd.

Lady Augusta's firm grip holds me in place. I ignore her hold and look over the room for Albert.

Could something have happened to him?

I continue my search as Lady Augusta speaks, "Lady Calderwood, what are you wearing?"

I notice Grange standing conveniently close to the crowd but not joining them. He stands by his mother, who looks concerned while he wears a smirk on his ugly face.

What if he did something to Evelyn, or to Albert while he was defending her. I should have come down sooner—I could have helped.

I begin to pull away from Lady Augusta, but she pulls me back. "I asked you a question, Lily. What are you wearing?" I look down, no longer remembering what I was wearing. "I specifically instructed you to be in black. How improper it is for you to wear colors during a memorial ball for your late husband."

"Lady Augusta." She balks back at the tone and volume of my voice. "Can you not see something has happened to one of our guests? I can change my dress if needed, but I must see to the individual if they are hurt." With that, I force my arm out of her grasp and turn from her.

"You never cared about him," Lady Augusta yells to me.

I turn back to her. "How dare you. The color of a dress I wear years after his passing has nothing to do with the love I hold for your son. If you care so much to know my heart, perhaps you should ask me. Instead of deciding yourself how I should act and feel."

I do not wait for her answer but turn toward the crowd, calling for Margo yet again while searching for

Albert among the guests. That is when I notice Evelyn and Lady Riley. Evelyn looks toward the center of the crowd, distressed, her mother stoic, holding her daughter close to her side.

Cold terror fills my body. The feeling I felt when losing Benedict comes rushing back. What if Albert… *No!* As my body begins to tremble with fear, I push through the remaining people blocking my way. *I cannot lose Albert.* Tears well in my eyes as I get closer to the answer I am so dreading.

Edward emerges from the crowd with his father, Lord Riley, close behind him. He spots me and places his arms on my shoulders. "Lily, have him moved to a private room at once." My legs shake, threatening to give out beneath me. *Albert…*

"We are going to fetch a doctor," Lord Riley continues.

Edward shakes my shoulders as I am frozen in place. The only movement from my body is the tears I feel falling down my cheeks. With a shaky voice, I ask, "Is it Albert?"

Edward relaxes his hold and quickly answers, "No, Albert is fine—it is his father, Lord Berry." Relief washes over me as I attempt to draw air back into my lungs. "But he needs to be moved. Now."

I shake my head to clear away the terrified thoughts that so quickly buried their way into my heart. As hostess to this evening and head of this household, I need to act.

Turning backward, I call Darcy, who, on Lady

Augusta's insistence came from the London townhome to assist in tonight's event. He and several of my men follow me to the center of the crowd to fetch Lord Berry. "He needs to be taken back to his private room at once," I instruct them.

When I reach Margo, she moves aside to reveal Albert kneeling next to his father, who has lost consciousness. His mother sits on the opposite side of her husband, holding his hand. Lord Berry's face is a deep red. Checking his chest, I am relieved to see the moments of his breath.

Kneeling down beside Albert, I ask softly. "What can I do?"

He does not respond verbally but leans into my touch.

Margo moves to Lady Berry, taking her hand as I do the same for Albert. The four of us follow behind the men carrying Lord Berry to his room in the west wing of the house.

As he is placed in the bed, Darcy directs his men to arrange chairs around him. We sit just as we were downstairs. Lady Berry on one side, with Margo trying to comfort her and Albert on the other, his hand locked onto mine.

Moments pass and Lord Berry's face seems to be returning to its natural color, but I notice Albert removing his own cravat. I suppose he is getting overheated. I move to open a window, but Albert holds onto my hand. With a gentle smile, I remain seated by his side.

It cannot have been an hour before a knock comes at the door. Margo rises to answer it. She cracks the door open slightly, it is clear in Albert and his mother's faces they are hoping it is the doctor. Unfortunately, that is not who is at the door.

"I demand to see Lady Calderwood this instant," Lady Augusta yells from the hall. Albert's head hangs as he finally releases my hand. He does not look up, allowing me to go to the intruder in the hall.

As I pass Margo, she quietly whispers, "I am sorry." I squeeze her hand in thanks and continue until I am outside the room. I close the door and walk a few paces away, hopeful that will keep this conversation from reaching the Berry family.

"You cannot ignore your own guests. What are you doing up here?" she asks.

This is an emotional day for her and her daughters, as it is for me. Each year, she gets progressively worse on Benedict's birthday, but this is crossing the line and my patience is wearing thin.

"A man has fallen ill in my home. I will stay by his side."

"You will do no such thing, you will change out of that mockery of a dress and return to your guests. At once!"

"This dress is Benedict's favorite color. It is one he would have preferred, that is why I wore it for him this evening. I believe prioritizing things he enjoyed over your orders is more important today. I will not change and quite frankly, I believe the party should end."

She gasps. "These people are nothing to you. And yet you choose strangers over your husband."

"They do mean something to me. I have room in my heart to love more individuals than just my late husband. If you would like to continue the party and act as hostess, you are more than welcome to. If not, I will instruct my staff to end the party immediately."

"I told Benedict you would make a poor wife, but he still married you. And look, I was right, you were no good as a wife and you cannot even make the effort to be an honorable widow. You are a disgrace to the Calderwood name." She waits as if to see if I will beg for her forgiveness.

I do not offer such penance and do not owe her any explanation. I walk back to Lord Berry's room without another look in her direction.

Albert looks up at me as I return to my seat beside his. He offers me his hand and I accept it.

33

Has it been hours? Minutes? I would believe it if days had passed since my father grabbed onto his chest and collapsed on the floor of the Calderwood Estate ballroom. Propping my elbow on the arm of the chair, I rest my forehead on my fist. The argument we had replays over and over in my mind. Each time I come to the end and relive that awful conclusion, I tighten my hold on Lily's hand. Her presence is the only reason for what little composure I am able to maintain.

My father demanding that I declare my intentions to marry a young girl I consider a sister this evening was preposterous, a misunderstanding. Harold Grange had a hand in this and it will cost him. If my father does not survive this ordeal, neither will Grange. I shall challenge him to a duel or possibly end him in a less gentlemanly way, as he deserves.

If only my father would believe his own son over the

word of a man whose name he cannot even recall. I tried to end it before it got out of hand. I suggested we discuss this later, after the event or better, when we all returned to town, in the privacy of our own home, but he would not have it.

Only the slight rise and fall of his chest is proof my father is still alive. But is he well? Will he survive the night? Day? Week? Or month? What will come if he does not?

I know what will come—I will become Lord Berry.

It is not the title I fear—it is the responsibilities that come with the title. I am certain I am more than capable of overseeing the estate, but it will require me to be more present at our residences, not to mention the hours it will take to manage it all. I am capable, but am I ready? Ready to let this lordship consume my life?

Since returning from her tiff with Lady Augusta in the hallway, Lily has continued to rub my back. The soothing motion is my solace as we wait for Edward Riley to return with a doctor. I steal a look over at her. Things may very well change after tonight. Her argument with Lady Augusta and my father's fate will most certainly have damaging consequences. Things will never be the same in our lives and tomorrow, we will need to face that reality. Remaining in her own chair, she places her head on my shoulder and snuggles into my side. I kiss her forehead in thanks. Much will need to be discussed, but not until we have answers.

The feeling of my mother watching me grabs my attention. Her knowing look tells me that our intimate interactions have not escaped her notice. She nods and smiles softly but gives no more reaction. Tears remain in her eyes while she takes comfort with Margo at her side. My mother has only interacted with my friend rarely at public events, but it seems she feels relaxed in her presence.

Aside from the condolences and small talk Margo offers, we sit in silence.

The sound of feet pounding the hallway outside the room causes each of us to jump to our feet. Surely, Lady Augusta could not manage so much noise. It sounds like a man running, no, multiple men.

The door flies open as Edward ushers an unfamiliar man inside, his father behind them. I release Lily's hand before we lift our chairs and move them against the wall to allow the doctor room to work. My mother stays where she is, with Margo moving to allow space for me to join my mother. Edward and Lord Riley huddle near the window with Lily and Margo.

The doctor is silent as he begins his examination. Once he puts his various tools down, he looks over to my father and asks for a description of the events, and then inquires how he appeared before the attack. I relay every detail to him, most likely sharing more intimate details of the argument than he needs for his evaluation.

The doctor nods. Once I finish, he states. "I believe this is heart-related."

"Will he be all right, doctor?" my mother asks, her voice shaking like the rest of her body.

"The next few hours will be the toughest. If he survives the night, he will have a great chance of recovery." My mother whimpers at his words.

"Is there anything we can do for him as we wait for morning?" I ask.

The doctor shakes his head, "Beyond keeping him here, in this comfortable state, I am afraid there is not much more any of us can do but wait. The rest is up to him now."

As the doctor begins to pack his bag, Lily moves toward him. "Would you be willing to stay here for the night?" she asks, and he seems surprised at the request.

Edward moves next to her, "We are happy to pay any amount you require to remain on call throughout the night, should you be needed."

The doctor smiles at Edward's offer of money. I will be sure to repay him and thank him for thinking on his feet when my mind is so clearly cluttered. "Yes, I can stay. However, I will need to get a letter to my wife."

"I will have everything you need arranged," Lily promises. "You are welcome to stay here for a moment while I prepare your room and find a carrier to post the letter to your wife." She moves toward the door but stops in her path to look at me. "I will be right back." I nod and watch her leave.

Mere minutes pass before she returns, as two women enter behind her. She begins introductions. "Everyone, this is Lady Edith Warren. She is the sister of my late husband, Lord Calderwood. She and Claire, my housekeeper, were waiting outside the door to see if they could be of any assistance."

"Oh, thank you both very much," my mother calls to them from her spot next to my father.

Edith speaks up. "Please allow me to show you to your room, Doctor." She looks at my mother. "We have the room three doors down on the same side as this room available for him. It is the last door before the staircase, should you need him." We all nod.

"There is parchment, ink, and quills in the desk, and I will be along momentarily to wait for your letter and personally see that it is on route to your wife as soon as possible," Claire adds.

"Why thank you, ladies." The doctor takes one last assessing look at my father and reiterates, "If you notice anything that seems out of the ordinary, please come fetch me."

Holding out my hand to him, I shake firmly, "Thank you, Doctor, this is greatly appreciated."

After they exit, Claire lingers. "Lord Riley, Mr. and Mrs. Riley. Would you like a room for the evening as well?"

Lord Eton is the first to answer. "Have my wife and daughter returned to Eton Cottage?"

"They have, sir."

"If it is all right with everyone, I would prefer to return there as well. I will come by in the morning to see if there is anything I can help with." His look lands on me as if for permission. I hold my hand out to shake his in thanks.

Margo answers next, "We would like to stay, but if you do not have the room, we can also return to Eton Cottage."

"You can have my room," Lily announces.

"Are you sure?" Margo asks.

"Yes, I do not plan to leave Albert's side this evening or tomorrow. It is free for the two of you."

"Can you please inform the Landons upon your return to Eton Cottage of the situation?" Edward asks.

"Of course," Lord Riley assures him. He looks back over my father, then to my mother, and finally stops at me. "I do hope to see him in better condition tomorrow."

I nod and thank him again for his assistance in fetching the doctor before he takes his leave.

Margo walks to my mother first, holding out her arms. Surprise crosses her face, but she quickly stands and hugs Margo. I cannot hear what she says, but she smiles. Edward rubs my mother's shoulder and encourages her to "try to rest."

My friends move to bid Lily and me a similar goodnight. "Send for us regardless of the time of night if there is anything you need," Margo insists. "We will return as soon as we wake in the morning." She pauses to look at my father once more. "If we can even sleep."

"Sleeping or not, I think it best to give you privacy at this time." Edward wraps his arm around Margo's waist and pulls her into his side. "Rest if you can. Tomorrow will be taxing."

As our friends leave the room, they hold the door

open for Edith, who is carrying a large, filled tray. She lays it on the small table. "In case you get hungry or need a bit of tea."

Lily releases my hand to go to Benedict's sister. She takes Edith's hands in her own, "Thank you, Edith." She sniffles. "Your kindness is a gift during this dark hour."

"It is my pleasure." Edith addresses my mother and me now. "Is there anything else I can get you this evening?"

My mother holds her handkerchief to her nose and shakes her head. "No, thank you, my dear."

"Thank you for everything you have done for us, Lady Warren," I tell her.

"Please, you may call me Edith, especially in such circumstances. I shall leave you for what remains of the evening, but I will return after sunrise." Addressing Lily directly, "If you need anything at all from me, please find me directly. I will come." She lifts her hand to wipe the tear that has fallen from Lily's eye before retiring herself.

The three of us remain in the room with my father for some time without speaking. Just waiting.

My mother clears her throat and I glance up to find her looking between Lily and me. We both fix our posture to sit straight up in our chairs.

Her voice is tired and cracks from hours of crying, but remains firm. "Am I to assume this has been occurring for quite some time?"

"Yes," I answer, not defensive. My mother deserves the truth without any attitude.

She looks at Lily. "How long?"

Lily steals a look at me, before I can decide if she wants me to answer for her, she does for herself. "Years." Her fingers tighten around mine. "We met the day your family attended my wedding to Lord Calderwood—were acquaintances following for years. When Margo Riley—then Eton—came of age, I became her chaperone in London society. It was at her first ball that I saw Albert again."

With a deep breath, she continues, "From that moment on, I felt a pull toward him, something stronger than I have felt with another person in this world. I did not know where it would lead at the time, but I knew I felt better when he was near. The friendship continued to grow over time, but then it turned into something even stronger."

My heart expands in my chest as I listen to her tell our story. "Albert is a patient man, a caring man, an exceptional man. Most days, I question if I will ever be able to reciprocate the devotion and affection he has shown me. I love your son, Lady Berry. Our situation is not ideal at the moment," she raises her free hand to the door, "as you can see, there are complications and tempers I must manage."

When Lily snickers at the tense situation she is in, my mother joins her. Lily continues, "I have also tried and failed to convince Albert to find a young bride for himself, someone without the tumultuous history I have."

"Never," I declare.

"I am thankful for his stubbornness in this matter." Lily lights up beside me before telling my mother in a serious tone. "I hope to see this predicament resolved in the future. That is my wish."

Hope sparks in my chest. Now is not the time to pressure her. I cannot allow such joy to consume me while my father's life is in question. I hold silent as we wait for my mother's response.

"I wish you had not kept this from me for so long." She looks at my father and sadness overcomes her once again. "I do understand why you kept it a secret." She looks up to us, the sadness removed from her features. "I am so very happy for you both and look forward to having you join our family, Lily."

With my mother's blessing, I pull Lily from her chair and into my lap. Her head rests naturally on my shoulder.

Even in such an uncertain time for my family, I have never felt more complete in my life.

I am not sure when we all fell asleep, but I wake up to the sounds of sniffles. The sound becomes clearer—someone is crying. My mother is crying. Lily stirs in my lap as I hear another sound, a masculine voice, moaning perhaps.

When my eyes finally clear, I see my mother perched over my father as he moves his legs beneath the blankets, his hand rubbing his chest.

"Nicholas, Nicholas!" My mother rubs his arms, then cups his face. "Nicholas, wake up."

Lily springs from my lap, "I shall gather the doctor."

Meeting my mother above my father, my deeper voice may be enough to wake him. "Father, Father!"

His eyes open slowly, blinking repeatedly.

"Oh, Nicholas, how do you feel?" He does not answer my mother fast enough, "Nicholas, say something."

"Teresa?" His voice is groggy and strained.

"Get me some water on a rag, Albert. No, do not move, Nicholas. The doctor will be here shortly." She continues rubbing his arms until I return with the damp cloth. She pats his head gently.

"Where are we?" he asks.

"The Calderwood Estate, you had an attack during the ball," she explains but thankfully does not elaborate. He is sure to remember our argument in time and most likely fault me for the rest of my days.

Though, I cannot truly blame him.

The door to the bedroom flies open as the doctor runs in, stopping at the foot of my father's bed. "Well, Lord Berry, what a happy introduction. So glad to finally meet now that you are awake."

The doctor moves to stand in the position I just occupied next to my father, not hesitating to begin his examination. Rather than waiting by my mother's side, I move back to stand against the window, still close enough to hear the doctor speak but far enough away to get some air. We all silently watch as the doctor takes his instruments from his bag. My father complains under his breath about being poked and prodded like a farm animal. Lily turns behind us to open the window, it is as if she knows my every thought. "Thank you."

Her hand finds mine again and she uses the other to wrap around my arm, snuggling against me while we wait.

"Well, Lord Berry, I am certain now that you will live from the attack you suffered yesterday." My mother lets out an audible sigh as the doctor speaks. "That is not to say you will be in perfect health moving forward. You will need great amounts of rest before returning to your daily schedule. At that, I would recommend modifying your previous routine."

"Modifying? I have duties I must attend to." Of course, it is not good enough to know there will be no permanent damage—he must insist on being in perfect health.

"Well, my lord. This type of attack, I believe, was caused by a strain on your heart. If you do not mind it, you will find yourself back in this very position. And the outcome might not be the same next time."

The doctor must sense his time here is complete. He begins to pack his bag. "I assume you have a family physician on staff?" he asks my mother.

"Yes, Dr. Baxter."

"Right, well, please give him my card. I will be happy to send a full report." He gives her the card before turning back to my father. "I must advise you to rest, in excess for now, and return to your modified duties when your physician gives his approval. Lord Berry, this is common among men of your age." He turns back to face me. "That is why you have an heir. It will be nothing for a young man like him to rise to the occasion."

My father grumbles under his breath, "Can I at least sit up in this bed?"

The doctor nods his head. "Yes, please feel free to sit all you would like." With his jacket in place, he bids us goodbye. "I wish you the best of health, Lord Berry, and the same to your family."

34

With Lord Berry awake and given such a positive evaluation by the doctor, I decide it is time for me to give the Berry family their privacy. I lean into Albert and whisper, "I am going to let the Rileys, Claire, and Edith know he is awake and well."

Looking between his parents and me, Albert nods and releases his hold on my hand. Lord Berry, being engrossed in conversation with his wife, does not seem to notice my departure. I consider that a gift as I quietly remove myself from the room.

Claire is standing against the wall opposite the door when I exit. "Morning, my lady. How is Lord Berry?"

I hold out my hand for hers, "He is well, awake, talking, and sitting." I share it with excitement. "I would like to let the Rileys and Edith know."

"Of course, should I bring some food and drink to

the Berry family, or do you think they would not want any interruptions just yet?" Claire asks.

"I do believe that by the time it takes for you to deliver the food, they would most welcome it."

"Then, off I go." Claire turns on her heels and walks in the direction of the kitchen.

I slowly move toward the opposite wing of the house, where both my bedroom and Edith's are located. Luckily enough, Edith is already on her way to visit the Berry family when our paths cross.

"Lily! How is he? Lord Berry?"

"Well, Edith. The doctor has come and cleared him that there is no immediate concern for his life. He is, however, to rest extensively, at least until he can see his own physician."

"How wonderful." She pauses. I notice her face change and her eyes grow serious. She looks around to see that we do not have an audience before she whispers, "I wanted to tell you, in private, that even in all the scuttle around last night, it did not escape my notice of your closeness to Mr. Albert Berry."

Defensively, I step back. Of course, I was aware today would bring change and that I would need to face the consequences of my actions with Lady Augusta, but having to face Edith, who has shown endless kindness, I grow weary. I open my mouth to begin reassuring her how much I loved her brother and that I will always have a place in my heart for Benedict, but she speaks first.

"Lily, please do not worry. I wanted to tell you how

happy I am for you and Mr. Berry. I do not know the man personally, but he is held in such high regard. And the way he looks at you, one cannot deny the love he feels." She grabs my hands. "I want you to be happy. In whatever way that comes to be with Mr. Berry. It will not change how I feel about you."

The tears flow like a waterfall from my eyes. The exhaustion certainly contributed to this, but mostly, it is a relief that overwhelms me.

She squeezes my hands tighter. "Oh, Lily. I am so sorry that you felt I would think otherwise, but I do not blame you, considering the other women in my family. Regardless of what transpires, please promise we will remain as is. Both family and friends."

"I would love that, Edith." I pull out of her embrace and wipe away the lingering tears from my cheeks.

"Is there anything you need from me, Lily?"

"Yes, actually, would you please take my place today as the guests are leaving? I want to remain with Albert."

"I will head downstairs directly. I shall call on you later should anything of note occur."

"Thank you, Edith...for everything."

With a soft smile over her shoulder, she leaves me. Turning I continue to walk to my bedroom to see Margo and Edward.

With the first official acknowledgment of the change that is coming today, I am happy to seek Margo's company. I need her help sorting through the endless thoughts of "what if" circling in my mind.

I knock on the door and immediately hear steps on

the other side as the door flies open. Edward stands there, still waiting for me to deliver the news.

"He is awake." I smile, watching Edward exhale as his hand moves to his chest. "The doctor does not feel his life is at risk any longer."

"Please come in. This is your room, after all." Edward moves from the entryway, Margo standing still as she listens from her position by the mirror.

"He did recommend great amounts of rest and seeing his family physician as soon as he can."

"How are Lady Berry and Albert?"

"Well, very happy that the worst is over, but I assume extremely exhausted too."

"As I assume you must be." Margo comes toward me to rub my shoulders.

"Lady Berry knows of Albert and me. As does Benedict's sister, Edith." I look down at my hands and clarify, "Both women were very supportive and comforting, but I need to decide what comes next." I look up at her. Into the eyes of a married woman, once a girl, who would beg me to braid her hair when she was sad because the crinkles it produced made her happy.

Edward calls from behind us, "I believe I should leave you ladies to talk. I will go check on Albert. And Lily, whatever may transpire, please remember, you have our full support."

I nod as my eyes begin to water again. He pulls the door open, "I shall find Claire to bring you both something to eat." Then he closes it softly behind him.

She waves her hand to my bed, "Shall we then?"

I laugh. I suppose we have spent many nights lying awake, talking together. Contemplating each and every big change we have faced in our lives. But most importantly, we faced them together.

Grabbing her hand, I pull her down onto the bed beside me. We lie shoulder to shoulder, staring up at the ceiling. I could draw the pattern of the cracks that have formed up there by memory. Thankfully, in all my years staying in this room, they never changed.

"Lord Berry is well. He shall live…for now," she starts.

"Yes, although it does seem Albert will need to take on more duties as the doctor gravely insisted that his father cut back on his daily schedule pertaining to the estate."

"I see." She pauses. "That may require Albert to be more regularly at one of his family's residences."

"Yes, the country estate, most likely."

"Is it a far distance to travel?" she asks.

"Hours away."

"And you say Lady Berry now knows of your involvement?"

"Yes, and has shared her support. Although we did not get into a particularly deep discussion." I suppose I had been so worried about Lord Berry's thoughts on us that I never considered how Albert's mother might react. Even during the distress around her husband, she showed great kindness.

That must be where Albert gets it from.

"Then you will likely be welcome to visit him if you

would like," she suggests optimistically. "Edward and I will accompany you if you do not want to make the journey yourself."

The beautiful thing about my friendship with Margo is as life goes on, we can rely on each other as we go through difficult times. I know she means each and every promise, but what if it is time for me to make such a grand change that I will not require such favors from her.

"Edith knows and reacted graciously, kindly, and encouragingly." The memory of the last meeting I had with Lady Augusta comes to the forefront, banishing the comforting memory of Edith's support. "I can be almost certain Lady Augusta has come to the correct conclusion."

Margo sits up and turns toward me with her legs bent and her feet behind her. "What was said?"

"She scorned me for leaving my guests unattended and demanded I return to the ball." She waits to hear my response. "I, in not so many words, insinuated that I cared for the Berry family…and loved Albert. And I told her to end the party."

Margo's hand covers her mouth in concern, but I watch as her eyes crinkle in the corner—happy, I suppose, to hear I stood up to Lady Augusta.

"She said I never loved Benedict and she always knew I would be a poor choice of wife for him. Yet, she did not expect me to be such a disrespectful widow."

Margo moves like she is going to stand from the

bed, I pull her back down next to me, but that does little to subdue her. "That vile woman," she shouts.

"Keep your voice down. We do not need that woman discovering me, slandering her name."

"How dare she say such a disgusting thing and to your face no less." She turns to me, "Benedict would never want you to be spoken to like that." I smile weakly.

I sure hope you are right.

"Lily, the love you have for your late husband is a grand love. I will never be convinced otherwise. Yet, I also feel the same about you and Albert. One does not cancel or diminish the other. And I know both men would want you to receive that love regardless of who was delivering it."

The tears return, this time at an overwhelming rate. I have to sit up to manage them, pulling a blanket from the bed to wipe it from my chin. Margo puts her arms around me and I can feel her deep breath as she begins to cry too. "Benedict loved you, and you love him, Lily. He would want you to find love again. I know that to be true."

I suppose I have felt that too, but only in my own thoughts, never sharing them with others. Never having to face the consequences I have been so much trying to avoid by keeping our love a secret. All at Albert's expense.

"When I came down yesterday, I heard yelling and then I saw you and Edward in the middle of the crowd. I thought something happened to Albert." I continue crying, now for Albert and the thought of losing him. "What if something happened to him?" I ask. "What if I have wasted years holding him at arm's length to protect the feelings of Benedict's family and my own guilt."

"Lily." She tries to soothe me, but we are beyond that.

"No, when I lost Benedict, it broke me, but I had no regrets. I spent each day of our marriage loving him fully. Last night, I realized if I lost Albert, I would regret so much of it." I sit up, "I do not want to continue my life like this for another moment, Margo."

"Tell me what you plan to do and how I can help." I place my hands in hers and hold them tightly to show my appreciation for her offer.

"I honestly have not a clue where to begin," I confess.

Three knocks, a moment apart, fill the room, then his voice. "Lily?" I smile. "Margo? Are either of you there?" Albert asks as we both sit up.

Margo leaps from the bed, "I think your first move has just presented itself," she whispers to me and opens the door as I sit frozen. As if my heart called to his, the moment I was resolved to have him, he came to me.

"We are, come in," Margo calls.

As Albert enters, my body relaxes. Seeking his company, that feeling of peace he brings with him is not a new occurrence, like an addiction that grows stronger with each taste. I need him every day, by my side, in my bed, and sharing our lives.

"Shall I check in on Lady Berry?" Margo asks Albert.

"Yes, she was asking for you. Edward is with her and my father now. As is Claire, she has quickly become a comfort to my father."

Grabbing her shawl, she turns to us and says, "See you shortly," and leaves us to ourselves. Alone in my room.

35

Without hesitation, Albert stalks toward me. Leaning up on my knees to greet him, he stops at the edge, catching my face in his hands. "I love you," he whispers but does not wait for my response as his mouth devours mine. Our tongues dance to meet each other. His hands move over my body. I need this man. *My man.* I fist his shirt and pull him down to the bed on top of me.

"Let me be your escape, your refuge, to rescue you from the endless worries and woes running through your mind." My voice is low in an attempt to comfort him, but my desperation still comes through. I need him just as much as I want to be his respite.

He lets out a sigh of relief before dipping his head to my shoulder to place gentle kisses on my neck. Wanting to close any distance between us, I wrap my free leg around him. One hand caresses his back while the other weaves through his long, soft brown locks. The feel of his body covering mine is comforting. All of my worry fades with him lying over me. His closeness is the only thing that has the ability to settle me.

His kisses begin to travel south. Still in my gown from the night before, he has very limited access to my chest. That does stop him from placing feather-light kisses on my overspilling cleavage while his hands grasp at the parts covered by fabric. His efforts leave me panting beneath him, longing for more.

As if he reads my mind, his movements continue down my body until he stands before me. I watch him, waiting, wanting.

He holds his hand out to me, "We need to get you out of that dress. Let me have the honor."

He pulls me to stand, and with our hands still clasped, he spins me so my back is to him. His fast fingers work to free me from the fabric. A dress that was not what Lady Augusta approved of, but I wore it anyway. I know deep down this act of rebellion will not be alone, my actions and choices will be my own from now on. A sense of relief floods my body. I feel the chill behind me as more skin is liberated from the tight garment. Albert continues his work. I find myself jealous of the corset getting so much attention from his skillful hands.

As soon as it is loose enough, Albert pushes the dress from my shoulders and down my body. He pulls me flush against his chest. Strong arms come around me as he explores my body. I come undone under his touch, shivering with need.

His lips graze my ear as I feel a stray strand of his hair brush my cheek. "On the bed." His grip moves to my hips and turns me to face him before he gently lowers me. When I feel the soft sheets touch my skin, I lay my body out, on full display for him while he dispenses his garments.

The sight of Albert's muscular form, bare in front of me, is a view I will never tire of. He does not hesitate, crawling over me, between my legs, as he doubles his efforts on my fully exposed chest.

I raise my lips to meet his, knowing what I am searching for. Albert repositions himself exactly where I want him. He brings his face up to mine and kisses me as he slides slowly and sensually into my body.

Our lovemaking today is so different from that last time in the library. That was rushed, rabid, frenzied, and impulsive.

This moment is about so much more than our lust and longing. This is a deeper expression of love and the role it plays in both of our lives. This is confirmation of our devotion to each other. This is an expression of the commitment, and the fierce connection we have. It is not rushed but a patient moment to bask in one another.

"I HAD BELIEVED myself at the height of exhaustion before coming to see you. Yet, after our shared passion, I fear I am even worse off. I worry I will not be able to move my body for days."

"Well worth it," I say with my head on his chest, his arm wrapped tight around me.

"Indeed, my love." His fingers play with my hair. "Thank you, I cannot recall if I told you that last night, but I want to say it again, Thank you."

"I wish I could have done more, Albert."

"You did everything, Lily. Without you there, I would have fallen apart. It was because I had you by my side that I was able to be there for my father, strong enough to stay at his bedside. Watching my mother weep over his unconscious body nearly killed me and would have if I did not have you."

I nuzzle closer against his body. "I was exactly where I was meant to be, where I belong...with you." Propping myself up on one arm, I want to look into his eyes. "I love you, Albert—"

Fists pound at the door, not heavy, but rapid. "Lily Calderwood, I demand a word this instant!" Lady Augusta's voice carries into the room.

Albert bolts from the bed, and the color drains from his face, but that could be from the exhaustion of last night and the amorous activity we just shared. He begins looking around and I realize he may be looking to hide. That will not do—those days are behind us. I nod to his clothes. He dresses quickly and I find a simple dress I can throw over my head.

I hold out my hand for him. The pounding on the

door continues as he studies my gesture. "Are you sure?" he whispers.

"More than I have ever been about anything." I smile at him as I move closer and grab his hand in mine.

I walk us to the door and open it to a red-faced Lady Calderwood. She opens her mouth to say something, but nothing comes out as she looks at Albert and down to our joined hands.

"Lady Augusta, you wanted to speak with me?"

Slowly, her gaze returns to mine, "Yes, I do." She nods toward Albert. "You may dismiss your male strumpet." Her voice drips with disgust.

Albert uses his other arm to pull me back, I had not noticed I leaned forward, hovering over her petite and fragile frame. "He is not my strumpet—he is my love and he will stay." Then I think better of it. Perhaps Albert does not want to deal with this interaction after the night he had. "If he wishes to." I turn to him, trying my best to share my understanding if he so chooses to excuse himself.

He squeezes my hand, "Always."

Turning back to Lady Augusta, "You may continue with what you need to say to me."

With a gasp at my forwardness, she stands straight. "You have disgraced this family and Benedict's legacy with the carelessness you showed for the event last night and a disregard for the many guests who traveled to attend when you did not return."

I feel Albert stiffen next to me, but he does not intercede. He knows this is my battle to be had.

"I am certain the guests will think me an honorable hostess. A man fell ill and was unconscious in my home. I saw to him and his health in every way possible. Would not each guest want to be treated the same if they were the ones confined to a bed?"

"I would argue that those guests would never know you were hosting, as some of them never even saw you last night. Which I suppose is a good thing that they did not have to bear witness to that ostentatious dress."

"Of course, they knew I was the hostess. It is my home," I insist.

"It is the Calderwood family estate." She leans in. "I curse the day my son shared our name with you. A name you did not deserve then and certainly do not today." She looks Albert over, "And to think you parade your lover around on Benedict's birthday as if to mock him!"

My body shakes with anger and she continues, "And you sit beside his father's sick bed as if they are your family. They are *not*! I am the one you should be waiting on, following around, and for heaven's sake, heed my directions."

I can not find the words to respond. I have given up so much time with Albert, to honor Benedict, the life we had together, to remain close to his family, to appease her. To stay with her in her grief. And she can accuse me of not doing enough...

"You missed your opportunity to apologize to your guests directly. Edith has graciously taken your place in seeing them off, but I expect you to write to each of them and apologize in great detail about how poorly you acted last night. I will send the guest list so you do not miss a single one. Do not seal them until I can read them." Relief fills me, knowing that the guests have left, especially Grange. It is for the best that he hides away after the scene he caused last night. Again, she looks over at Albert. "You will need to find something else to occupy your time today. *She* will be busy."

"I will not," I correct her.

"Excuse me?"

"I will not be writing an apology to any of the guests."

"Need I remind you that my position ranks over yours?" Her pointer finger is now jutting from her fist, getting closer and closer to me.

"You need not, but I did not act poorly or in a state that would require an apology. I may have given more attention, staying at Lord Berry's bedside through the night, than I would have some of the guests. Yet, believe me when I say, I certainly would have provided every service to anyone in such a need."

"You foolish girl!"

Something shifts as Albert steps a hair closer to me. Everything falls into place. She grows angrier, her hands in fists at her side, her face growing red. Yet, my feelings head in the opposite direction.

"Lady Augusta, last night was a reminder for all of us within the Calderwood family. Life is precious and can be taken in a moment. I am thankful Lord Berry will recover as I am thankful for the reminder it gave that we all must live every day to its fullest."

I chance a step closer to her, never breaking the connection with Albert, who remains planted at my side. "Benedict would want you to be happy. He loved you so deeply. I truly believe he would never want you to spend years of your life mourning him."

"You know nothing," she spits back.

I step away. Try as I might, Lady Augusta may never find peace with Benedict's death, but that is her journey and decision to make.

"Then, if that is all, Lady Augusta, I have nothing more to say on the subject and I would like to check on Lord Berry and then get some rest."

Without waiting for her answer, I close the door on her and turn the lock.

36

We barely make it to the bed before another knock sounds on the door. I move Lily behind me. I held back at Lady Augusta, letting Lily get her points across, but now I will not let her return to continue that senseless tirade.

A gentle voice comes through, "It is Claire. Can I come in?"

"Yes," Lily calls out over my shoulder then I move to unlock the door.

"I passed Lady Augusta in the hall. I cannot imagine you had a pleasant exchange." I move to help Claire with the tall stack of bedding in her arms.

Lily's head falls, "You imagine correctly."

"Well, pay her no mind. I brought new bedding for you. With Mr. and Mrs. Riley staying here last night, I thought you may like some fresh sheets to rest your heads on this afternoon."

"Thank you, Claire, but we need to check on Lord Berry."

"I just came from his room. All is well and you both need rest, just as I told Lady Berry. With the guests gone, I have cleared the room next to Lord Berry for her to sleep. The young Rileys are taking their leave to Eton Cottage but wanted me to tell you they will be back for dinner."

Lily and I look at each other. It seems Claire has taken care of everything. "Perhaps we should try to sleep," I suggest.

Lily moves to help Claire dress the bed as I remove the old sheets, placing them in the corner for washing. Once she has finished, she moves to the windows, pulling all the curtains down. It does not completely block out the sun, but it is dark enough for two people as tired as Lily and I are to sleep.

"Rest well, you two. I shall be back to wake you for dinner." Before we can argue, Claire rushes from the room.

"Let us rest, my love." I pull her into bed with me and my body responds, needing her close. A lustful look fills her gaze, yet as our heads hit the pillows, her eyes grow heavy. The fatigue wins out this time, and I follow behind her into a restful sleep.

SITTING at the grand dining table at the Calderwood Estate, I find myself at ease more than I have in weeks.

Lady Augusta and her daughters took their leave hours ago. Even in the presence of my stoic father, who refused to stay confined to his bed a moment longer, insisting he join everyone for dinner. To his right is my mother, smiling brightly, never looking away from him for too long. Watching closely for any reason she may see that would warrant him returning to his bed.

Lily is seated next to my mother at the head of the table. I am on her other side. I catch my father looking between us on more than one occasion, but he has yet to question it. Unable to tell if he is simply suspicious or if my mother confided in him.

Beside me is Edward Riley with his wife, Margo and his sister at the end. Evelyn insisted on not only staying longer at Eton Cottage but to coming this evening for dinner.

Conversation is scarce, but I believe that is only due to the wild evening that proceeded, during which none of us found time to eat properly. Forks and knives clink against the porcelain plates as a serenade to our feast.

"Will you be staying for an extended time, Lord Berry? For your recovery?" Evelyn asks my father.

He softens at her question. Please let us hope it is not because he still thinks she could be a prospective wife for me. Let it just be the charm the young girl exudes. "I am hoping to return to our home in the country first thing tomorrow."

"So soon?" Lily asks.

He turns to her with the same gentle expression, "Yes, I greatly appreciate your hospitality, Lady

Calderwood, but I feel it would expedite my recovery to be in the comfort of my own home."

"Of course," she answers.

I wait for my father's insistence that I will need to join him tomorrow in his return to the Berry Estate but it never comes.

Light discussions continue as if nothing had been amiss last night and if we were all a cordial family enjoying dinner together. How I want to enjoy it without suspicion, but like all things, I am cautious for it to take a negative turn at any moment.

Long after everyone eats to their fill and the dishes are cleared away, I overhear my mother, "I do believe that has been a great first step in your recovery, dear, but I think we best get you back to your room now. We can prepare for our departure in the morning."

"Yes, right you are." He stands and holds my mother's chair out for her. "Thank you again, Lady Calderwood. I am sure I will see you once more in the morning before we depart. Goodnight, everyone." With my mother's arm locked in his elbow, they slowly walk out of the dining hall.

"That was pleasant." Lily's hand rests atop mine.

"It was." Still surprised myself.

"Wonderful meal, Lily," Edward calls.

"I am so glad you have your home to yourself again." Margo shares Lily's relief. No one speaks of Lady Augusta and her outbursts, but collectively we are all elated there is not a chance of any more.

Lily laughs lightly, "As am I."

"Well, we better be off before the sun begins to set." Edward stands and moves to help Margo and Evey out of their chairs.

"Can we expect to see you both tomorrow? Give you a break from hosting duties?" Margo asks.

"That would be wonderful. We can have a game night," Evey suggests.

I look to Lily, allowing her to answer for us.

"We shall be there."

After seeing our guests to their horses and watching them race back to Eton Cottage, Lily asks, "Would you care to join me for a short walk, Albert? I know it is a bit chilly, but I could really stretch my legs. I need some fresh air."

"That would be lovely, my dear. Let me gather our coats."

BUNDLED UP, the cool fall air brushes our cheeks as we walk away from the grand home. Pinks and oranges fill the horizon as the sun begins its descent. Lily is tucked closely to my side, one gloved hand wrapped in mine, the other wound around my arm. Our hips meet side by side as our steps fall into place.

Looking at Lily, she seems distracted, most likely recalling all that has happened since the ball.

"Are you well, my love?" I ask.

She pulls away from my body, completely stopping in her tracks and turns to me. "Albert."

"What is the matter?" Worry floods me.

"Let me finish." She teasingly swats at my chest with a devilish grin.

"All right, darling. Please proceed." I bow in a grand gesture.

Her mouth opens and drags in a big gulp of the chilly air as her chest puffs out, then returns as she releases the air.

"Albert, I do not deserve you, but I will spend every day trying to earn the gift of such a grand love."

I open my mouth to argue that it is I who is undeserving of her love, but she holds up her hand in protest, and I stop, allowing her to continue.

"In the moments when I heard screaming and then I could not see you in the crowd, I broke down, thinking that I might have lost you." Her voice cracks as tears gather above her bottom eyelids. "My heart stopped, my body revolted against my attempts at moving, my world began to crumble."

She is only arm's length away, but it is too far. My need to comfort her is fighting against me as I try to honor her wishes and allow her to finish what she has planned to tell me.

"When I reached you...I will never be able to explain the relief I felt at seeing you. It is shameful to admit the ecstasy that washed over me with your father lying beside you motionless. But I do not regret it. I am only sorry that it took such a disastrous event to help me see how wrong I have been for all these years."

An ounce of doubt comes to mind. *Could she be*

ending this? I will not be able to live without her. No, I squash that down to hear what else she has to say.

"You are my bright spring mornings that invoke new hope. You are the warm summer days that make me feel comfortable and relaxed. You are my fall evenings, bringing out the beauty of life like the perfect sunset. You are my winter nights, strong and an unshakable force."

I swallow deeply, moisture forming in my eyes, matching hers. She closes the distance between us, holding my hands in hers.

"Albert Berry, I love you. Will you marry me?"

Infinite emotions come over me.

Elation.

Bliss.

Joy.

Euphoria.

Delight.

Glee.

Comfort.

Security.

Lily's face falls, and I realize I have not answered her.

I pull her hand to my lips and I kiss the glove that stretches over her knuckles. "It would be my greatest honor."

With tears of joy streaming down our cheeks and giggles of elation coming from Lily, I pull her close, my lips colliding with hers.

It is as if my world is suddenly brand new. She is the

only woman I have loved in my entire life, but now it is so much more. I am kissing, devouring my fiancée. Her hands move from my chest to wrap around my neck.

I pull my soon-to-be wife flush against my body. Exploring her mouth with a new vigor and purpose.

She is the first to break our kiss. I do not know if I ever would have pulled away if she hadn't. We both gasp for air, having forgotten to breathe during our embrace. "Should we take this inside?"

"Indeed we shall." I lift her into my arms and carry her back into the house with every intention of spending the night making love to my fiancée.

37

While I have every intention to move forward securing my new life with Albert, I want to be respectful and share my plans with Lady Augusta Calderwood and her daughters in person rather than in letters. To make the journey easier for them, I asked to meet with them at the Calderwood family's townhome.

After arriving in London yesterday with the company of our friends Edward and Margo, Albert and I spent our first evening dining at the Riley house. After sharing a delicious meal with the extraordinary company, we all parted ways. Albert returned to his bachelor's lodgings while I ventured to the Calderwood townhome alone. While ideally, he would have stayed with me, for now, our love is still concealed from the staff there. Once I receive Lady Augusta's reaction, I will know better how to proceed.

Now, I listen as the rain outside hits against the

window of the sitting room. I am prepared for this discussion to be an absolute disaster, but maybe she will be so happy to be rid of me that she will take the news in stride.

Before traveling from the country, I sat with each member of my staff at the Calderwood country estate to inform them of my decision to marry Albert and that they would most likely be reporting to Lady Augusta or her daughter Amelia from this point until Benedict's nephew is old enough to manage the estate on his own. Tears filled my eyes as I shared the news. These people have been with me since I was a young bride wildly out of my element when I found myself a widow and when I found love once again. How can I repay all they have done for me? And now I feel as though I am abandoning them.

Claire is aware of all that is happening, but I have yet to have a personal conversation with her. I am still at a loss to find the right words to thank her, let alone how I will say goodbye.

"Your guests have arrived." Claire settles the final plate of pastries on the small table that sits between mine and an empty chair. It's my hope that Edith will select that chair. While it is not directly next to me, it sits on my side, opposite the sofa that I assume Amelia and Lady Augusta will occupy.

I take a deep breath, "Thank you, Claire. I am ready." She nods and leaves to get them.

Edith and I have grown closer in the past few weeks than I ever hoped we could be. After her show of support on the night of the ball, we have been writing to each other regularly. I now understand that she never reserved her affection for me, she was simply busy. With so many young children, her attention was directed toward them, as it should be. Now, with the children past the most difficult ages, she has the time to share how she has always cared for me.

Thankfully, Edith's friendly face is the first one to enter the sitting room. Following close behind are her mother and sister. I rise from my seat to welcome them.

"Good afternoon." I slightly bow in greeting each of them as I address them individually. "Lady Augusta, Amelia, Edith. Thank you for coming."

Edith is the only one of the three that meets my eye and returns the greeting. I stand firm in front of the chair I plan to occupy. Edith shares a smile with me before taking the seat beside me, as I hoped she would. The smile, a clear sign, shows she knows what I have brought them here for.

"I must say, Lily, I was pleasantly surprised by your invitation." Amelia finally looks at me with an odd sense of entitlement to her. "After your poor display at the ball, I had not expected you to be considerate enough to seek a reconciliation with us."

She thinks I brought them here to apologize. I try my best to hold the polite smile in place on my face, but I feel it slipping away. Lady Augusta notices my inability to find my words.

"Speak up." I feel my heart begin to race at her directive. "You may apologize to us, as you should have that day. And do not think I have forgotten your refusal to apologize to the guests you ignored. I still expect you to write a letter to each guest."

I steal a glance at Edith. Her eyes close briefly before finding my gaze and shaking her head slightly.

With a deep breath, I picture Albert and the future I am about to have with him. The thought of his support and love reminds me I am strong enough to do this. To fight for the future we will have together.

I take one more look at the three faces in front of me. Each reflects features they shared with Benedict. I think of him. My husband loved fiercely and lived with an unmatched vigor. I picture him at the front of the room, standing with his arm resting on top of the fireplace. This is not the legacy he would want left after his death. The most important women in his life, sitting opposite each other with such animosity between them. I will not remain under Lady Augusta's thumb any longer. The fun and light life we had together will never be forgotten. It is his mother who has made every conversation and event in his honor about his death and absence in our lives, not the man he lived as each and every day. I choose to fight for the love I had with Benedict and the life filled with love we both wanted for each other.

"While I am sorry for the health issues Lord Berry experienced the evening of the ball, I do not apologize for the actions I took to prioritize his comfort or insistence that he received medical care."

"How dare you." Lady Augusta's eyes are wide as

she grips the armrest on her right and leans in my direction. "You bring us here to remind us of your poor hostess behavior on the night you are to honor your late husband. And then you have the nerve to mention the family name of your lover."

"Your lover?" Amelia asks.

"Amelia." Edith squares a look at her sister.

"Are you not close friends with Lady Berry? I thought you would have been by her side when her husband fell ill in your family home." I should not have said this—it is petty of me to bring up her poor actions toward her friend in a discussion such as this, but I could not stop myself.

"Teresa is aware of the duties that come with being the lady of such a house. I am sure she understands where I was needed."

"You came to the room. You could have checked on her then. Yet, you pulled me into the hall, demanding I leave her side," I argue.

"Oh, do not pretend you were there for a friend of mine. No, you took any chance you could to get your hands on Teresa's son." She shakes her head and continues, "She was raised better, should have instilled better morals in her son than to be jumping from bed to bed with who knows how many widows he visits."

"He does not visit with other widows." This is not how I wanted to broach the topic, but it seems we have found ourselves here anyway. I square my shoulders and straighten my back. "Albert and I are together in a serious courtship. We have been for years, keeping it a secret to preserve your feelings."

"Foolish girl." Lady Augusta laughs as she rolls her eyes. "He has persuaded you to keep it a secret. I am sure that is what he tells every other woman whose bed he warms."

"Mother," Edith says in my defense. "Let her finish."

I continue. "Having been together and faithful to each other for years, I have taken enough time to come to this decision." Amelia and Lady Augusta sit silently, waiting intently for my next word. "Albert and I have decided to marry."

"Congratulations, Lily." Edith is the first to speak. Most likely in hopes of setting the tone for the other's reactions.

"You will do no such thing." Lady Augusta sits still as stone in her seat. Amelia has yet to add her opinion, waiting for her mother's next words.

"Pardon?" I ask.

"You will not remarry. Keep your lover, flaunt him all over the country. I do not care what happens out there. You will not associate with him or his family while in London ever again."

I shake my head, "Lady Augusta, y—"

This time, she raises her voice, "And you will never think of disrespecting my son in such a devastating way ever again. He loved you, and you have forgotten him to such a degree that you have now decided to renounce his name and replace him as your one and only husband?"

"Mother, you are taking this too far." Edith's defense is much appreciated.

Her mother rises from her chair and scolds her daughter. "I am not sure what has gotten into you, Edith, but you are not to speak again unless it is in defense of the brother who would have done so much more for you."

"That is not true, Mother." Amelia gasps at her sister's defiance, Edith continues. "I was closest to Benedict as children and into adulthood. He would have never wanted her to miss a second chance at love. Just as she made every day they had together the best he could have for his life."

I move closer to Edith, keeping my arm at my side and grab onto her hand. I hate that I waited so long to get this close to her only to begin my departure from this family. Regardless of my name, I will always consider her a sister.

"You are just as silly as her, but I should think you know better than to encourage such disrespect." Lady Augusta points at Edith as she reprimands her.

"I can assure you, my love for Benedict lives within me and remains just as strong as it ever was. No one can replace him, but I truly believe he would want me to be happy."

"Inconsiderate girl," she scolds me and begins to walk slowly toward me, with Amelia close behind. Edith stands firm next to me as her mother continues. "As the matriarch and head of the Calderwood family. I forbid you to take such brazen and disrespectful action.

You will live the rest of your days as a Calderwood, just as my son intended."

With my emotions firmly locked away, not allowing her false accusations to penetrate what I know to be true. I am doing what Benedict would want for me, what I want for my life. "I am sorry that you feel this way, Lady Augusta, but I will be proceeding with my marriage to Albert Berry."

"We will see." She turns quickly on her heels and walks out of the room.

Amelia is next to approach me. "If you are to marry into another family, I will be taking control of the Calderwood properties in the interim while we wait for the rightful Lord Calderwood to claim them."

"Of course. I ask you to permit me time to gather my things and I will vacate soon after."

"You have a fortnight," she insists, clearly not torn up at all about seeing me out of the family as quickly as possible. "And remember, aside from what you brought into the marriage and your personal effects, everything else there belongs to the estate."

I hear Edith groan next to me but answer Amelia directly, without emotion. "Of course."

Amelia takes her leave. Edith, with her hand still in mine, walks me over to the loveseat where her mother and sister were just sitting and pulls me down next to her.

"You will always be family to me, Lily. I wish you every day of happiness with your new husband."

Tears begin to fill my eyes, unable to hold back my

emotions any longer and knowing Edith is a safe space to let them out.

"Please do not cry over them. It is their own unhappiness they are taking out on you. My mother has suffered the loss of her husband and son, never knowing how to cope with either. My sister has never known a day of happiness in her own marriage. Quite frankly, you are doing her a great favor by giving her an excuse to take a new residence far away from her husband without causing concern. She should be thanking you."

"Thank you, Edith." We sit together for a moment longer until I can regain my composure.

"Now, if it is not too much to ask..." Edith begins.

"Anything, Edith."

"I would love to be present for your wedding and visit you and your kind husband when you establish your new residence."

"Of course," I reassure her. "We are family, after all."

38

I had expected our time in London to be filled with emotions. I just did not know which emotions to expect, given the individuals we planned to speak with about our upcoming wedding.

Elation fills the air as I share the news with my parents. I assume I am receiving a much better response than Lily is having at the moment telling Benedict's family. My mother is far more surprised than I had expected her to be now that she is aware of Lily and me. Perhaps she was just understanding of Lily's position and did not expect such news. Hell, I had not either.

"Oh, Albert!" My mother's embrace is comforting and unmoving. She holds me tight in her arms as tears dampen my shoulder. "I am just so happy for you...for you both."

"Thank you, Mother." I maintain our hold, waiting until she is ready to release me.

My father clears his throat behind her and she

moves, as interested as I am to hear what he will have to say. Since I spoke the words of my engagement to Lily, my father's reaction was completely overshadowed by my mother's. Now that I have a chance to look him over, I see no signs of the anger or disappointment I have come to expect from him.

"It is a great relief to hear you are finally settling down and taking a wife." I wait for him to say more. "Now we know why it took so long. You were being strung along by a woman—I had just guessed the wrong one."

"Nicholas," my mother scolded his harsh comment.

"Apologies, Teresa." He looks at me and, with what appears to be genuine regret, says, "I am sorry, Albert." My mother smiles at him. Perhaps my own love has been distracting me, but something does seem to have changed between my parents. They are not suddenly an affectionate couple as Lily and I are, but it does feel there is something gentler and caring between the two.

"How soon do you plan to wed?" My father returns to our conversation.

"We have not settled on any arrangements yet. Lily is visiting with the Calderwoods at present to share the news of our engagement. She wishes to be respectful by informing them directly, then we shall decide on a date for the wedding." My chest tightens at the thought of Lily on the receiving end of what is sure to be constant beratement from Benedict's mother, Lady Augusta.

"Did you not think to join her?" my father asks.

"She requested to do this alone," I answer and recall

how I have countlessly pleaded with her that I should be by her side since she decided how to tell them. Yet, she was insistent. I suppose Claire will be there, and Edith has shown her affection for Lily as of late. Surely, she will step in if her mother and sister become unreasonable.

"Will Lily be vacating the Calderwood properties immediately?" my mother asks, her eyes creased with worry.

"I believe that is one of the items they will be discussing today."

"Would it be helpful for me to call on Lady Augusta?" My mother is too kind. After the way Lady Augusta acted the night of the ball refusing to so much as check on my mother during that entire ordeal, she does not deserve any kindness.

"I do not believe that will be necessary." Or a good idea. "Lily is prepared for the changes that this will bring about, including the loss of her residence both in London and the country."

"She is welcome here." Surprisingly, it is my father who makes the offer. I did not think he was so generous. "I do not believe any of her family remains in the country, am I correct in that?"

"Yes, her parents and elder sister reside in Wales. Contact between them is quite scarce." If she received more than two to three correspondences a year from them, I would have gone to her father, and asked for her hand. But that is not a requirement for widows, and I am certain Lily's is the only permission I need to marry her.

"Would she like to stay here?" my mother asks with hope in her eyes.

"She may. I can certainly extend your offer." I look over to check the clock. It is still early afternoon and Lily is not expecting me until dinner. Hopefully, by then, her dealings with Lady Augusta will be concluded. She may want to spend as much time as she has left in the Calderwood townhome. It has been one of her residences for so much of her life.

While I do not worry about Lily's decision, that does not mean it is coming without any cost to her. She is losing both her homes and her staff, who, in the country especially, have become like family to her. I need to be sure I offer enough support to her every step of the way.

"And where will you reside after the wedding?" My father pulls me out of my worry.

"We have not decided on that yet. I have some ideas, but I will need to seek her opinion on each and move forward from there." We are not in a position that our friends found themselves in when dealing with Harold Grange. There is no haste in our need to marry, at least none that I am aware of at this moment. If she does face any adversity from the Calderwood family, we will discuss the best way to move forward together.

"Your mother and I would be happy to make the country estate our permanent home. You and Lily can have this townhome. Taking a step back, as the physician had instructed, would include less travel. For as long as you need."

Well, it truly does seem the health episode did have a great effect on my father's heart. In more ways than one. I do not want to question his goodwill, so I simply say, "Thank you."

"Of course, she is to be a Berry soon. This place will be just as much hers as it is any of ours." My father nods and stands. "I will be in my study if you need me any further."

"Nicholas, you are not to be working," my mother calls after him.

"I will simply be making preparations should Albert and his new bride wish us to give them privacy and head to the country sooner than planned." While his tone remains purely stoic, his words and gestures are far more than I could have imagined him capable of.

My mother notices my surprise, and I ask. "Is he truly so changed by my finally marrying?"

"You knew how much he wanted you to wed."

"Yes, but I always thought his displeasure with me was far more rooted than that."

"It seems you may have been wrong." She stands. "I need to make sure he does not overexert himself." She leans down and kisses my forehead. "We could not be happier for you."

I watch her leave the room and relax in my seat. Recognizing the settee, I glide my hand across the familiar fabric. Although I have endless memories with its twin that lives at the Calderwood family's country home, excitement fills me at the thought of replacing it with this one, in what will be Lily's new home.

Checking the clock again, I still have a couple hours before Lily expects me to return for dinner. I rise and look around the room, now with new eyes and considering for the first time what it will be like to have Lily here.

As my wife.

I walk each hallway into every room, picturing her enjoying her morning tea by the front window, sneaking down to the kitchen when she gets thirsty in the night, entertaining Margo and Edward when they visit, and hosting parties and balls when she chooses.

Yet one major thing will be missing, the staff at her country home who have supported us and kept our secret so loyally for these past years. She will miss Claire terribly—I will miss Claire.

Maybe Lily would not enjoy being in the city so much, but I am certain she will at least accompany me on my visit. She will need to take residence when I become Lord Berry and she becomes Lady Berry. But what if she wants something different until then... similar to Edward and Margo living permanently at Eton Cottage until they inherit one or both of their titles.

So many options I must discuss with my soon-to-be wife. Truly, I do not have a preference as long as I get to be by her side every day and night without any interruption.

39

THREE WEEKS LATER...

My rest begins to fade as my body stirs under the blankets. While it is not particularly sunny, I can still make out the minimal light fighting to make its way past the dark curtains covering the large window in my bedroom at Eton Cottage.

I stretch my arm out for Albert but do not find him. Only a letter that has been left on his pillow. I sit up and blink a few times to wake my eyes. There is no seal on the letter. I suppose we no longer need our discreet seals, especially once we are married in a fortnight.

The room is still too dark to read. I go to the window and pull back the curtain before I move to sit on the oversized windowsill, a feature I have always loved about Eton Cottage. I wonder if the Berry family country estates will have the same.

My Dearest Lily,

If you should wake before I return, be assured I will not be gone long. I would not leave your side if it were not of the utmost importance. And what could be more important than arranging a gift or two for my betrothal?

With all my love,
Albert

How silly of me to consider missing our secret seals. They represent a time when Albert and I could not send each other such love letters for fear of being discovered. Looking at his name under his declaration of love fills my heart more than I imagined possible.

Is this what marriage to Albert will be like? *I think it will be.* I hold the note to my chest, but this time, it is not to hold on to his words until we can meet again. It is to remember how happy I am to be his.

Where should I put this letter? I want to keep it, but I should put it away.

Wait, no. There is no need to hide these.

I leave the letter on top of the nearest trunk. The room is somewhat cluttered with my things. Well, this room and two other spare rooms. As I am currently between homes, Margo has offered to board me until Albert and I officially decide on a residence.

I've told him I will be happy anywhere, but I am not sure if he believes me. With our wedding planned to take place in London, we will most likely reside at the Berry family townhome. Yet, I can tell he has other plans for us, perhaps a smaller country home to be close to Eton Cottage. But I will not question him for fear of spoiling a surprise he may be planning.

Although, when I think of it being too close, I worry about how I will feel about seeing the Calderwood Estate. After sharing my wedding plans with the women of the Calderwood family, I took my final leave of their townhome the following day. Not having spent too much time there, I was able to pack my personal belongings fairly quickly.

Claire returned with Albert and me to the country estate. That was a far more excessive undertaking, both physically and emotionally.

My clothes are the first to be packed as they are the items most clearly mine. Edith volunteered to act as the Calderwood family representative to make sure I do not take with me anything that belongs to the family.

I do not request anything I do not feel is rightfully mine, but I am certain Edith is more in agreement with me than her mother or sister would have been. I keep my wedding band and some small pieces of jewelry that Benedict had custom-made for me. A few paintings I had brought with me when we married, my painting supplies, and of course, the boxes filled with Albert's letters under my bed are packed up with my other items.

The last place I go through is the library. I sigh as I enter my favorite room, knowing very well I will most likely never step foot in here again. With a cart in front of me, I walk through the rows and remove the many books I have purchased and Albert has gifted me since living here.

When I finish, I meet Edith at the door way.

"Why are there so few books?" she asks, looking down at the stack of at least ten books in the cart.

"These are the only ones I can claim as my own," I confirm.

"Are there others you long to have?" she asks.

"Certainly, ones that were Benedict's favorites, others I would read to Margo, and ones I would read alone. But they were here when I arrived and undeniably belong to the Calderwood family."

She places her hand on the cart handle next to mine. "We must get those too."

"But, Edith—"

"I can tell you with absolute certainty that my mother and sister have never read a single book in this room." I suppose, based on my interactions with them over the years, that is believable. "Now, let us gather the rest of your books."

"Thank you, Edith." I begin my second walk through the shelves with her close by my side.

"I look forward to seeing them in your new library when I come to visit you."

"I look forward to hosting you," I answer.

Most of my clothes and a few smaller items were sent ahead of us directly to the Berry townhome in London. The more valuable things I worried about sending without my supervision. We will see them moved when we leave Eton Cottage for the city in a few days' time.

I spent my final day at the Calderwood Estate with the staff. Albert and each of my dear friends, Margo, Edward, Mr. and Mrs. Landon, and Evelyn, helped me to prepare a large dinner for us to have together. We shared memories and stories from the years, remembering Benedict throughout and honoring my new life with Albert as well. We laughed, we cried and at times, we laughed so much it brought us to tears. It was not that I wanted to leave them, but it was the perfect way to say goodbye.

Claire was different. She was more to me than a housekeeper—she was a confidant, a support, a friend, a sister. I still spend my nights tossing and turning, trying to think of how I can bring her with me. It would be unfair to dismiss Lord Berry's housekeeper or ask Claire to assume a lower position.

I did, however, ask her to remain my friend. She received an invitation to our wedding, but I am still waiting for her reply. I understand she has much work to complete as she is welcoming a new employer into the estate and it would most likely be difficult for her to request a day off for an event Lady Augusta is so strongly against.

Dressed and ready for the day, I leave my room and make my way downstairs. The dining room is filled with commotion. I have so enjoyed my stay at Eton Cottage, having my friends just steps away. I have found instant comfort in staying at this cottage. I suppose it's always felt like another home for me.

Looking around the table, I notice an unexpected smile.

"Claire!" I run to her, pulling her into my arms as soon as she stands.

"Lily." She returns my hug. "I want to come and deliver this in person." She pulls a letter from her pocket and holds it out to me.

I open it quickly and read the writing as quickly as possible. "Your response. You are coming to the wedding!" I squeal with joy, more excited than when my parents confirmed their attendance.

"I would never miss such an important event," she reassures me. "I do, however, have to get back now." Her face falls.

"Is everything all right, Claire?" Panic fills me. Sure, Amelia and her son are not my favorite people, but if they are treating the staff poorly, I must do something.

"Everything is just as it should be. Do not worry, Lily." She smiles, "I just miss you."

"I miss you too, Claire."

"Please write to me when you can," she asks.

"Yes, I certainly will."

Claire turns to everyone else at the table and thanks them for their hospitality before taking her leave.

I sit in the chair that Claire was occupying next to Mrs. Landon. Her husband is seated next to her at one head of the table. On his right is Margo and the empty seat next to her I can only assume belongs to her husband, who is carrying two bowls of oatmeal. A sweet scent fills the room. He places the bowls in front of his wife and sister, who sits across from me.

"Good morning, Lily. Would you like some oatmeal?" Edward asks.

"Yes, it smells delicious."

"Cinnamon?"

"Of course."

Edward nods and returns to the kitchen.

As I finish my oatmeal, Albert returns in a great mood.

"Hello, my friends!" He leans over my chair to kiss my cheek, "Hello, my love."

"And where have you been?" I ask.

He moves to the chair beside me. "Planning a surprise for you," he says plainly as if it will not fill me with curiosity.

"And when will I find out about this surprise?"

"When I decide to share it with you." He laughs to himself. "Within the next month."

"Hmm...I suppose I can wait," I jest.

"I am so glad to hear it." He smiles and leans over to kiss me again.

"I thought Eddy and Margo were bad on their honeymoon. You two are not even married yet and cannot stop." Evelyn rolls her eyes.

"One day, you will feel and act in exactly this way, Miss Riley," I tell her. "And when that happens, all four of us will be present to mock you."

Everyone laughs, but Evelyn's smile is forced as her cheeks grow rosy with embarrassment. She clears her throat and stands. "I think I shall prepare for our outing now."

"Outing?" I ask.

"We are heading into town today," Margo says with a mischievous smile on her face.

I turn to Albert, "Does this have to do with the surprise that kept you occupied this morning?"

Albert opens his mouth to answer, but Margo cuts him off. "Something like that." Albert lets out a low laugh and winks at me.

After we finish eating, our friends rise around us then move toward their rooms to prepare for their excursion as Albert and I clear the table.

When we are finished cleaning up, we move to the foyer to wish them a nice day. I notice Albert is near Evelyn. They are both talking in hushed voices. I assume they are speaking about this surprise I have heard so much about, but then I notice Evelyn roll her eyes, much in the way she does to her brother. Still whispering, I can hear a change in Albert's tone.

While trying to be respectful of their private conversation, I wonder if I should interject to settle it.

"Everything all right over here?" Edward beats me to it.

Evelyn lets out an exacerbated and overdramatic

huff. "Yes. There is nothing to concern *either* of you." She moves past the two men, calling to the rest of her party as she exits through the front door. "I will be in the carriage."

We all look around in silence at each other. Mr. Landon is the first one to speak. "Good thing we have experience with raising a temperamental young lady." Mrs. Landon, Albert, and I all burst out in laughter. Edward wisely tries to hold his in by pushing his lips together and tilting his head away from Margo's view.

"Do you mean me?" she asks, pretending to be affronted.

"No, darling." Mrs. Landon barely gets the words out before her laughter continues.

"Well, you all enjoy your joke. I will be outside with someone who understands my passion and whimsical way of life." She smiles in a playful way before going toward Evelyn, who is waiting in the carriage.

As my laughter subsides, the Landons and Edward bid their farewells and head out to the carriage.

I turn to Albert. "What is the matter with Evelyn?"

He shakes his head and sighs deeply. "Nothing too concerning. She has her brother's unwavering romantic qualities and seems to have absorbed Margo's impulsive rational."

"A dangerous combination." I shiver at the thought.

"Yes, if it gets out of control. I am hopeful she will see reason before we need to worry." With the carriage out of sight, Albert grabs my hand and leads me back inside.

"Looks like we will have to find something to occupy our hours until they return," I tease Albert. "What ever will we do?"

Albert pulls me against his chest, wrapping his arms around my waist. "We will do everything I have thought about doing to you since I reluctantly left your side this morning." Without a moment to speak, his lips are on mine, consuming my thoughts and meeting every desire I have.

40

Today is the day Lily becomes my wife.

This morning, I wake up elated knowing that from this day forth, Lily will be my wife.

If she had never married me, if things had never changed, I would have loved her just as fiercely as I always have. But today, we are finally able to share our exceptional, beautiful, fantastic love with the world. Today is a gift, one I never quite let myself covet for too long, always determined it would forever be out of my reach.

Lily and I arrived at the church with many of our closest acquaintances. We repeat the vows and speak aloud a vow we have shared over and over with each other in private. Forsaking all others and loving each other until death do us part.

As she speaks those words, I know she is thinking of Benedict—I do too. Seeing her in this dress, I quickly recall the day we met, and today, she is once again just as happy. At that moment, my guilt regarding Benedict evaporates. If this were reversed and I was the man to marry her first, I would have been thankful to Benedict for caring for her after I was gone. Lily deserves to be shown such devotion, even if it cannot be from me.

Now, my wife and our guests are gathered at the Berry family townhome in London. Endless congratulations are offered to me from familiar faces. How glad I am that we kept the guest list small. Then I catch a glimpse of Lily in a white gown, talking with my mother and Mrs. Landon.

I stand still as my mind pulls me from the present and back to the first time I saw Lily and the white dress she wore that day. It was so much different from the silhouette she chose for today. The memory of complaining to my father and loudly voicing my displeasure for having to be there loud enough for the young bride to overhear my cruel words. Then, instead of calling me out for my childish complaining, she offered me cake in hopes it would make my day a little better.

In truth, since that day, I have found she makes everything better. I swear I fell in love with her then.

"Hem-hem," a soft voice whispers behind me, pulling me from my memory and back to the present, my wedding day. I turn to find my wife, with the brightest blonde hair loosely pinned back with flowers placed throughout. A simple yet elegant white gown covers her thin frame. In her white-gloved hands, she holds a small plate with a piece of cake.

"Perhaps some cake would improve your experience, Mister...?"

My face heats with recognition. Though we never spoke about that day, she remembers.

"Mr. Berry, Mr. Albert Berry." She walks closer, with the plate still held out in front of her. "And you are?" I ask.

Her smile grows, "Hello, Mr. Berry. I'm Lily—Mrs. Berry now."

I step forward, closing the gap between us. "I do not believe we had this cut yet, Mrs. Berry. How did you acquire a piece?"

"I took it from the back of the cake when no one was looking. It was necessary."

"Necessary?" I ask.

"Yes, you see, my new husband is not particularly fond of weddings. That is how we met, actually. But I know a piece of cake helps. So I had to steal for him."

"I can assure you, Mrs. Berry. I am very fond of this wedding." I take the cake from her and place it on the table, and then, without reservation, I kiss my wife.

A mixture of cheers and awkward coughs fills the space around us. We break apart and Lily covers her mouth, embarrassed at just how intimate our kiss grew in mere moments.

Margo and Edward approach and Lily whispers "sorry" to them.

"No apology needed, Lily." Margo giggles. "But if you plan to forget you have guests again, I recommend moving it to a dark corner or, even better, a closet."

"At the very least, grab us and we can stand in front of you to block your lustrous displays," Edward scoffs mockingly.

"Thank you, but I imagine we will be able to contain ourselves for the remainder of the festivities," Lily says as she straightens the front of her dress I wrinkled in my passion.

"Speak for yourself, dear wife. I will make no such promises." I move to kiss her again, but she turns away. Calling my name as if scolding a small child. As if that could stop me. Her evasive move only gives me better access to her neck. I take my chance and nuzzle into the exquisite skin right above her shoulder. She melts to my touch and I decide to have mercy on her. I can hold back for now, but later, I will do no such thing.

"Let us return to our guests," Lily pleads with little conviction in her voice.

"Of course, my love."

My parents were elated to have the wedding celebration in our home. My father's mood continued to get progressively better as time grew closer to the wedding. I still cannot be sure if it was his close call with death or learning I have found someone and shortly after planned to marry. With both events taking place so close together, I suppose I will never know, but I truly do not care for the reason. My mother has never seemed happier and that is most important. She smiles at me as my father whisks her around the room in a dance. I see her mouth *slow down*. He nods kindly, his movements becoming more restrained, but he never lets her go.

We continue to mingle over the next hour, enjoying the company of those closest to us. However, one guest in particular goes to great lengths to avoid me each time I begin to make my way toward her. Evelyn Riley and I have not spoken since I saw her at Eton Cottage a fortnight ago. I insisted she share her situation with Arthur Landon with her brother and new sister-in-law.

She argued that she did not tell them because it was not a situation and there was nothing to tell. Yet, I know from our previous talks she felt very strongly about the young man not too long ago. Could something have happened that changed her mind about the musically inclined young Mr. Landon? Or could it have progressed out of her control and she is afraid to tell Edward?

I do not want to betray her trust, but I fear I will need to share this with her brother since she clearly has no intention of doing so anytime soon. But not today—cornering a young woman who is clearly trying to avoid me would really dampen the atmosphere of my wedding celebration.

"Shall I steal another piece of cake for you, darling?" I turn toward my bride, puzzled at her question. "You look particularly broody at the moment."

"Not at all." I pull her into my arms. "Just contemplating something."

"What are you contemplating?" Lily asks,

I do not wish to burden her with my concerns for Evelyn, so I share another item I have been debating in my mind. "When is the best time to announce the gifts I have for you to our guests."

"Gifts, as in multiple?"

"Yes." I grin at her. "I suppose now would be the perfect time." I release her from my embrace but continue to hold her hand. "Can I have everyone's attention?" I ask loudly, and it works. All eyes are on us.

I clear my throat, "First, on behalf of myself and my beautiful bride, I would like to thank you all for sharing this significant day with us. It is all the more special because each of you is in attendance."

Cheers and clapping come all around us.

"Now, I do believe it is time for me to share the honeymoon destination I have selected for us."

Lily's eyes widen with excitement and intrigue.

"We will spend the coming months traveling throughout the United Kingdom of Great Britain and Ireland during our extended holiday. Of course, our journey will not begin for six weeks' time." I glance over at Edward and Margo. "That should give us plenty of time for privacy and to visit with friends before our departure."

Lily throws her arms around me and squeals with elation. "Albert, I cannot believe we will be gone for so long!"

Quietly, I say to her, "One day, we will have our titles and the responsibility that comes with them.

Unable to travel for months or even a year if we would like. Now is the time to do so."

She nods and blushes when I bring her hand to my lips to kiss her knuckles. Then I turn back to our guests. "While travels will be exciting, we will need a place to live once we return." I turn to my parents. "Lord and Lady Berry have graciously offered to permanently move to the Berry family country estate and leave this beautiful townhome for us. A generous offer, but I feel this London home should be shared as needed."

My mother and father nod knowingly at me.

"I have purchased a small estate in the countryside, not more than an hour's walk and an even shorter ride to Eton Cottage, so we can be near our dear friends."

"You did?" Lily asks with surprise in her eyes.

"I did, I hope you are not cross that I did that without including you. I assumed you would be happy to live in the country privately before we become Lord and Lady Berry."

Tears fill her eyes. Her endless admiration for Eton Cottage confirmed she would enjoy a residence similar and nearby to her friends. "Yes. I want nothing more."

"Oh, and one final matter I resolved without your counsel," I say, trying my best to fake a concerned look.

"I can not imagine what it could be." She laughs.

"Staffing for our new estate." I look through the crowd until I meet Claire's gaze. She smiles back at us when Lily follows my gaze and realizes where I am looking.

"Claire?" she asks with excitement in her voice.

"Not just Claire." I share hints at what I have done.

Her face falls with surprise.

"While it is a little estate, I do feel like we will need a large staff. So, I offered positions to those who were employed at Calderwood Estate," I tease.

"How many accepted?" she asks. Tears no longer sit in her eyes but fall from her face as Claire makes her way toward us.

"Let's just say Lady Amelia is currently looking for an entirely new staff for her son's country estate."

Lily's jaw drops just as Claire approaches. When she is close enough, Lily hugs Claire fiercely. "I can not believe it to be true."

"Believe it all, Lily. Each of us accepted to work for you and Albert without hesitation."

Lily pulls back and asks Claire, "What did Amelia do?"

"She was not particularly happy, but given you two will be on your honeymoon, we each offered to stay until our positions have been filled. Then, as we are relieved, we will move into the new Berry Estate and begin preparations for your return."

"I am just so happy," Lily whispers.

"Your husband is a wonderful man, Lily." Claire smiles back at me. "Enjoy your celebration and rest assured, your new home will be waiting for you upon your return."

I take this chance to raise a glass to my new bride.

"To Lily!" I call, and it is echoed back at me by our guests.

She kisses my cheek before borrowing my glass and calling, "To Albert!" Again, it is echoed back.

Then we lean in, our foreheads touching and together we whisper, "To us."

COMING SOON

ARTHUR AND EVELYN'S STORY

Disparity and Devotion

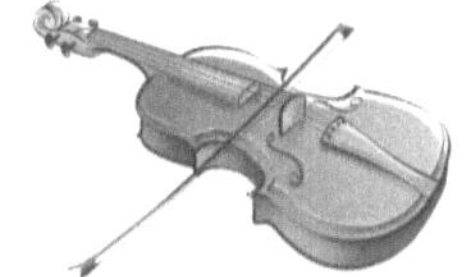

E.G. Verot

ACKNOWLEGDMENTS

Just about a year has passed since writing my first acknowledgments for my debut novel and the first in this series, Hostility and Heartstrings. At that time, I had one goal, to publish this book to have on my bookshelf. That was the only goal. Although it was a daunting task, it felt obtainable. What has happened since, has been an experience I could have never imagined.

Thank you. I say it a lot, but only because I don't think it is enough to convey just how much I appreciate the individuals, who were strangers to me before starting this journey, but have now become my safe space. The Eton Cottage series is built on found family, and the book community is the perfect example of that. Thank you.

To everyone who read H&H and fell in love with Albert instantly. When writing that, I too was smitten with Albert, but knowing he had so much support made this book all the more fun to write.

To the guy playing guitar in the room across from me, thank you for being just as invested in my characters as you are every beautiful note you play. It is your words and encouragement that make the journey so much more than it would be if I did it alone.

To my friends, who have embraced my change from teacher to author. Thank you for your support and interest in my books, always listening when I go off about a new book or changes to a story. It is your kindness, humor, and love that inspires my characters.

To my editor, partner in this author journey, my friend, and fellow cat lover, Cassie, thank you for making me a better author with each and every step in this process. From alpha reading to proofreading, you are the only one I could do this with. I've said it once, I will say it again, and many more times in the future, I could not do this without you.

To my author friends: Taryn, Maggie, Cait, Megan, Penny, Samara, and Marian. Thank you for beta reading when you can, providing exceptional feedback, bouncing ideas around, answering my endless questions, offering venting space and most of all believing in me. I am so very grateful to have to have the support and friendship of such amazing individuals.

To my beta readers, Alyssa and Amber. I cannot thank you enough for the time you have taken out of your lives to support me and provide invaluable feedback. In addition to you both, thank you to Whitney and Fern, I greatly appreciate the social media love you have shown for me and my books. Thank you to Cambria for the stunning graphics you have created for my books, your talents are unmatched and so very much appreciated! Most of all, thank you for your friendship. I am so very lucky to have you in my life.

To my family, thank you for your excitement when I mention my books and display your copies proudly. Thank you to those who, on my request, skipped those spicy chapters, Mom, Michael and LT. For those who read them anyway (Nana, Aunt Barb, and Danna), I'm sorry, this is the spiciest book yet, please just don't tell me if you've read them. Thank you for your love and support.

Lastly, I want to thank Lily Calderwood. As we all face struggles throughout our life, I find the loss of loved ones is where I have the most difficulty. When overwhelmed with grief and a voice very similar to that of Lady Augusta filling my thoughts, I was able to lean on Lily and let her be my strength. If you ever find yourself in this position, think of Lily, holding your hand.

ABOUT THE AUTHOR

E.G. Verot spends her days in the world of education but her evenings reading, writing, and loving books of all flavors and spices. She has a TBR list longer than she cares to admit. She has been longing to share the characters from her daydreams with you for many years. She lives in the Northeast area of the United States and looks forward to the winter weather all year. When she is not reading, she can be found spending time with her pets, crocheting, and enjoying her life with loved ones.

egverot.com

For more information on E.G. Verot, her social media accounts, and the Secrecy and Swooning playlist, please visit https://linktr.ee/e.g.verot

The Director DILEMMA

Semi-retired, famed, British romance film director Henry Brooks finds himself in quite a predicament. When his playboy public persona threatens to risk his chance of directing Pride & Prejudice, he searches for a way to convince the studio to hire him.

Where will he find a Jane Austen fan that can help him turn his public image around?

When Lucy moves to London for a fresh start at the age of thirty-seven, her only companions are her fictional boyfriends. Yet, in the land of Jane Austen, that surely will be more than enough. After a chance encounter at a coffee shop, she befriends a group of twenty-somethings, and suddenly London is starting to feel like home.

When her new friends invite their father to join them at the coffee shop one night, Lucy can't take her eyes off the handsome older man in front of her. That is until he opens his mouth. She should have known not to consider him—he isn't a fictional man, after all. To make matters worse, he even teases her for her love of romance novels. Until he needs her help, that is...

Will Lucy be willing to help Henry improve his image to appeal to Jane Austen fans like her?

If it means a new adaptation of one of her favorite novels, it might be worth the aggravation...for Jane.

www.ingramcontent.com/pod-product-compliance
Lightning Source LLC
Chambersburg PA
CBHW030102310726
48970CB00004B/1114